ACRE

ACRE

by

Tom Grundner

Fireship Press
www.FireshipPress.com

Acre - Copyright © 2010 by Tom Grundner

ISBN: 978-1-61179-153-2

BISAC Subject Heading:
FIC014000   FICTION / Historical
FIC032000   FICTION / War & Military
HIS015000   HISTORY / Europe / Great Britain

Address all correspondence to:
Fireship Press, LLC
P.O. Box 68412
Tucson, AZ 85737

Or visit our website at:
www.FireshipPress.com

1.0

DEDICATION

To
Raymond Cecil Durbin
and Jack Isaac Pulley
The real Cecil and Isaac

Who knew that those long childhood walks to the Clawson
Shopping Center—ferociously debating topics we
knew absolutely nothing about—would prepare us
so thoroughly for our respective careers, and for
a lifetime of friendship.

Chapter One

"Do you know what I will do when I get back home?" Captain Joseph Moiret gave a short rueful laugh as he tried to tidy-up his now filthy uniform.

"First, I will find a case of the finest wine, the largest wheel of cheese, and the prettiest maiden in all of France. Then I will take all three up into the mountains and find the coldest stream I can locate. I will then lay down in it—and never get up."

"Not even for the wine or the mademoiselle?" Asked his friend, Captain Horace Say.

Moiret thought about that for a moment. "And I will never get up except for brief periods of necessity."

Captain Say's mirth was cut short by a shrieking sound coming from on top of the city walls just in front of them. Both men looked down wishing that somehow, in some way, those sounds would stop. The heat and the thirst were bad enough, but those noises could only be made by men whose souls were being shredded a piece at a time.

About a month earlier Bonaparte, with an army of 13,000 chosen men, left Egypt to forestall a possible counter-invasion by the Turks, and to add the region of Syria to his

1

conquests. The French fleet had been destroyed by Nelson at the Battle of the Nile, and it was thought that Bonaparte was now trapped. The British owned the Mediterranean. No ship, French or otherwise, could sail on it without risk of British interception. Not only did that cut off Bonaparte's communications with Paris, it cut off his supply lines and his ability to easily move troops and equipment.

The problem was that Bonaparte did not see himself as being ensnared. He saw the situation as an opportunity. As he said to his officers the night they learned of the French naval defeat: "The sea, of which we are no longer master, separates us from our homeland, but no sea separates us from either Africa or Asia."

His staff was not immediately sure what he meant; then it dawned on them. Bonaparte intended to conquer the eastern Mediterranean *by land!*

The trek had been a trying one. Leaving Cairo on February 5, 1799, they had crossed 60 miles of desert, marched north to the sea, then turned east. The first significant town they came to was El-Arish. It fell after a few days of siege, when the defenders agreed to surrender in exchange for parole, an agreement that they would no longer fight in the war. Bonaparte granted it, a decision he would later regret.

The second town on their route, Jaffa, was proving to be more obstinate. Bonaparte surrounded the town and sent in a delegation with his usual surrender demands. Instead of complying, the Turkish governor, Abdallah Bey, seized the messengers, dragged them up on the city walls, and proceeded to torture, castrate, and kill them, one at a time, in front of the entire French Army.

It might be said that this action was not well received by the French soldiers.

As the last screaming man was ushered into silence by a decapitation, bugles started sounding and drums started beating in the French camp. It was the call for a full scale assault. Bonaparte had had enough—and so had the men.

"It's about time!" Captain Say spat as he threw down a small stone with which he had been playing.

"No, it's past time," Moiret replied, and both men leaped to their horses.

The two were almost identically dressed. Both wore the bright red coats and white piping of General Kléber's 75th Infantry Demi-Brigade—the Invincibles. But Moiret had a sky-blue collar, Say a black one, and those collars determined where the two men would go. Moiret was an infantry officer and went to his men. Say was an engineer and went to the wall.

When all was ready, a single word came down from Bonaparte to his line generals—Reynier, Kléber, Bon, and Lannes. From these men, the word was relayed to their demi-brigade commanders, and from there to the battalions. It was only one word; but it was all that was needed. Attack!

A multicolored wave of enraged humanity threw themselves against the walls of Jaffa. They were beaten back. They launched themselves again. Beaten back again. The defenders then sortied a company of cavalry, but they were met by an equal number of French cavalry and turned back into the city.

Horace Say was working with some of Caraffeli's engineers and sappers to figure out a way to undermine the town walls. Suddenly, with a thunderous crash and a huge cloud of white dust, a portion of the wall collapsed. Say had no idea why. It certainly wasn't because of anything they had done; but the French troops began to pour through the breach nevertheless. From that point on, it was a slaughter.

It is not unknown for men in battle to work themselves into a murderous rage; but these soldiers were in that state before the battle had even begun, due to the treatment of the surrender delegation. They took it out on anyone they could find.

Anyone male was killed, and it didn't matter what age he was. Anyone female was raped; and, again, age didn't matter. Anything that could be plundered—was.

Say went through the breach about an hour after the initial breakthrough, and what he saw would haunt him for the rest of his life.

He wandered down one street and up another, but the scene was unchanging. Doors were broken down and houses were on fire. The smell of bodies scorched by the flames was everywhere. Dead fathers were heaped upon dead infants. Raped daughters were piled upon beaten and bloody mothers. The screams of the women were drowned out only by the shouts of the victors as they argued over plunder. The smell of blood and smoke was everywhere.

When asked whether the rape and pillage should be curbed, Bonaparte said no. It was a city that deserved to die horribly, as a lesson to all the other cities in the Levant. It was a clear message: This is what happens when you torture and kill our representatives. This is what happens when you resist French might.

The destruction of Jaffa went on throughout the evening and into the next day—everywhere except in one spot. Several thousand holdouts were located in a walled caravansary in the middle of town. Bonaparte sent two of his aide-de-camps to negotiate with them, Eugene de Beauharnais, Josephine's seventeen-year-old son and Bonaparte's stepson, and Captain Jean-Louis Croisier.

The two young men proceeded to the caravansary with an interpreter, and asked to speak with their leader. A head soon appeared in the window of a tall building behind the wall.

"I am Captain Beauharnais. You must know that your position is hopeless. This town is completely in the hands of the *l'Armée d'Orient*. I order you to surrender!"

"We cannot; and we will not."

"Why can you not?"

"We have seen what your troops have done, Captain. You have gone mad. You will kill us all if you get the chance. Well, monsieur, you might kill us, but not without a fight. It will take thousands of your troops to storm this place, and we will take hundreds of your men with us in death."

Beauharnais turned to Crosier. "He's right, Jean-Louis. Those walls will not be easy. What do you think? Should we grant them amnesty to get them out?"

"I don't know. You heard what the Général said when he was asked about showing mercy to this Godforsaken town."

"Yes, but he also spared those soldiers back at El-Arish on condition of parole."

A thousand conflicting thoughts were rushing through the head of the teenager. What would the General do? What would he want? Is it really *my* decision? He knew that his stepfather had been disappointed in him up to this point. He didn't say anything, but Eugene knew. Whenever Napoleon spoke to him, he could see in his eyes the thought: *You will never be what I had hoped you would be.*

At that moment, he made his decision. He would show his stepfather that he could indeed make the decisions of a man.

He called to the soldier in the window. "Will you surrender if we guarantee your safety?"

"Our safety? Under what terms?"

"Each of you must swear that you will not take up arms again against France. You will be allowed to return to your homes and your families, but you must not return to war against us."

"And by what authority do you make this promise?"

"Do you see this yellow augulette around my shoulder?" He said, pointing. "I am the senior aide-de-camp to Général Napoleon Bonaparte, Supreme Commander of this army. I speak in his name."

The head disappeared inside the building. Obviously, the defenders were discussing the matter. Five minutes went by. Ten minutes. Fifteen. The unbelievably intense sun was baking the two Frenchmen, and there was not a breath of breeze to be found anywhere. Eugene was futilely swatting at a fly that refused to leave him alone when the head reappeared.

"We accept your terms. We will lay down our arms and come out through the south gate."

Eugene Beauharnais was beaming. He had successfully defused a delicate situation and saved countless French lives in the process. He would take these prisoners back to his stepfather in triumph—living proof that his judgment could be counted on.

Unfortunately, Captain Beauharnais had failed to ask one rather important question of the enemy negotiator. "How many of you are there?"

They began to stream out of the gate, hundreds and hundreds of them, and still they came.

* * * * *

Bonaparte was alerted by the sound of men buzzing outside his tent. He was finishing some dictation to his secretary, Louis Bourrienne, and couldn't be bothered to see what was going on. Just as he was dismissing Bourrienne, however, his stepson and Captain Croisier entered the tent. Both saluted, but Beauharnais spoke.

"Mon Général, I have returned from the caravansary and settled matters there."

"Have you indeed?" Bonaparte leaned back in his chair, amused by the spectacle of his stepson, playing soldier. "And how was the matter settled?"

"I have... er... we have captured their entire force, sir. We hold them as prisoners for your inspection."

Bonaparte's face suddenly grew serious. He leaned forward. "And how many of the enemy have you captured?"

"We have not counted them all yet, but there are thousands."

Surely, Bonaparte thought, *this young fool must be mis-*

taken. It's merely the fevered imagination of a young man on his first campaign; but still, I had better check it out.

"Show me," he said and strode out of the tent, followed by the two young officers.

Bonaparte took three steps and stopped, dumbstruck. He found himself looking at over four thousand enemy faces. They were all seated on the ground, hands tied behind their backs, with a look of somber resignation.

His eyes grew wide and the color left his face. After a long moment, he pivoted around, grabbed his still radiant stepson by the arm and pushed him back into the tent. Croisier followed, alarmed.

"What have you two idiots done?" Bonaparte demanded.

"Done?" Beauharnais replied. "I have told you, sir. We captured thousands of the enemy, without the loss of a single French life."

"Have you? And what do you propose I do with them? Do I have the food to feed them? Do I have the men to escort them back to Egypt? Perhaps I should send them back to France aboard the ships we don't have, as a present for the Directory?"

Beauharnais face was beginning to flush. "Sir, I would suggest you let them go, like you did at El-Arish. I have obtained their parole. They'll not fight us again."

"You imbecile! Half those men were *at* El-Arish. They're the men we paroled the last time!"

* * * * *

Three nights later Bonaparte called his senior officers in for a meeting. He had a problem—a big problem—and he needed their help to think it through.

His aides had commandeered the house of the local pasha for his headquarters, although they had the devil of a time finding a suitable western-style table that they could all sit around like Christians.

At precisely 8:00 PM, Bonaparte entered the room and looked over his assembled staff. Along one side of the long table were the four line-generals. First was Jean Louis Reynier, 28 years old, a former gunner with a quick temper. Next to him was the rock-solid Jean Baptiste Kléber, 46, the former architect; normally even tempered, he could be unbelievably brave if the situation called for it. To his left was Louis André Bon, 41, the lifelong soldier and proud grenadier; and to his left was Jean Lannes, 30, daring and talented, but undisciplined. He was Bonaparte's personal project.

At the far end of the table was Joachim Murat, Bonaparte's brilliant cavalry commander. Thirty-two years old, he was a flamboyant dresser, and referred to as "King Dandy" by his men—who adored him. Across the table from the line-generals was the infantry Brigade chief Jean-Baptiste Bessières, artillery commander Dammartin, and the scholarly, one-legged, Louis-Marie Caffarelli, one of the finest military engineers of his day.

Bonaparte opened the meeting.

"I need not go into why I've called you here. As you all know, we are now *blessed...*" he spat out the word while casting a withering glance at Beauharnais and Croisier, who stood petrified in the corner, "...we are now blessed with exactly 4,138 captured enemy soldiers.

"Unhappily, I must decide what to do with them. To do that, I would like your opinions. Gentlemen, speak freely. I want to hear any and all ideas."

Nothing was said for a long moment, each general waiting for the other to go first. Bonaparte waited them out. Finally, the cavalry commander, Murat spoke up.

"Général, we can't keep them here with us. Why not send them back to Egypt where they can be properly confined?"

"And how would you do that? Caffarelli asked. "There are over 4,000 prisoners and we're in the middle of enemy territory. How many of our troops could you send to escort them without fatally weakening the army as a whole?"

"It's even more than that," chimed in Kléber. "How would you feed them on the journey? We have no excess food to give them, and we stripped the countryside bare on our way here."

"Is there any hope that the remainder of our fleet will come to reinforce us?" Lannes asked. "They could take them back to Egypt."

Bonaparte spoke. "I've been watching the horizon ever since we've been on this coast. I keep hoping to see French sails, but I am afraid we cannot depend on our navy for any assistance."

Silence reigned again.

General Bon spoke up. "Why not release them on parole, like we did at El-Arish?"

"Because they would be back at our throats within a week," replied Reynier. "Breaking an oath to a Christian is not a sin in their eyes. Indeed, it's a badge of honor. As soon as they are out of sight, they would head to Acre, or join the Bedouins in the mountains of Nablus to harass our rear and right flank. It would be their way of thanking us for our generosity."

Lannes spoke again. "Then maybe we could absorb them into our army. We could integrate them with our soldiers."

No one even commented on this suggestion. It was too stupid.

There was another long pause. Bonaparte continued looking at them, saying nothing. The silence was becoming uncomfortable, when finally Reynier spoke.

"I don't understand this. Why are we all dancing around the obvious solution like a group of old women?"

"And what obvious solution might that be?" Bonaparte asked.

General Reynier, the hot tempered 28 year old, the

youngest man in the group, looked Bonaparte straight in the eyes and said evenly, "We must kill them."

This brought an eruption of commentary from every member of the group. Bonaparte restored order.

"Gentlemen, please. One at a time. Général Kléber, I believe you had something to say."

"Général, we cannot do that! Those men surrendered with arms in their hands. They were in a strong defensive position. We have no right to induce men to abandon their means of defense, and then—three days later—decide to kill them. It's not only contrary to the rules of war, it's contrary to the laws of humanity."

The room grew silent again. No one dared to move. Bonaparte stood up and slowly walked over to the map table. He was looking down, playing with a pointer, but no one thought for a moment that he was studying a map.

After several long minutes of deliberation, his head came up and he stood erect. A decision had been made. He locked his hands behind his back, and gently rocked back and forth, as he quietly gave his orders.

"Gentlemen, I have no choice." He fixed Beauharnais and Croisier with a stare as if to say: See what you two have done. "They must die. Every one of them. Starting first thing tomorrow morning."

* * * * *

General Bon could have had his choice of a dozen different horses. He chose a coal-black mare, because her color seemed fitting. Bon was selected to carry out the executions. He had been a professional soldier his entire life; and it was thought that there was very little in the way of horror that he had not witnessed. That might be true, but it did not make the current task any easier.

The mare was skittish as he tried to mount her. The groom settled her down with a few soft words and the general swung into his saddle. After a moment, with a sigh, he signaled to one of his aides, who signaled to the regimental Sergeant-Major, who caused the drummers to begin their staccato tattoo. At precisely 8:00 AM on March 10, 1799, members of a special detail formed in front of the French encampment.

Bon had three demi-brigades under his command, the 4th, the 18th, and the 32nd. Rather than task any one battalion, from any one of the demi-brigades, he selected men from throughout his command. Light-green jacketed soldiers from the 4th were mixed with the red coats of the 18th, who intermingled with the brown coats of the 32nd. The men did not officially know the task for which they had been assembled, but the campfire rumor mills had been working overtime the previous night, and they had a pretty good idea.

The makeshift battalion, over 1000 men, formed a hollow square and marched to the large pen where the prisoners were being held. A large number of prisoners were led inside the square, and the entire group set off for the sand-hills to the southeast of Jaffa.

At first, there was confusion among the prisoners. "What's happening?" "Where are we going?" Their destination soon became obvious however and, to the amazement of the French soldiers, a strange calm came over the Turks. There was no pleading. There was no outrage. There were no complaints. No one tried to bust through the French ranks. They simply marched along, silent and composed. It was Allah's will that they should die in this manner, and they were servants of the Prophet. Who were they to object or resist?

They soon arrived at the seaside. The prisoners were divided into small groups and led out of the square. Group after group were taken to the beach, lined up, and shot. The bodies soon began to mount, making the executions more difficult, so periodically the shooting would pause. French soldiers would go in and bayonet anyone still alive, while other men were tasked with hauling the bodies away and placing them in a huge pile. The shooting would then begin again.

Not all the prisoners, however, were taking their demise stoically. Some begged. Some pleaded. Some tried to hide themselves under the bodies of their already dead comrades; and some rushed into the water to swim out to a collection of rocks that were located not far off shore.

The shooting stopped again. The French soldiers laid down their arms in the sand and gave the Egyptian sign of reconciliation to the men who were clinging to the rocks. They came back ashore—and were shot as soon as they reached it.

The pyramid of bodies was growing higher and higher. French officers became alarmed at the amount of ammunition that was being consumed, so they ordered the men to bayonet the prisoners instead. They did. The sand was now slippery with blood, which was running far faster than it could be absorbed.

By late afternoon, the prisoners had all been dispatched; and the enormous mound of bodies was left to rot in the hot Syrian sun. Visitors said that Jaffa had the stench of death for years afterward.

* * * * *

Nelson was trying to identify the odor that was lightly drifting through his cabin. He finally settled on lilac. *Yes, that was it,* he thought. *Lilac, like the shrub that grew so well in the alkaline soil of his native Norfolk. I wonder if she knew that when she scented the paper. Could she have known it was my mother's favorite flower?*

He stood up, walked to the back of his cabin, and looked through the gallery windows at the measureless sea. Normally that had a calming effect on him. Normally he would have opened several windows to welcome in the sharp sea air; but not today. He wanted the smell of lilacs to linger.

The *Vanguard*, along with the other ships in his squadron, was making slow progress. They had defeated the French fleet at what some of his officers were calling the Battle of the Nile, and others the Battle of Aboukir Bay. The French were defeated, yes, but not without cost. The damage to his ships was considerable, and progress was slow. He would not allow his squadron to travel any faster than the slowest and most heavily damaged of his ships, of which the *Vanguard* was one.

Nelson felt almost as damaged as his vessels.

During the battle, a piece of langridge shot gashed his forehead. A flap of skin fell over his one remaining eye and he was convinced he was going to die. "Berry, I am killed," he said to his flag captain, Edward Berry. "Remember me to my wife." They hauled him below where the surgeon declared it a superficial wound and stitched him up. Nelson would not believe him, however, and convened a hasty conference in the bread room with his chaplain.

Nelson lived, but was paying the price. The wound, now infected, ached. He had blinding headaches which, when added to his perpetual seasickness, made him sometimes wish the shrapnel had taken off his head. He had had headaches before, but they were nothing like these. They seemed to come from deep within his forehead and radiate out so that, at times, he could barely even see. There was something terribly wrong, but he would never tell anyone about his symptoms. Not ever.

But maybe there was a light to be seen in the darkness of this damnable pain, he thought. Weeks earlier he had sent Captain Hoste in the sloop *Mutine* with dispatches announcing his victory. He gave explicit instructions that he was to stop at Naples with the news. That order had born fruit. Earlier today a packet ship had found them and two letters lay on his desk as a result.

He walked back over to his desk, sat down, and picked up the first of them. It was from Lady Emma Hamilton. He smiled at the curious misspellings and grammatical errors, but was very much attuned to what he perceived as the message behind the message.

NAPLES
September 8, 1798

MY DEAR, DEAR SIR, How shall I begin, what shall I say to you. 'tis impossible I can write, for since last Monday I am delerious with joy, and assure you I have a fevour caused by agitation and pleasure. God, what a victory! Never, never has there been anything half so glorious, so compleat. I fainted when I heard the joyfull news, and fell on my side and am hurt, but now well of that. I shou'd feil it a glory to die in such a cause. No, I wou'd not like to die till I see and embrace the Victor of the Nile.

How shall I describe to you the transports of Maria Carolina, 'tis not possible. She fainted and kissed her husband, her children, walked about the room, cried, kissed, and embraced every person near her, exclaiming, *Oh, brave Nelson, oh, God bless and protect our brave deliverer, oh, Nelson, Nelson, what do we not owe to you, oh Victor, Savour of Itali, oh, that my swolen heart cou'd now tell him personally what we owe to him!*

You may judge, my dear Sir, of the rest, but my head will not permit me to tell you half of the rejoicing. The Neapolitans are mad with joy, and if you wos here now, you wou'd be killed with kindness. Sonets on sonets, illuminations, rejoicings; not a French dog dare shew his face. How I glory in the honner of my Country and my *Countryman!* I walk and tread in air with pride, feiling I was born in the same land with the victor Nelson and his gallant band. But no more, I cannot, dare not, trust myself, for I am not well. Little dear Captain Hoste will tell you the rest. He dines with us in the day, for he will not sleep out of his ship, and we Love him dearly. He is a fine, good lad. Sir

William is delighted with him, and I say he will be a second Nelson. If he is onely half a Nelson, he will be superior to all others.

I send you two letters from my adorable queen. One was written to me the day we received the glorious news, the other yesterday. Keep them, as they are in her own handwriting. I have kept copies only, but I feil that you ought to have them. If you had seen our meeting after the battle, but I will keep it all for your arrival. I coo'd not do justice to her feiling nor to my own, with writing it; and we are preparing your appartment against you come. I hope it will not be long, for Sir William and I are so impatient to embrace you.

I wish you cou'd have seen our house the 3 nights of illumination. 'Tis, 'twas covered with your glorious name. Their were 3 thousand Lamps, and their shou'd have been 3 millions if we had had time. All the English vie with each other in celebrating this most gallant and ever memorable victory. Sir William is ten years younger since the happy news, and he now only wishes to see his friend to be completely happy. How he glories in you when your name is mentioned. He cannot contain his joy.

For God's sake come to Naples soon. We receive so many Sonets and Letters of congratulation. I send you some of them to shew you how your success is felt here. How I felt for poor Troubridge. He must have been so angry on the sandbank, so brave an officer! In short, I pity those who were not in the battle. I wou'd have been rather an English powder-monkey, or a swab in that great victory, than an Emperor out of it, but you will be so tired of all this. Write or come soon to Naples, and rejoin your ever sincere and oblidged friend,

Emma Hamilton

The Queen has this moment sent a Dymond Ring to Captain Hoste, six buts of wine, 2 casks, for the officers, and every man on board a guinea each. Her letter is in English and comes as from an unknown person, but a well-wisher to our country, and an admirer of our gallant Nelson. As war is not yet declared with France, she cou'd not shew herself so openly as she wished, but she has done so much, and rejoiced so very publickly, that all the world sees it. She bids me to say that she longs more to see you than any woman with child can long for anything she may take a fancy to, and she shall be for ever unhappy if you do not come. God bless you my dear, dear friend.

My dress from head to foot is alla Nelson. Ask Hoste. Even my shawl is in Blue with gold anchors all over. My earrings are Nelson's anchors; in short, we are be-Nelsoned all over. I send you some Sonets, but I must have taken a ship on purpose to send you all written on you. Once more, God bless you. My mother desires her love to you. I am so sorry to write in such a hurry. I am affraid you will not be able to read this scrawl.

Nelson put the letter down, smiled, and thought, yes indeed my dear. Naples is precisely where we are headed. He then took up a second letter. It was from his wife, Fanny.

Dearest Horatio,

The weather is very fine; nice clear sky, which helps to cheer us. I was determined to see if I could write without tormenting you with my anxieties, every day produces hopes of hearing from you...

He could read no further. He set down the letter from Fanny, picked up the letter from Emma, and began to read it again.

* * * * *

Spencer Smith was bored. He had seen it all before—many times. Lucas Walker was examining the walls,
interested in their general antiquity; and Sidney Smith was
captivated by the exhibits. However, Susan Whitney was in
another world. She was awestruck by what she was seeing.

Topkapi Palace was the home of Sultan Selim III, the
ruler of the vast Ottoman Empire. It was situated in Constantinople, on a peninsula that jutted into the Bosporus,
and consisted of four courtyards, and the harem.

The harem and the fourth courtyard were completely off-
limits to anyone except the Sultan, his personal servants, and
the eunuchs. In front of that, the third courtyard was accessible only if the person was personally summoned by the Sultan, and even then, they usually got no further than the audience chamber just inside the gate. In front of the third courtyard was the second, where most of the day-to-day governmental activities took place; but even then, you couldn't get
into it unless you had some specific business.

The first courtyard, however, was the largest, and it was
open to anyone. It was bordered on the north by the walls of
the second courtyard, and on the south by a wall that ran the
entire width of the peninsula. It was, in effect, a large city
park. It was known by various names, such as the Court of
the Janissaries or the Parade Court, and it included a mixture of both public and governmental buildings. Included in
this mix was the Hagia Irene, often erroneously translated
into English as the Church of St Irene. That was where
Walker, Whitney, and the two Smiths were taking in the
sights.

The church had been built on the foundations of an old
Roman temple by Constantine I in the mid-fourth century.
As such, it was almost as old as Christianity itself. Over the
years, it had suffered its share of wear and tear, as well as
restoration and repair. In 1435, however, after the conquest

of Constantinople by Mehmed II, it was enclosed within the walls of the Topkapi palace. Having little use for a Christian church on their grounds, it was used by the Janissaries as an armory, then as a storehouse for war booty, and finally, in 1725, it became a military museum.

It was the weapons exhibits that had Sir Sidney's attention. Walker was mildly impressed by a building that has been in continuous usage for almost 1500 years; but Susan was rendered speechless by the architecture.

The building was a massive stone structure laid out in the shape of a cross. Inside, at the top of the cross, was a two story high narthex, and each arm held a two story atrium. Where the cross pieces intersected was a magnificent dome. But the thing that attracted Susan's attention was the half dome that formed the top back wall of the narthex. There, staring down at the world for the past fifteen centuries, was a rough cross carved into the stone. It was not elaborate. In fact, it was quite the reverse; but in that simplicity was its power.

"Lucas, would you look at that?" Susan said softly.

"Look at what?"

"Up there. That cross on the back wall."

Walker studied it for a moment, his head tilted slightly. "Yes, it *is* rather crude isn't it? You'd think they would have taken better care in carving it."

"No, no. Don't you see? That's its beauty. In the midst of this glorious soaring building there is that simple, unadorned cross. It's like it's saying: forget all your foolish pretensions. Just live with a simple faith—the faith of a child."

"It looks like it was carved by a child."

"Walker, you are *such* a barbarian. I am serious. Try to imagine the person who carved it. I mean, here he was, a mason working on the first Christian church to be built in Constantinople. He wanted to put some sort of symbol in place, but what symbol should he use? Remember, this was 360 AD. Christianity was still sorting out what it believed and didn't believe. The New Testament as we know it had not been pulled together. So, what symbol should he use? The fish? The Chi-Rho monogram? The trefoil? The Star of David? Even the pomegranate had been used as an early symbol of Christianity. No, he chose the cross. He wasn't sure if it was the correct choice, but he chose it anyway."

Walker had a look of wonderment on his face. He had seen Susan Whitney swear like a bosun, drink like a Coldstream Guard, fire a naval gun like a gunner's mate; and then turn around and hold a scared sailor tenderly in her arms as he lay dying. *Now,* he thought, *she turns into some kind of philosopher-poet. Is there no end to...*

He was about to say something when his thoughts were interrupted by the penetrating sound of high-pitched instruments, the banging of drums, and the clashing of cymbals. The four hurried out of the church and saw one of the great sights in the empire. The Sultan was emerging from his palace.

Hundreds of Janissary warriors, the Sultan's elite guard, were marching down the road leading from the Gate of Greeting. Leading them was a mehterhane band playing their peculiar brand of music. The boom of the davul, [1] combined with the squeal of the zuma, [2] which was assailed by the blaring naffirs, [3] jingling triangles, and crashing cymbals.

As the Janissaries came down the road, strings of them would peel off to stand by the roadside as an honor guard for the sultan. Janissary officers, with their strange shoulder epaulettes curving upward like the horns of a bull, were issuing orders to sergeants in their bright red uniforms with long horsetails flowing from their peaked caps. The rank and file were standing at rigid attention in their short turquoise jackets and gold laced pants. Their rectangular caps rose high on their heads, terminating in a long flowing piece of white

---

[1] Base drum

[2] A kind of loud oboe

[3] Trumpets

cloth that ran halfway down their backs. That white cloth, a tradition that went back to their founding, was the identifying sign of a Janissary.

Before long, the first members of the imperial procession began to appear.

It was led by a senior Janissary officer, a *segban-bashi*, riding a prancing horse with a gorgeous silver inlayed saddle with fur trim. Behind him were about 50 *peiks* carrying razor sharp halberds. Their normal duty was to run in front of the sultan, to clear away the crowds; but, with the Janissaries lining the road, there was little need of that today.

Next came the Grand Vizier and other important officials. Behind them, and surrounding the sultan, were a group of *kapici*—the doorkeepers—with huge headdresses of white feathers. From a distance, those headdresses made it seem like the Sultan in his chair was riding on a cloud.

Behind the Sultan was the Sword-bearer or *Silihdar*, followed by the Chief Black Eunuch or *Kislar Agha*; and behind him were two of the more important pages—the *Chokadar*, [1] and the *Sharabdar*. [2]

Throngs of people, from every social strata were lining the roadway to behold the magnificence of Sultan Selim III.

"Where's he going?" Susan asked Spencer Smith.

"I have no idea, unless possibly there is... yes, that's it. There's a jereed game today."

"A what? Walker asked.

"A jereed game. See how the Sultan and all the principal members of his court are dressed in green?"

"Yes."

"That's because the Sultan is a cabbageman. A big supporter, in fact."

Sidney Smith was as confused as everyone else. "Spence, I

---

[1] Bearer of the royal robes

[2] The cupbearer

think you're going to have to begin at the beginning on this one."

"It's a game called jereed—basically a mock war game. It's been played among the Turks for almost a thousand years. At the moment, there are two main teams, each named after a vegetable, the *Bahmiaji* and the *Lahanaji*, the Blues and the Greens. The Sultan is a big fan of the *Lahanajii*, which takes it's name from the word for cabbage, which is why everyone is in green."

"Do the Blues ever dare win?" Susan asked.

"Oh yes, in fact they're currently leading the series. Not even the Sultan would interfere with a jereed game. If he did, he might lose his throne. The people take the game rather seriously."

"So, how's it played?"

* * * * *

Within twenty minutes the four had made their way over to the jereed field, which was to the east of the palace, about halfway between it and the lapping waves of the Bosporus. It was a flat area 76 yards wide by 142 yards long. The perimeter of the field was outlined in white chalk dust, along with two large rectangular zones at each end. Spencer Smith explained that the field had been seeded with grass specially imported from the Central Asian steppes, the homeland of both the Turkish people and the game itself.

The field was already ringed with spectators. The wealthier were under brightly colored canopies being tended by multiple servants and slaves. The poorer classes were sitting on the ground, sharing slices of roast lamb and a kind of cheap wine smuggled in from the island of Bozcaada. The atmosphere was filled with a carnival-like excitement.

Along one side of the field there was elevated seating for the Sultan and several hundred members of the court. Spencer Smith, through his position as the British ambassador, was able to bluff his way past the attendants and secure the group some of those prime seats.

Not long after they had sat down, the Sultan arrived, settled into his box, and waved his hand for the pre-game rituals to begin.

In front of the Sultans' seating area, the band started playing a series of complicated rhythms and melodies known as the *at oynatma havası*. As they did so, two lines of horsemen appeared from the far end of the field riding side-by-side in a *rahvan*—a delicate style of walking a horse so that the rider is not shaken. All the men were dressed in the traditional garb of *Sipahi* cavalryman, red *şalvar* [1] decorated with gold lace, and brown bowl-shaped helmets. The only thing distinguishing them was that one line was clad in bright green silk tunics, the other in a deep blue. Leading them was the head referee known as the *çavuþ*, followed by three assistant referees, all notable former players. The first man in each line, the captain, proudly carried his team flag.

The two lines continued to midfield, did a 90-degree turn, and moved to stand before the Sultan and the crowd. The assistant referees peeled off and galloped to their places, the band stopped playing; and the *çavuþ* began to introduce the players, one at a time, with a word of praise for each. After being introduced, each rider galloped to his respective team's box at the end of the field. When everyone had been introduced and the teams were in their boxes, the *çavuþ* dropped a white flag, the band started playing *Cirit havası*—jereed game music—and the contest began.

A single rider emerged from the green team, their youngest and least experienced member, who trotted down to the blue team at the other end of the field. When he got about 25 or 30 yards away, he shouted the name of a blue team player and threw his *cirit* at him—a short javelin, about a yard long, an inch in diameter, and blunted at one end.

---

[1] Loose trousers

The named blue player then took off after the rider that challenged him, who was now racing back to the safety of the green team's box. The blue rider, however, was trying to throw his javelin and hit the challenger. If he could do so, or force his adversary out of bounds, his team would score one point. If the opponent could catch his javelin in midair, he would score the point.

Once the green challenger made it to the safety of the box, one of his teammates would take off after the person who had been chasing him. The blue rider would then do a screeching 180-degree turn, and try to get back to his lines without getting hit. Once there, one of his teammates would take off after the green pursuer, and so it would go, back and forth.

Walker, Smith, and Whitney were quickly caught up in the contest. It was like watching a complicated ballet being performed with 1200-pound animals. The horsemanship was stunning, with riders literally performing acrobatic feats in the saddle to avoid being hit, while racing their horses at top speed.

The green team initially surged out to a comfortable lead, but lost points on two occasions when a thrown javelin hit the opponent's horse instead of the rider, and once when one of their riders fell off his horse while trying to pivot underneath his neck to avoid a throw. Disaster struck, however, early in the second 45 minute half, when a green rider turned to see whether his opponent had thrown, and caught his javelin in the side of his face, shattering his jaw. Along with losing the services of the rider for the rest of the game, he fell off his horse, thus costing the green team yet another point.

Spencer Smith turned to see how the sultan was taking this reversal, but was surprised to see him paying no attention to the game whatsoever. He was in an animated conversation with one of his generals as a courier arrived and handed him a message. He read it and threw it at his general, while shaking a finger at him.

"Sidney, sit tight until I get back," he murmured to his brother. "Something's wrong."

Sidney followed Spencer's gaze and just nodded, saying nothing.

Spencer Smith slid out of his seat and walked as causally as he could over to where Mustafa, the Sultan's favorite cousin, was seated. Mustafa was close enough to the Sultan to overhear what was going on, and friends enough with the British ambassador to tell him.

After a few minutes, Spencer Smith returned.

"Sidney... all of you... get back to your ship and be prepared to get underway at a moment's notice."

"What is it, Spence? Why's the Sultan so agitated?"

"Bonaparte has broken out of Egypt and is leading an army through the Levant. There are confirmed reports that he has taken El-Arish."

"El-Arish?" Walker asked. "He's coming up the coast? But why? Surely he's not crazy enough to march on Constantinople."

"Don't be so sure," Spencer replied ominously. "There are some very good reasons why he might do it—and why he just might succeed."

Chapter Two

In effect, HMS *Tigre* was nothing more than a floating gun platform. It was 183 feet long and 49 feet wide. It weighed over 3000 tons, and could spread almost 26,000 square feet of sail. All of it had one purpose, and one purpose only—to convey 80 guns from point A to point B, fire them, and wreak death and destruction on the enemies of England.

To accomplish this task, the *Tigre* required manpower—lots of it. Although no navy ship was ever fully manned, she had over 600 men and 100 marines. That manpower required food and water, the guns required powder and shot; and the ship itself required spare yards, miles of rope, extra canvas, spare anchors, and on, and on.

As a result, the HMS *Tigre* had been a beehive for the past two days. She took on dozens of casks of beef, 700 bags of bread, 20 casks of flour, 975 oranges, over 7,000 pounds of peas, 2000 pounds of rice, and 1000 pounds of sugar.

Two hundred and nineteen tons of fresh water was shipped, along with—via special permission of the Sultan—2800 gallons of wine, and 6700 gallons of a kind of Turkish beer. Her gunpowder supply was topped off with an additional 338 barrels, and over 1000 shot of various types were added to her shot lockers.

Complicating matters further, every pound of that material had to be stored, but it couldn't be stored in just any fashion. A ship was like a two-axis balance board. Put too much weight forward, and her bow goes down, which causes her to plow through the water like a haystack. Put too much aft, and she becomes difficult, if not impossible, to handle. If you put too much to starboard or larboard she will list, and be in danger of capsizing in heavy weather. At the same time that this balancing act is going on, the articles have to be stored so that the most important items, the things used most often, are easily accessible.

Ultimately, the provisioning of the ship, and the stowage of the materials, was the province of two people—the first lieutenant and the purser. The first lieutenant was there to make sure everything was stowed properly and the ship remained balanced. The purser was there to make sure that every thing he ordered—and paid for—got to the ship in the proper quality and quantity.

While all this was going on, Sir Sidney Smith was in his cabin, reading a newly arrived set of orders, shaking his head, and reading them again. Three knocks sounded on the door, thumped with all the authority that a teenaged marine guard could muster, followed by the words: "Sir, the First Lieutenant."

"Come," Smith replied.

Lieutenant Edward Jekyll Canes opened the door, but did not come in all the way. "Captain, your brother is approaching the ship in a launch."

"Ah, good. I was expecting him. I'll be up directly to greet him. Meanwhile, find Lieutenant Wright and..." Smith thought for a moment. "And Colonel Phélippeaux, and bring them here to my cabin. I'll want you here too."

"Aye, sir." And within a few minutes the group had been assembled.

John Wesley Wright was a lieutenant in His Majesty's Navy—this week. In fact, he was a master intelligence officer who assumed whatever civilian or naval rank he needed, when he needed it, to accomplish whatever mission was at hand. He had been conducting intelligence operations with Sir Sidney when they were both captured at La Havre. He stayed with Smith during his imprisonment in the Temple prison, and helped him run the *Agence de Paris*—Britain's primary spy ring in France—from his cell. [1]

Louis Picard Phélippeaux, better known to his friends as just "Picard," was a royalist guerrilla fighter who engineered Sir Sidney and Wright's escape from their Paris prison. For that, he was awarded the rank of Colonel in the British Army; but, more to the point, he personally knew Bonaparte. They were schoolmates at the elite *École Militaire* in Paris and had grown up together. They hated each other then; and they hated each other now. But the important thing was that he knew how Bonaparte thought; and, to Sir Sidney, that was invaluable.

The meeting was being held aboard the *Tigre*; but it was Spencer Smith who called it, so he rolled out a map of the eastern Mediterranean, gathered the group around Smith's chart table, and began.

"Well, gentlemen, I've gathered as much information as I could. I got most of it from the Sultan's foreign minister and then confirmed at least the essential details with the Russian ambassador. Russian intelligence, by the way, is surprisingly good in this part of the world. John Wesley, you're going to have to find out how they do it someday."

John Wesley Wright was sitting in a chair, his elbow on the table, his head propped in his left hand. He just nodded and smiled as if to say: *I already know how they do it.*

Spencer Smith continued, "You all know about Nelson's victory at the Nile. With the destruction of the French fleet, we assumed Bonaparte was trapped in Egypt. Unfortunately, Bonaparte didn't see it that way.

---

[1] See *The Temple* - Book three in this series

"What you need to understand is that our two nations see things very differently. It's like there is a battle going on between a whale and an elephant. Whenever we have a victory at sea, we go wild with delight. The elephant, however, looks at it differently. For him, the whale's triumphs are mildly interesting, but not all that important. For the elephant—for France—it's what happens on land that matters.

"Late last year, while still in Egypt, Bonaparte made overtures to Ahmed al-Jezzar, the Pasha of Acre, to assist him in his various projects. While Jezzar Pasha is not exactly the Sultan's most loyal subject, he declined Bonaparte's offer. Instead, he sent 4,000 troops down to take over the fortress at El-Arish, keeping another 8,000 in reserve. At the same time, Bonaparte learned that a second Turkish army of about 8,000 men was beginning to gather under Mustafa Pasha, on the island of Rhodes.

"These events set off warning bells with Bonaparte, as well they should. If the Turks were going to send an army down the coast, he didn't want to be in Egypt when it arrived. He wanted to meet them on the way, and not be pinned between the arriving army and the remnants of the Egyptian Mameluke army that was still holding out in Upper Egypt. It would be far better to take on the two Turkish armies one at a time—defeat Jezzar Pasha's forces first, then worry about the group on Rhodes.

"So, in early February of this year he set off from Cairo with 13,000 soldiers on a brutal march up the coast. On February 20, after a three day siege, they took El-Arish.

"And that, gentleman, is all I know."

"So what's Bonaparte going to do next?" Lieutenant Canes asked.

Spencer Smith just shook his head. "I don't know, nor does anyone else; but here are some possibilities."

Smith leaned over the chart table and pointed to a spot the map. "Bonaparte is here in El-Arish," he began, "and he can do one of three things.

"First, he can stop in El-Arish, strengthen the fortress there, and wait for the Turks to come to him."

"That will never happen," Phélippeaux interrupted. "Bonaparte would never fight from a fixed location. He needs to be in the open—maneuvering and attacking. He'd be lost trying to defend a stationary fort."

"Then there is a second possibility," Smith continued. "He could head his army to the northeast, through Syria, and pick up the Silk Road."

"The Silk Road?" Sidney Smith asked. "To where? China? If so, I hope he does."

"No, not China. India. The French have long coveted our presence there, and a branch of the Silk Road runs right into central India. If you were to couple the French Army with those of the local Indian rulers, who already hate us, there would be nothing we could do to stop them."

The room went silent as the enormity of that possibility set in. After a moment, Sidney Smith got the presentation in motion again.

"You said there were three possibilities, Spence. What's the third?"

"The third is even worse than the second. Look here." He pointed to the map again. "He's already in El-Arish," Spencer Smith started moving his finger up the coast as he called out the cities. "Gaza, Jaffa, Caesarea, Acre. If he takes Acre, the only other fortified city of any consequence is up here at Aleppo. Following the existing roads, it's about 290 miles north of Acre, but it's also a good 75 miles inland. That means we can't support the defenders by sea; and if he takes Aleppo, he's got us. He can swing east and head his army to India, or he can swing west and head to..." Smith swung his finger across Turkey, stabbed it down, and said, "Constantinople!"

"Oh, come on, Spencer. You can't be serious." Sir Sidney remarked. "He's going to take Constantinople with 13,000 troops? I know Bonaparte's good, but no one is *that* good. It can't be done."

For the first time John Wesley Wright spoke up. "No, Spencer's right. By the time he gets to Constantinople, he won't have 13,000 men. He could easily have a quarter million or more."

"How?"

Wright reached across the table to point to the map. "This route is lined with hundreds of tribes and petty kingdoms. All of them are fiercely independent, and none are very happy about being under the Sultan's rule. If Bonaparte can show that he can defeat Turkish armies—not just the Mamelukes in Egypt, but mainline Turkish armies—they will go over to him in droves."

"Quite correct," Spencer Smith continued. "And if he takes Constantinople, he'll pick up even more troops. At that point, again, he can head off for India, like Alexander the Great, or..." he moved his finger slowly along the map, "enter Europe by the back door.

"Now, think about that for a minute. Think about Bonaparte returning to Europe at the head of a half-million or a million man army—from the east! The Austrians would fall first, and Russia and Prussia would be too intimidated to do anything about it. France would own Continental Europe. Then, with a secure path back to the Middle East, they could set up a system of governance that stretches from Sweden to Egypt. And, with that in place, how long do you think *England* would last?"

The room was again deadly silent.

"What can we do?" Canes asked.

"I don't know what the Admiralty is going to do," Sidney Smith replied, "but I know what I am about. I am being sent to Alexandria."

He walked over to his desk, picked up a sheet of paper, and tossed it on the table. "I got these orders from Admiral

Jervis, by way of Nelson. They want me to relieve Troubridge and take over the blockade of Alexandria.

"Isn't that wonderful?" he added sarcastically. "We know where Bonaparte is, and I am being sent to where he isn't."

"I don't understand this whole thing," Phélippeaux injected. "Who exactly is your boss, Sidney? Is it Admiral Jervis? Admiral Nelson? Or who?"

"That depends on what day of the week it is. My original orders were to report to Admiral Jervis, who is in command of the entire Mediterranean; but I was to operate in the eastern Mediterranean, which is under the command of Nelson. At the same time, I was appointed minister plenipotentiary to the Porte in Constantinople, which outranks either Jervis or Nelson, at least in diplomatic matters; and privately I was told that my assignment to Jervis was only for show, and under no circumstances would I be under the command of Nelson. In addition, I have another set of orders that states that... wait I have it here..."

Smith went over to his desk again and rummaged through some papers in a drawer.

"Here it is: I am to '...take command of such of his Majesty's ships as he may find in those seas (the Levant) unless, by some unforeseen accident, it should happen that there should be among them any of his Majesty's officers of superior rank.'

"Then let me throw in another level of complexity. Sultan Selim III has placed me in charge of all Ottoman forces, whether at sea or on land.

"So let's suppose I am in a situation where Admirals Jervis and Nelson want me to do one thing, but the proper diplomatic solution would be to do something else. And let's say to do any of those things I need ships, but I arrive in a location which has a more senior officer who doesn't want to give them up, or wants me to do a third thing. I am a King's officer and must obey my superiors, or do I? As a diplomat, I outrank all of them; and as Commander-in-chief of the Turkish forces, I could literally start my own damn war, quite independent of Naples, Gibraltar, or even London."

Phélippeaux just shook his head and muttered "*Incroyable.* So what are you going to do, Sidney?"

"I am going to do whatever I think is right," he replied softly. "Whatever I think is right."

* * * * *

On Thursday, February 21, 1799, a rat died. As world events go, this fact would not normally be considered remarkable; but this was no ordinary animal. Indeed, technically, he wasn't a rat at all. He was a jird, a type of rodent related to the gerbil family; but, by whatever name, he was very, very, sick.

The bright sun of noonday had passed and it was dusk. The animal had lain under some rocks for most of the day, waiting for the cooler night temperatures, and the disguise of darkness, to forage for food. Today was different, however. For the first time in his life, he had no desire to leave his rocky lair. He had no desire for anything. His head pounded, and his stomach hurt, and he seemed to ache all over. Even breathing was becoming difficult.

Still, the timeless urge to forage was forming in his brain—a brain that had been hardwired for a million years to do little else but eat, sleep, and reproduce. It was a need that could not be denied so, as darkness fell, he set out; but he knew he would not be going far. His head was swimming, and he was having trouble focusing his eyes. Nearby he spotted the outlines of a tent. If he could just make it under the loose folds of canvas near the ground, he could rest for a bit.

First, his nose entered. A few sniffs later came his eyes, and he could see the inside of the tent was empty. Over to his right was a canvas rectangle lying on the ground. He knew from experience that inside that canvas was straw, and maybe that would have to do for tonight's meal.

He started gnawing on a corner, but didn't get far. Suddenly, he felt something let go deep inside of him, and a gush of blood poured forth from his mouth. He fell to his side, his legs making futile running motions. The blood did not stop and, in less than a minute, he was dead.

Inhabiting the animal's body, embedded deep within the thick fur, was a colony of fleas. They knew something was wrong, but had no idea what it was. Instinctively, however, they knew that their home was no longer viable, and it was time to leave.

By ones and twos, more than a dozen fleas leapt off the dead jird on to the canvas rectangle. Some stayed on the surface, others found a new home in the straw, others found accommodations on a field mouse that was hiding in a corner.

Shortly after midnight, an unknown private laid down on the canvas mat. Exhausted from a long workday, he quickly fell asleep.

The fleas were delighted. They had a new home; and Bonaparte's army had the plague.

* * * * *

The sound of the 24-pound guns going off deafened the ears, and the force caused palpable vibrations to radiate through the hull of the wooden ship. For the past 20 minutes, a ragged volley had been dropped on to the city of Alexandria, to little effect. All at once, the guns stopped, and men scurried to secure them.

"And that is basically what we do every day, Captain Smith." The speaker was Thomas Troubridge, captain of the *Culloden*, and about to be relieved by Smith as commander of the Alexandria blockade.

"We shell the city and the harbor for 15 to 20 minutes each day, just to let them know we're still here; and we make sure no one gets in or out of the port without our permission—and no one gets that permission."

"Altogether, how many ships do you have for the blockade?"

"Five. We have my ship, the *Culloden*, of course. Then we have the *Theseus*, 74, Captain Miller; the *Bulldog* and the *Perseus*, both bomb-ketches, Captains Drummond and Oswald, and the 22-gun store-ship, *Alliance*, Captain Wilmot."

"How many will I have?"

"Two."

"Two?"

"Well, two real ships—your own *Tigre* and we'll be leaving you the *Theseus*."

"How am I supposed to blockade Alexandria with two ships? What happens if we need to go to Rhodes or somewhere for provisions, or take on water?"

"Two was all that Admiral Nelson thought you would require." Troubridge's voice had turned frosty. He and Nelson were old friends; and clearly, Nelson's views of Sidney Smith had spread to his cronies.

Troubridge, when he was first appointed to command the *Culloden*, participated in the Battle of Cape St. Vincent. This was the battle at which Nelson first showed sparks of heroism, not to mention common sense, by disobeying Admiral John Jervis' orders and throwing his ship in front of the fleeing Spaniards. This act won the battle, and made John Jervis an Earl—the Earl of St. Vincent—even though he was miles away at the time. It also won Nelson the undying patronage of Jervis.

Troubridge was also with Nelson at his disastrous attack on Santa Cruz, and was with him at the more recent Battle of the Nile. Smith was tempted to counter Troubridge's supercilious attitude by asking him about the Nile; but he decided that would be too cruel. Troubridge had run his ship aground just as the battle was starting, and thus missed the whole thing. It was still a sore point with him.

"Oh, we'll leave you a few others. You can have the store-ship, the *Alliance*, and you can keep the ship you captured on your way down here, the *Marianne*."

"But the *Marianne* only has four guns."

Troubridge ignored the statement and continued, "And you can have the *Torride*."

"What's the *Torride*?"

"See for yourself. She's over there, anchored just aft of the *Bulldog*."

Smith reached in his pocket and took out the small folding telescope he always carried with him. Taking off the initialed brass caps, he looked over to where the *Bulldog* and the *Perseus* were anchored. "I don't see anything," he finally said.

"It's right there in plain sight," Troubridge said irritably, as if Smith was an idiot. "Right behind the *Bulldog*."

Smith looked again more closely. "*That* is a ship? I thought it was a captain's gig."

"Yes, it's a ship."

"How many guns does it have?"

"Two."

"And so, I am to blockade Alexandria with two third-rates, a store-ship, a captured sloop, and an attack canoe."

"That was all Admiral Nelson thought you..."

"...yes, thought I would require." Sidney Smith finished the sentence for him. The two men glared at each other for several long moments, then turned to stare at the waves crashing against the Alexandria breakwater. Smith finally broke the silence.

"I guess I just don't understand."

"What's that?"

"I don't understand your attitude toward me. It's common knowledge that Nelson and I don't exactly get along; and I know you've been his friend for many years. But... Is that it? The enemy of my friend is my enemy."

Troubridge looked hard into Sir Sidney's eyes. "You really *don't* understand, do you?

"Understand what?"

"What you did to Nelson."

"What I did?" Smith was genuinely astonished. "I've done nothing to him—nothing at all."

"Smith, you've been sent out here and given command of the Levant—including this blockade. Did you ever stop to think about that from Nelson's viewpoint?"

Smith waited for Troubridge to go on.

"Nelson has three responsibilities: the support of the Neapolitans, the blockade of Malta, and the blockade of Alexandria. Then you come along. You not only take the Alexandria blockade away from him, but you become the commander of every British ship in the Levant."

"And what do you expect me to do?" Smith shot back. "Shall I tell the Admiralty they've made a terrible mistake? That I can't handle the job? That I am not ready for this kind of responsibility? Or perhaps I should just flat disobey my orders? I tell you, sir, I have never done that and I never..."

"Smith, you're *junior* to Nelson! Don't you see it?

"In the whole Mediterranean there's only one place that really matters—Egypt. It's where Bonaparte is. It's where Nelson might have the chance to take Bonaparte on, head-to-head—a situation was that made possible by his victory at the Nile. Now, suddenly, all that has been taken from him and given to a man who is so far beneath him on the seniority list as to be laughable.

"I tell you, no man—other than perhaps the Earl St. Vincent—no man has as good a claim to the command of the Mediterranean as Nelson. Yet, here you are."

"Well, if he's so damned outraged, why doesn't he resign—or at least threaten to?"

"He did! You didn't know that, did you? I've seen copies of the letters.

"Nelson wrote St. Vincent and offered his resignation. I believe the letter opened: 'I do feel, for I am a man, that it is impossible for me to serve in these seas with a squadron under a junior officer.' And he requested permission to resign as soon as a replacement could be found."

"What did St. Vincent say?"

"He talked him out of it, of course. He said that, for the sake of the country, he must remain where he is. But he went on to say that he should feel free to use you in any way he wished; and, knowing Nelson's magnanimity, he was confident that Nelson would mortify you as little as possible."

"Please pass on to Admiral Nelson that I shall sleep easily knowing of his magnanimity."

"You see, that's what I am talking about. The damnable arrogance you have toward your superiors."

"But that's what *you* don't seem to understand, Troubridge. Nelson is my senior—not my superior."

"Nelson defeated the French at the Nile, or did you somehow miss that?"

"Yes. He defeated 13 anchored ships, with a maneuver that he didn't even order. Tom Foley on the *Goliath* thought it up, and did it without Nelson's authorization. When Foley got between the French ships and the shoreline, Nelson was as surprised as the French."

"He still commanded a fleet that defeated the French in an even fight—13 ships against 13 ships."

"Correct, and have you ever thought about *that*?"

"What do you mean?" Troubridge demanded.

"Do you remember back in '93? The Siege of Toulon? I paid my own way—bought a ship, in fact—to get there and participate. Before we pulled out, I volunteered to destroy the French ships that were still in the harbor and burn their warehouses."

"Yes, I know that. What of it?"

"Do you remember what was said afterward? Let me

quote from memory one of Collingwood's letters: 'No preparation was made for the destruction either of ships or arsenal; and at last perhaps it was put into as bad hands as could be found—Sir Sidney Smith...' And from Nelson himself: 'Sir Sidney Smith did not burn them all. Lord Hood mistook the man: there is an old song, Great talkers do the least, we see.'"

"Must I repeat myself? What of it?"

"Have you ever thought what would have happened if Nelson had been facing 23 ships at the Nile and not 13?"

"You're babbling like a lunatic."

"Am I? On that day in Toulon, I volunteered to do what no one else would do. I went in with a small force and burned ten French ships of the line, and God knows how much in the way of supplies. Suppose I hadn't done that? Suppose those ships had still been intact when the French eventually retook Toulon. They would have been *at the Nile*, Troubridge! It would have been 23 French, against 13 British. Nelson would not have been the hunter, he would have been the *hunted*."

"You're still an arrogant bastard."

"Yes, I am. You've got me there. I plead 100% guilty."

Smith turned away, placed his hands on the quarterdeck rail, and gazed again at the Egyptian coast. After several moments, he spoke again, his voice much softer this time.

"Troubridge, throughout my whole career I've only asked one thing of people—either support me, or get out of my way; and yet my career has been one unending string of people who will do neither.

"A moment ago, you asked me to put myself in Nelson's position. All right, now I ask you to put yourself in mine.

"I told you that Nelson is my senior, not my superior, and I meant it. I doubt if you will ever find two men more evenly matched in terms of talent. Now imagine the soul-shattering frustration of a person, with that level of talent, who has to do everything—and I mean everything—*despite* the system and not because of it. Imagine a life spent having to overcome an endless line of people like St. Vincent and Nelson. I am right—demonstrably right—repeatedly; yet, instead of receiving their support, I get their condemnation and contempt.

"How do you think you might be shaped by such a situation? Might you become bitter? Might you become cynical about your senior officers? Might you perhaps become what some people would call arrogant? Tell me, Troubridge. Tell me how you would react? What kind of man might you become?"

The silence on the quarterdeck was broken only by the screech of a seagull high overhead.

* * * * *

The oars of the small boat were softly creaking as Nelson looked around. There were at least a dozen other boats that he could see, all filled with officers and men from the ships in his squadron—all headed for the piers at the far end of the Bay of Naples.

The moon was half full, but it's light was intermittent as patches of low cloud cover moved across the sky obscuring it. When the moon was covered, Nelson found himself in a world gone black—black sky, black water, black mood. The choppiness of the waves, and his resultant seasickness, did nothing to help his disposition.

The whole scene put him in mind of another, similar, night. It was a year and a half earlier when he led the British forces in an amphibious invasion of the island of Tenerife. It was a fiasco from the very beginning. The Spanish general commanding the island's defense, Antonio Gutiérrez, anticipated Nelson's every move. When the 700 British troops got to shore they were cut to ribbons by everything from cannon fire to musketry issuing from rock formations and house windows. Included among the casualties was Nelson himself. A musket ball took away a large piece of his lower right arm, requiring that much of the rest of it be amputated. The stub of that arm was aching again, as if to remind him of that disastrous night.

But his mission this evening wasn't to attack an island. It was to rescue the royal family of the Kingdom of the Two Sicilies. Nelson rewrapped his boat-cloak more tightly around him, stared off at the lights of the city, and thought about his situation.

He had arrived in Naples in September as a conquering hero, and settled into court life. He quickly learned that the true power in the Kingdom was not the King, Ferdinand IV; it was his wife, Queen Maria Carolina. She, in turn, was strongly influenced by her close friend and confidant, Lady Emma Hamilton, the wife of the British envoy to Naples, Sir William Hamilton.

The Queen was the sister of Marie Antoinette of France, who had been guillotined during the Reign of Terror. Because of that, she had an undying hatred for the French Revolution and everything connected with it. Nelson's victory at the Nile, and his presence in Naples, gave her the license she needed to act on that hatred.

The Kingdom of the Two Sicilies consisted of the southern half of the Italian peninsula, plus the island of Sicily at the toe of the Italian "boot." The dividing line on the peninsula was just south of Rome, and Rome was under French control.

This was an intolerable situation to Maria Carolina; so, shortly after Nelson's arrival, she and Emma Hamilton decided that a blow should be struck against the French occupying forces in Italy. As Nelson's victory drove the French from the Mediterranean Sea, now was the perfect time to drive them from the Italian peninsula.

Nelson absolutely agreed with them, and could not understand Ferdinand's reluctance. He wrote St. Vincent, "War at this moment can alone save these kingdoms." And later, "This country by its system of procrastination will ruin itself.

The queen sees it, and thinks as we do...," the "we" being himself and Emma Hamilton.

Fortunately, help was on its way. A general, Karl von Mack, was dispatched by the Emperor of Austria to take over command of the Neapolitan army. When he arrived, however, he had bad news. The Austrian King was reluctant to commit his forces unless the French moved on either Austria or Naples first.

For King Ferdinand, that ended things. The idea was to get the French caught between two pincers—the Austrians attacking from the north, and the Neapolitans from the south. If the Austrians were out, the plan was dead.

It was not dead for Nelson, however.

He told the King that one of two things must happen. He had a choice. Attack and trust to God for his blessing on a just cause—or remain quiet and be kicked out of his kingdoms. Ferdinand folded, and ordered his army into action.

It was a disaster. On 29 November, they attacked Rome, and by early January, the Neapolitans were in full flight. General Mack surrendered himself to the French, for fear of being killed by his own troops.

Ferdinand was now in a panic. The French Army was only days away. The city's intelligentsia favored the French, but the majority of his subjects were perfectly willing to defend Naples to the death. Indeed, the previous day they had hung a suspected French spy before the Palazzo Reale to show their loyalty. That the man was a court messenger carrying a letter from the King to Nelson made no difference.

Ferdinand wanted out of Naples; but the question was how to do that. The logical option was to flee to his palace in Palermo, Sicily. In that Sicily is an island, and Nelson and his ships were at hand, he knew he would be safe there. So, several days previously, the royal treasury was quietly taken to the Palazzo Sessa, where Emma Hamilton arranged for it to be smuggled out to Nelson's ships. The only thing that remained was to get the royal family—and Emma—out of there.

"The royal family and Emma," Nelson thought. "Especially Emma." And his spirits revived.

His boat was approaching the Neapolitan Naval Arsenal basin. He was landed, but all the other boats were ordered to lie off the quays. He walked up the incline of Strada Toledo, past the arsenal, to the Piazza del Palazzo Reale. Off to his left the palace was completely lit-up, a sure sign that a party was in progress.

The occasion was a reception being held for the Turkish envoy; but that was just a cover. The idea was for Nelson, the Hamiltons, and the royal family to be seen at the party. They would spend several hours circulating, talking, dancing, and generally having a good time, as if they did not have a care in the world. Then they would separately drift away. And, that's exactly what they did.

Just before midnight, Nelson met Sir William and Emma Hamilton on the piazza at the southeastern corner of the palace. They cut around the back of two government buildings and arrived at the quay where Nelson's boat awaited them. As he helped Emma into the boat, he felt the extra squeeze she gave his hand and noted the concerned look on her face. She knew, as did Nelson, that the more dangerous part of the mission was now at hand.

He needed to get the royal family out, but it had to be done in secrecy. If anyone knew that the King and Queen were fleeing the city, they would be stopped; and once the word got out, there would be riots.

Nelson was joined by several heavily armed sailors, and ordered the Hamilton's boat to cast off. The group walked back to the Palazzo Reale; but instead of going through the front entranceway of the palace, they skirted along its side. Arriving at an obscure doorway, he was challenged by a courtier standing in the shadows. Passwords were exchanged and Nelson was allowed into the palace. He left his sailors at the doorway with drawn swords, and orders that they were to defend the door with their lives.

The courtier led Nelson into a cellar where a hidden door was opened that led to the vast network of secret passages that riddled the palace. Traversing several narrow, slippery, stone staircases, he soon found himself emerging into the apartments, where the royal family awaited.

The Queen immediately rushed over to him and, with tears in her eyes and gushing expressions of gratitude, embraced him. There was no time for that, however. He led the royal family, ten people in all, with no ladies-in-waiting or other attendants, down the staircases, out the hidden doorway, and back to the quay, where they were loaded into the waiting boats.

The boats got underway and passed through a screen of still more boats. These latter had carronades in their bows that were loaded and pointed toward shore to provide cover in case anything should go amiss.

Nothing did. All was quiet. There were no cries of alarm, no torchlit mobs, no cavalry racing to the waterfront.

At the same time, another naval operation was in progress.

A Neapolitan officer by the name of Francesco Caracciolo had arranged for a similar, but much more difficult, evacuation to occur at several locations along the Bay of Naples. Included in these groups were British citizens, French royalists, various members of the Neapolitan nobility, assorted ambassadors, and key members of the court. Some two thousand Royalists were spirited away under the guidance of Caracciolo.

When dawn broke, the people awoke to a bay that was unaccountably devoid of both British and Neapolitan ships. They were all well on their way to Palermo, and the people of Naples were left to face the French on their own.

* * * * *

The same bright half-moon was shining on another small boat operation that was being conducted some eleven hundred miles away.

John Wesley Wright adjusted his entari [1] and tightened the folds of his sarik [2] as he looked up at the night sky. He had hoped there would be more cloud cover; but things were what they were and he knew no amount of hoping would change them.

He lowered his lean frame into the boat to be rowed ashore where he would be inserted into Alexandria on the first of several planned intelligence gathering missions. Next to him was his interpreter. Wright spoke numerous languages fluently, but he was not confident of his Turkish. He could understand it well enough to get by, but he felt his pronunciation left much to be desired, so the interpreter was needed in case they got into a jam. Next to the interpreter was a special red lantern. It was constructed to give off a directional beam that they would use to signal the ship when they wanted to be picked up.

Sir Sidney Smith stood on the quarterdeck with his hands locked behind his back, watching as the muffled oars of the cutter began working and the boat slipped into a curtain of darkness. Soon Lucas Walker and Susan Whitney silently joined him in staring out over the choppy moonlit waves. They started talking about everything and nothing, as old friends will do—their discussion fueled by the beautiful Egyptian night and the countless stars overhead. After a while, the discussion turned to John Wesley Wright.

"He's quite a guy, isn't he?" Walker asked.

Smith laughed. "You don't know the half of it. In fact, I am not sure if *I* know the half of it; and he and I were in the same prison cell for two years."

"Tell me about him."

----

[1] A loose coat
[2] Turban

"John Wesley? He's an enigma, to be sure; but I can tell you this. I don't know that I've ever admired, or trusted, a man as completely as I do him." Smith caught himself. "Present company excepted, of course."

Sir Sidney, Lucas Walker, and Susan Whitney had been together since the Battle of the Chesapeake back in 1781, during the American War. Their friendship had been forged in countless scrapes where the only way they had of staying alive was by trusting in the courage, skill, and integrity of the other two. Walker and Whitney knew what he meant.

"I heard that he was originally born in Ireland," Walker prodded, to get the discussion restarted.

"Yes, indeed," Sidney replied. "In the south. Cork to be exact. His father was an army captain, the paymaster of the 6th Royal Veteran Battalion."

"So, he was destined to be an army officer?" Susan asked.

"Oh no, quite the reverse. Remember, his father was a paymaster—very little in the way of rushing around screaming 'charge.' No, John Wesley was destined to be a businessman. After he completed his schooling, he was packed off to Russia to learn everything he could about the Baltic trade."

"Russia? Why on earth was he sent there?

His father knew that the Royal Navy had a bottomless need for wood, canvas, and cordage to keep its fleet afloat. Add to that the public's need for food, furs, and other goods from that area, and he knew there were fortunes to be made. He wanted John Wesley to make one of them."

"So what happened?"

"Two things, really. First, it turned out that our friend is a bit of a freak."

"In what way?"

"You know how little kids seem to pick up languages so easily. It's effortless for them. Then somewhere along the way they lose that acquisition ability and, as adults, have a terrible time learning new languages. Well, John Wesley never lost it. I think he can master a language in less time than it would take us to learn how to ask directions to the nearest privy."

"How many languages does he speak?"

"All of them, near as I can tell," Sidney replied. "I know he can read, write and speak French, Spanish, Gaelic, German, Russian, Dutch, and Swedish flawlessly; and I've heard him converse briefly in a couple of other languages that I couldn't even identify.

"Take tonight, for instance. He's going ashore on an intelligence mission, but he insisted on taking an interpreter with him. Why? Because he's convinced that he still has a slight accent to his Turkish pronunciation. A slight accent, mind you. I mean, to me the whole language sounds like someone clearing their throat of phlegm; but he perceives a slight accent."

"You said there were two reasons. What's the second?" Walker asked.

"The second isn't a reason; it's a person. William Wickham. Lucas, I know you've met him; but Susan, you haven't.

"Back when John Wesley was in Russia, Wickham was the assistant to our Ambassador to Switzerland. That's how he met Wright... on a diplomatic trip to Russia.

"But it seems that the good Mr. Wickham is something more than a mere Assistant Ambassador. He also runs all of our spy networks in Europe, but he does it in a rather unusual way. Instead of just shoveling cash and bribe money in all directions, he recruits and trains selected people to be what he calls 'operatives.' These are very talented, very intelligent, and very skilled young men, who have a flair for adventure, and the personal discipline and sheer guts to be a spy."

"Is that what people are referring to when they... well, I've heard people say that Britain is developing something they're calling the 'Secret Service.' Is that Wickham?"

"It is indeed.

"Anyway, John Wesley Wright met all of those requirements, plus he had this additional capacity for languages, so Wickham recruited and trained him.

"I first met him the same time you did—back when we were all on the old *Diamond*."

"Well, that brings to mind something I've been meaning to ask you for years," Susan said. "Back at Le Havre, when you decided to cut out the *Vengeur*... what in the world were you and Wright doing going in at all? Royal Navy captains—in your case the commanding officer of a frigate—do not go gallivanting off on cutting-out expeditions. They send lieutenants and midshipmen for that kind of thing."

"Wright was disguised as a midshipman," Sidney lamely replied.

"You're avoiding the question."

"I know. That's because I can't tell you."

Susan opened her mouth to reply, but then realized the significance of what Sidney had just said. She stopped to consider her words, then continued.

"Sidney, when you and Wright, and this one over here," she said, gesturing toward Walker, "...when you three were captured at Le Havre, the French held you for over two years. They said you were a spy, and thus did not qualify for exchange like an ordinary prisoner.

"So, was that true? Did you go into Le Havre harbor that night to cut out the *Vengeur,* or were you on a spying mission?"

Smith didn't say a word. He just shrugged his shoulders with a slightly sheepish look on his face.

Susan was about to press him further when a voice called down from the maintop. "On deck, thar."

"Deck aye!" Smith replied, glad to be free of the conversation.

"Capt'n, thar's a light comin' from shore... seems ter be a signal'a some sort."

"What color is it and what's it doing?"

"It's red, sor. It seems ter flash three times, then pause, then flash three more times, an' on like that."

Smith immediately grew concerned. "That's Wright!" He said, and started calling for the boat crew. He dispatched them with Midshipman Janverin and orders to get to the pickup site fast. Then he returned to the quarterdeck where he started pacing.

"Sidney, what's wrong?" Walker asked.

"That's the signal for a pickup. The problem is, he wasn't scheduled to give it until just before dawn. Something must have gone wrong. Terribly wrong. Wright would never break off a mission for any reason less than that."

Walker glanced over at Susan Whitney and started to speak. "I know," she said with a sigh. "I'll go get the surgery ready." She grabbed a passing midshipman, told him to rouse out the loblolly boys—the nursing assistants—and continued to the orlop deck. There she would pull together the operating table, adjust the lights, lay out the instruments, and do the hundred other things that were necessary to greet the horrific realities of war.

Smith and Walker said nothing, as they stood with their eyes boring into the darkness. The Egyptian night was no longer a gentle friend. It was a malicious impenetrable black cloak that was keeping them from seeing what was happening. The cutter finally appeared and pulled up to the starboard side where Wright scrambled up the steps that had been built into the hull.

Emerging at the foot of the quarterdeck, he whipped off his turban, climbed the quarterdeck ladder, looked for Sir Sidney, and rushed over.

"Sidney, Bonaparte's on the move."

A bit of color drained from Sidney Smith's face. He knew Bonaparte would have to do something, sometime; but he hadn't expected it to occur so soon.

"When did it happen? Where's he going?"

"Just a few days ago.

"You know he had taken El-Arish on the 20th. On February 24th or 25th—I get conflicting reports—he surrounded Gaza, and they gave up without a fight. On March 3rd he arrived at Jaffa, and had it conquered by the 7th. I understand it was a rather messy affair. The latest report was that they were packing up, preparing to move again."

"And this is reliable information?" Smith asked.

Wright simply said, "Yes." And gave no elaboration as to how he knew it was reliable.

Sidney Smith thought for a moment, looking out into the darkness, then said to Lieutenant Canes, his first officer, "Mr. Canes, I desire you to take Mr. Wright's boat over to the *Theseus*. Give Captain Miller my compliments, and inform him that I wish to speak with him immediately."

"But Captain, it's past midnight."

Smith glanced at his coveted French pocket watch, "Yes, 12:08 to be exact. Now *go!*"

Turning to Walker, "Lucas, be so good as to locate Picard Phélippeaux and have him report to me in my cabin. Then you can disassemble your little house of horrors on the orlop. You'll have no business tonight; but I make no promises for the coming weeks. Mr. Wright, you're with me."

Within the hour, four men were hunched over a spread-out map of Syria and the Levant. John Wesley Wright, still dressed in his Turkish garb, was completing his presentation.

"Thus, there's no doubt in my mind," Wright concluded, "that he's headed for Acre. If he takes that city, I see nothing between Acre and Constantinople that can even slow him down. He must be stopped; and he must be stopped there!"

"How's that to be done?" Captain Ralph Miller asked. "Where could we possibly get the troops to do it?"

"What about the army that the Sultan was going to send down the coast?" Phélippeaux asked.

"No good." Wright replied.

"Why?"

"Bonaparte took El-Arish, Gaza and Jaffa."

"So?"

"That *was* the Sultan's army."

Miller continued, "Well, we can always send the *Marianne* for help. She's a nimble little sloop, and very fast. Send her to St. Vincent in Gibraltar or even Nelson in Naples. Just tell them Bonaparte's on the move, and we need troops and more ships. I am sure they'll send help."

Smith thought about it for a moment, as if weighing the probability of that happening, and then came to a decision.

"Perhaps we'll do that," he said, "but first we have to get to Acre to see exactly what the situation is there. Therefore, tomorrow morning at first light, John Wesley, I want you to go aboard the *Marianne* and head for Acre. You'll get there first. Make contact with the Pasha. Tell him Bonaparte is coming, if he doesn't already know it, and so are we. Tell him we plan to make a stand at Acre.

"Picard, I want you to go aboard the *Theseus*. Ralph, tomorrow morning, also at first light, I want you to go to Acre as well. Picard, you're a military engineer. I want you to examine the city and tell me if it's defensible.

"I'll spend tomorrow with the *Tigre* lobbing shells into Alexandria right on schedule. Then tomorrow night, we'll quietly depart. When I get there I'll want reports from all of you."

After everyone had left, Sidney Smith dowsed the candles and walked to the gallery windows along the back wall of his cabin. He opened several to admit a breeze into the now stuffy room. The breeze was spiked with the tang of salt air, but the night seemed gentle again.

* * * * *

Dr. Dominique-Jean Larrey pulled the sheet over the still warm corpse and slumped back in the hard wooden chair. He had lost track of the number of men on which he had performed that ritual. Dozens? Hundreds? Even though he was the chief surgeon of the *l'armee d'Orient*, he was completely helpless in treating the plague.

He looked down and saw a flea emerging from under the dead man's sheet. As he flicked it away, he wondered for the thousandth time: What could be causing this illness? How is it transmitted? What can I do about it? Damn it! What can I *do*?!

His thoughts were interrupted by one of the junior physicians. "Dr. Larrey, there is a Général here to see you." He followed the young man out of the makeshift hospital building and blinked rapidly as his eyes adjusted to the bright Syrian sun.

"Dr. Larrey, may I introduce you to l'adjudant-Général Grézieux."

Larrey was still trying to get his eyes accustomed to the light as he held out his hand to the uniformed figure in front of him. "Good day, Général."

"Good God, doctor!" he said sternly. "What are you about?"

Larrey's eyes had cleared; but now he was wondering if his ears were working.

"What am I about? I am not quite sure..."

"You, sir, might have the plague. People who might have the plague do not touch other people—not here, nor anywhere in the civilized world!"

Larrey was momentarily speechless; but he was rescued from his confusion by a another voice coming from his left— the voice of General Bonaparte.

"Grézieux, if you're that worried about the plague, you will surely die from it." He then turned to Larrey. "Good afternoon, doctor. I see you've met my advance party." He cast a disdainful glance over at Grézieux.

"I've come to visit my sick men; and I'd like you to show me around."

For the second time in as many minutes, Larrey doubted his hearing.

"Are you sure you want to do that, sir? I rather doubt that the plague is transmitted by proximity; but, on the other hand, no one really knows how it *is* transmitted."

"You keep referring to it as the plague, doctor; but I have it on good authority that it is *not* the plague. Rather, it's simply a fever that has buboes associated with it."

Bonaparte delivered those last sentences in a noticeably louder voice, as if he wanted the others around him to hear. Larrey was on guard.

"May I ask who made that diagnosis, Général?"

"None other than your superior, Dr. Desgenettes, the physician-in-chief of the army. Now, if you would be so good..."

There was nothing to do but comply, even though he had no idea what was going on.

They entered the hospital, once the home of a wealthy merchant, and walked along corridors, into rooms, along patios, and through the great hall. Bonaparte stopped to talk with those few men who were conscious, even shaking hands with one of them. He rapidly passed by those beds containing forms that were completely covered with sheets.

At the conclusion of the tour, he thanked the doctor and returned to his headquarters. By nightfall, the French camp was abuzz with talk:

"Did you hear? It's not really the plague."

"The Général himself went to the hospital, and even shook hands with some..."

"Yes, he shook hands with every one of them."

"...shook hands with every man, and even kissed one on the cheek for his heroism. If it was the plague, you think he would'a done that?"

By exposing himself to the sick, Bonaparte removed the terror of the disease from the soldiers—and even from some of the patients. It was important that they not think about the plague or any other sickness, for the following day they would be marching to Acre.

Chapter Three

Jezzar Pasha was in a hurry; and if he was in a hurry, everyone was in a hurry. He didn't know when Bonaparte and his army would be arriving. He only knew he didn't want to be in Acre when it happened.

His formal name was Ahmed al-Jezzar. Ahmed was his given name; al-Jezzar meant "The Butcher." He earned the nickname when he was a young captain under Ali Bey for his treatment of those enemies who were unfortunate enough to fall into his hands. He liked it so much that he incorporated it into his formal name.

It was a well-earned epithet, as nothing delighted him more than to see body parts flying off of living humans. When he deposed and murdered his predecessor and best friend, Dahr al-Omar, he decided to take vengeance on those who had supported al-Omar. Noses and ears were cut off, eyes were gouged out, and some even had their feet shod with horseshoes and were made to walk around town. Earlier, when he was governor of Beirut, he decided to rebuild the city's walls. While doing so, he had a number of Greek Orthodox Christians built into the wall alive, with just their heads exposed, so he could enjoy their torments and pleadings as they slowly died over many days.

At the same time, he was no fool. He could be brave as a lion—if it was virtually assured he would win; but nothing terrified him more than fighting if there was even a remote chance that he might lose. That was why, today, he was running.

"You idiot! I did not tell you to pack that!" Jezzar Pasha screamed at the man, who was now trembling uncontrollably. He knew that potentially he was only seconds away from death.

"I said the valuables must go first. Is the treasury packed? No! Are my personal valuables packed? No! And yet you run around here like a fool packing clothing." Jezzar Pasha was about to give a command to his guards to take the man away. This could quite possibly mean his death, and the man knew it. But before Jezzar could give the order, a voice sounded from the door.

"Your highness, I beg leave for this unworthy servant to enter your presence."

Jezzar turned to the doorway. "Yes Farhi," he said with disgust in his voice, "get your misbegotten face over here. What is it? Can't you see I am busy?"

From the doorway, a bent man shuffled over to Jezzar Pasha as quickly as he could, folded his hand across his chest, and bowed with the deepest humility. He was Haim Farhi, Jezzar's chief advisor. When Jezzar referred to his "misbegotten face" he was not exaggerating. Farhi was blind in one eye and was missing the tip of his nose, along with his left ear. All three items were removed several years earlier, on a whim, by Jezzar Pasha.

"What is it, you fool?"

"Sire, there is a British naval officer here to see you."

There were dozens of things Jezzar Pasha might have expected to come from the lips of Farhi, but this was not one of them.

"A British naval officer? Here? In Acre?"

"Yes, sire. If you would be pleased to go to the window you will see a British ship in the harbor."

Jezzar walked over to an opening in the thick stone wall of his palace. He shielded his eyes from the sunlight glaring off the water, looked for a moment, and said, "A ship? You call that a ship?"

"It is but a messenger ship, your highness, carrying this envoy."

"I will see him. Meanwhile, all of you—out! Out! And take that trash with you." He kicked over a neatly folded pile of exquisite clothing. "Farhi, you stay."

Within a few minutes, the room had been cleared of both people and disorder. Jezzar Pasha was sitting on a large, thick cushion that was embroidered with gold thread in an array of intricate designs. He had on a white turban with a large ruby in the center, and a robe; both were made of the finest silk. The robe was bright red, with gold tigers in various aggressive postures. Around the robe was a white sash, and stuck into the sash was a ferocious looking scimitar with a gold and jewel encrusted hilt. He was looking as regal and as warlike as an overweight 60 year old potentate could look.

John Wesley Wright walked through the entranceway in a full-dress lieutenant's uniform, with a bicorne hat tucked neatly under his arm. He strode up to where Jezzar Pasha was seated and executed a minimally polite half-bow, the kind of thing that would be offered by one person to another of equal rank. Haim Farhi was astonished. Jezzar Pasha was speechless, but soon recovered.

"I am surprised to see a British officer at my court," he said through clenched teeth, "and even more surprised at the casualness with which you approach me. Farhi, translate that."

"There is no need, my Lord. I understand you quite well," Wright replied in only slightly accented Turkish.

Jezzar shot back. "If you speak our language, you must understand something of our customs. Do you understand the insult you have offered with your bow? Is there some reason why I should not, this minute, cut off your ears and sentence you to live the rest of your life as a galley slave?"

"If you would similarly cut off the ears of King George III of England, and His Highness Sultan Selim III, then you may do so, sire. I await your pleasure." Wright said it with such confidence that Jezzar Pasha was taken aback.

Jezzar studied Wright for a moment. He could deal with references to this King George person; but invoking the name of the Sultan was another matter entirely. He knew he must be careful. Very careful.

Haim Farhi knew it too, and decided it was time to defuse the situation. "Captain... er..."

"I am not a captain. I am Lieutenant John Wesley Wright."

"Yes, Lieutenant Wright, may I welcome you to the court of his highness Ahmed al-Jezzar, Pasha of Palestine, Valdi of Sidon and Damascus, Protector of Acre, and Sultan Selim III's most humble servant in the Levant. I have no doubt that you must be tired from your strenuous journey. I beg of you, please be seated and let us offer you some refreshments."

"The hospitality of his highness is legendary. Thank you." Then, without invitation, Wright strode across the priceless rug that lay before al-Jezzar, to the cushion on Jezzar Pasha's right, the seat of honor, and sat down as if it was his natural place. Farhi suppressed a gasp; but Jezzar grew even more worried. This *farangi* was either completely mad, or a person of extreme importance. Until he knew which it was, he would have to treat him with respect.

Farhi fluttered his hand and three servants appeared with silver trays. One tray was filled with börek, a delicate layered pastry, filled with feta cheese. The second tray contained three small demitasse coffee cups and three glasses of cold water. The third servant carried a copper pot with a spout and a long wooden handle. Both Farhi and Jezzar Pasha were curious as to whether the *farangi* knew how to drink Turkish coffee properly.

Wright first accepted the glass of cold water and took a long sip. This was to freshen his mouth so that he might better taste the coffee. He then took the tiny demitasse cup and held it with his fingertips, as the next servant poured. The cup had no handle and the coffee was extremely hot, so this was the only way the cup could be held without burning your hand and dropping it. When all had received their coffee, the tray of pastries was placed on an ivory-inlayed mahogany table between them, and the servants departed.

Over the next hour, everything except the business at hand was discussed. The plate of pastry was eventually replaced with a hookah, with which the men enjoyed a leisurely smoke. Finally, Wright began the discussion.

"Sire, I am here on behalf of Commodore Sir Sidney Smith; and I speak for him. Commodore Smith, in turn speaks for His Majesty King George III, and His Majesty Sultan Selim III. I have urgent issues I wish to discuss with you on behalf of Commodore Smith—and both rulers."

"You may speak."

"I believe this conversation would best be conducted in private," Wright said, glancing over at Farhi.

"That miserable worm before you is what passes for my chief advisor. You may speak freely."

"As you wish.

"I am sure your highness is aware that French forces, under the command of a General Napoleon Bonaparte, have invaded your territory, and are, even as we speak, headed here to Acre."

"Yes, and if he shows up he will be crushed. His army will be destroyed to the last man. Their bones will bleach in the sun for..."

"If he shows up," Wright interrupted, "Acre will not last three days."

Jezzar Pasha fell silent. He knew the man was right; that's why he was packing.

"Nevertheless, I have come to offer you a way to save your city and your pashalic."

"And how might you do that? Will you call upon your Christian God to send down a host of armed angels?" Jezzar said, his voice dripping with sarcasm.

"Yes, something like that.

"Tomorrow an 80-gun British ship of the line will be arriving. In two or three days, a second 80-gun ship will arrive. On board the first vessel will be Colonel Picard Phélippeaux. He is one of the world's finest military engineers. On board the second will be Commodore Sir Sidney Smith, who I personally believe is Britain's finest Admiral.

"Both ships will be filled with guns, shot, powder, and sailors who are expert in the use of all three. In addition, both ships will have contingents of marines, who are experts in land warfare.

"We mean to stop this General Bonaparte here at Acre."

Jezzar thought about this turn of events for a moment. "And what do you want from me?"

"We want your cooperation. First, when Colonel Phélippeaux gets here, we want you to allow him free access to all parts of your city and its defenses. We want him to make an assessment as to what needs to be done to strengthen Acre; and we want you to give us whatever assistance is needed to make those necessary repairs.

"Second, we want you to place the defense of the city in the hands of Commodore Smith—that includes command of all your troops and other assets. You will be nominally in charge, of course, and you will get all the credit for the victory; but Commodore Smith must be allowed to use your troops in whatever manner he sees fit."

"I will get credit for the victory? And what if you lose?"

"We will not lose."

"Lieutenant, do not make me repeat myself. It is tiresome. What if you lose!"

"We will have command of the seaward approaches to Acre at all times. There are simply no significant French ships in this end of the Mediterranean that can challenge us. If things should go badly, we can evacuate you by sea."

"And why should I not simply 'evacuate' myself right now?"

"That would not be wise."

"Because?"

"Sire, the Sultan put you in charge of his territories in the Levant. You are charged with administering those territories, collecting taxes, and *defending* them." Wright placed special emphasis on the word "defending."

"You speak of removing yourself from this situation? Pray, sire, tell me where you would go? No, let me rephrase that. Tell me where you *could* go, where the Sultan could not locate you?

"No matter what place you pick, sooner or later a *hashshashin* will find you. You will be in your bed one night, asleep, thinking you are safe, and suddenly you will feel a knife at your neck. Within a few seconds you will be suffocating on your own blood as you try to breathe through a cut throat."

Jezzar Pasha was lost in thought. The fingers on his hands were intertwined on his belly as he rocked back and forth on his cushion. After the better part of a minute, he looked at Haim Farhi, then at Wright, and quietly said:

"*Öyle olsun.*" Let it be so.

* * * * *

Bonaparte stood on a small rise, and looked back at his army trailing off into the distance. *It's like a colossal multicolored snake*, he thought, *slithering along the coastal wastelands of Syria.* Escorting the snake were small groups of brown ants—Murat's cavalry—dashing here and there, off to the side.

The weather had been beautiful during the five-day, 60 mile, march from Jaffa. Temperatures were around 70 degrees during the day and 50 degrees at night. However, what surprised him the most were the wildflowers. They seemed to be everywhere, springing up in their annual defiance of the hot summer months that were to come.

There was something very odd about the tranquility of the scene before him. Here were France's finest troops, the elite of the *l'armée d'Orient*, an entity that had no real purpose other than to pillage, kill and conquer. Yet, here also was this same army moving along like it was part of a slow-moving but stately ballet. He had trouble holding both concepts in his head at the same time.

He turned and looked off to the north, the direction in which they were headed, and marveled at the dignity of the long, low, range of hills known as Mount Carmel. This was the place where Elijah built an altar to Yahweh, and challenged 450 prophets of Baal to see whose God was greater. Following Yahweh's victory, Elijah had the prophets slaughtered at a brook called Kishon, a brook they would soon be crossing on their way to Acre.

Bonaparte was not an adherent of any particular religion. That allowed him to be whatever he needed to be at the moment. Christian, Muslim—it made no difference to him, and he understood none of it. However, Mount Carmel was filled with history, and history was something he understood and appreciated.

He knew he would not be afforded the luxury of reverie for long, however. In the near distance, three riders were racing his way from the direction of Mount Carmel where he had sent a scouting party. This brought him back to the present with a jolt. He sighed once, and then mounted his horse to meet the riders.

"Général, we have just been around to the other side of

Mount Carmel," the young lieutenant said breathlessly.

"And..."

"And there are British warships in the harbor before Acre!"

Bonaparte just looked at the man, speechless.

"Two of them, sir. They look to be 70- or 80-guns each."

Bonaparte continued to stare; then suddenly spurred his horse in the direction of the hills.

It was five miles to a convent at the foot of Mount Carmel, and just beyond that was a little spit of land that jutted into the Mediterranean. From there the entire bay could be seen, and to there Bonaparte was now racing—his staff and orderlies strung out behind him like the tail of a comet.

Upon arriving at Cape Carmel, he brought his horse to a halt, and took in a sight he never expected to see. There, firmly anchored in the placid waters of the Bay of Acre, were the *HMS Tigre* and *HMS Theseus*. Swarms of small boats were going back and forth from ship to ship, and between the ships and the land. He could see cannon being hoisted up the sheer walls of the city and swung into place. He could see fortifications being built, and a long narrow moat being restored. Everywhere there was activity.

His staff soon caught-up with him and were as shocked to see the British as he was. After several long moments of silence his stepson, Lieutenant Beauharnais, ventured, "It is but two ships, sir. We can handle them."

Bonaparte slowly turned and looked at him like he had just spoken in Swahili. Then in a low, quiet, menacing voice he said, "Be... silent. You understand nothing about what you're seeing.

"Murat! Where's Murat?"

"Here, sir," he answered, nudging his horse over toward Bonaparte.

"Pick three of your best men—I want the fastest riders, on your fastest horses. Send them down the coast to find our

63

support ships, and head them off! I don't care how they do it, but they *have* to stop them. They have our siege train on board—artillery, cannon, powder, shot, and battering rams—everything! If they try to come here, those damned British ships will snatch them up. Tell the ships to go back to Jaffa and we'll bring the materials overland. Now, go!"

Riders were dispatched, and they found the French flotilla. The three riders stood on shore waving and screaming at the top of their lungs for the ships to stop. The men on the ships waved back—and remarked at how friendly the army had suddenly become.

* * * * *

There is no way of knowing who was more shocked—the lookouts on the *La Foudre,* or those on the *Tigre*—when the *La Foudre* rounded Cape Carmel and saw the *Tigre* anchored in the middle of the bay. Earlier that morning the *Theseus* had been sent on a reconnaissance mission, leaving only the *Tigre* before the walls of Acre; but the *Tigre* was all that was needed.

The crews of both ships sprang into action immediately. The *Tigre* tied a buoy to their anchor line, released it into the water, and set all sail. The *La Foudre* spun on her heals and headed out to sea, while frantically signaling the other ships in her flotilla. Her sister ships broke and ran, but there was very little they could do.

The flotilla was headed north, with a "soldier's wind" behind them. They couldn't go east, that was where the landmass was. They couldn't continue heading north, that's where the *Tigre* was; and they couldn't head south, because they would be sailing directly into the wind. The only thing they could do was head west. They knew it, and so did the much faster *Tigre.*

There really wasn't much to it. The *Tigre* would come up on the slowest, or the unluckiest, of the French ships and fire a single shot, just to demonstrate that they were in range. The Frenchmen would fire a single shot in reply, for honor's sake, then surrender. The *Tigre* would quickly transfer an officer and a handful of men to take charge of the prize, then head off for the next ship.

All the French vessels were between four and eight guns. The *Tigre* was 80 guns. Resistance would have been insane, and the *Tigre* just rolled them up.

The first ships to fall were the smallest ones: *La Marie Rose* (4-guns, 22 men) *La Dame de Grace* (4-guns, 35 men) and *Les Deux Freres* (4-guns, 23 men). Next came *La Dangereuse* (6-guns, 23 men) and *La Negresse* (6-guns, 53 men). And finally, after a bit of an extended chase, *La Foudre* (8-guns, 52 men). By 8 o'clock in the evening, Smith had them all, except for a small corvette and two even smaller gunboats which had escaped in all the confusion.

In one three hour period, he had added six ships and 32 badly needed guns to the naval side of the coming fight; but what was more important—he had Bonaparte's siege guns! These were huge cannon that, given enough time, could punch holes in the thickest walls—holes big enough to drive an army through. Smith not only had Bonaparte's guns, he had his shot, and powder, and all the miscellaneous supplies that go with them.

It was a very satisfying day.

* * * * *

In Naples, the night was not hot at all, in fact, it was quite pleasant outside; but the temperature inside the room had soared because of the number of people who had gathered in it. Little thought was given to discomfort, however, as Lady Emma Hamilton was about to strike another of her famous "attitudes," and the crowd was entranced.

Emma was standing in Sir William's Etruscan Gallery, a room of antiquities her husband had unearthed and summarily appropriated over the years. She stood alone amid the graceful columns, broken statues, and sarcophagi, looking like she had just stepped off of the side of one of her husband's numerous antique vases.

She wore nothing but a simple white peasant-style garment—simple, loose fitting yet somehow vaguely erotic. Her long hair flowed freely down her back; and her bare arms, tanned to a golden brown by the Mediterranean sun, were accentuated by the elegant gold bands that she wore on each arm. Her only props were a couple of shawls and an occasional Greek urn.

With nothing more than this, she would move from one silent tableau to another, changing posture, position, and gesture, leaving the viewer to guess which character she was creating. Was it Daphne's Flight from Apollo? Or, the Tragedy of Deianira? Or the Death of Cleopatra? One scene seamlessly flowed into another like a slow-motion kaleidoscope. One moment she would be standing, then kneeling, then seated, then reclining. Her expressions would move from happy, to sad, to teasing, to penitent, to alluring, to threatening, to fearful. Each pose seemed to grow naturally out of the one before it, and the effect was hypnotic.

Her repertoire finally ended. The last pose—Britannia Welcomes Her Conquering Hero Home—was held an especially long time as she made direct, almost passionate, eye contact with Horatio Nelson. This was an allowable gesture, however, as this was yet another of a seemingly endless parade of parties honoring Nelson; but he could read her eyes, and they were both clear on the message.

Emma eventually dropped out of character to the thunderous applause of the party-goers. After absorbing due credit, she quieted the crowd.

"My friends, thank you for that wonderful gesture of applause; but we are not here tonight to honor *me*. No indeed, we are here to honor the greatest of Britannia's sons—Admiral Horatio Nelson."

This reignited the crowd. Nelson gave his best boyish smile and briefly waved in acknowledgement.

"So, please, allow me the honor of finishing this evening with a slight variation of a song that I know you all know."

Emma composed herself for a moment, turned to Nelson, and began singing in an astonishingly beautiful voice:

> See the conquering Hero comes!
>   Sound the trumpets, beat the drums,
> Spoils prepared, the Laurel bring,
>   Songs of Triumph to him sing.
>
> See our gallant Nelson comes,
>   Sound the trumpets, beat the drums,
> Spoils prepared, the Laurel bring,
>   Songs of Triumph, Emma, sing!
> Myrtle-wreath and roses twine
>   To deck the Hero's brow divine!

The crowd erupted again. It was the perfect ending to a perfect spring evening.

As the crowd broke up into smaller groups, Nelson received his well-wishers in an appropriately modest fashion, yet noticed a movement near the main entrance to the room. A young man in the green coat and gold trim of a Neapolitan officer entered the room, looked frantically about for the King, and quickly moved to him. Sir William Hamilton also saw him enter, and edged over to eavesdrop on whatever the news might be. After a moment, the King turned and said something to Sir William, who signaled to Nelson with his eyes to meet him out on the balcony.

"There is news from Cardinal Ruffo. The King wants to meet with you and me in the library in 20 minutes."

Nelson went back to the party and flitted from one group to another. He wanted to remain socially mobile so that if he were to disappear in a few minutes, no one would particularly notice. While making his rounds, however, he was wracking his brain to remember everything he could about Cardinal Ruffo.

Fabrizio Ruffo was a nobleman's son, but was largely raised by his uncle, Tommaso Cardinal Ruffo, who was then dean of the College of Cardinals. Through his uncle's influence he became involved in Vatican affairs, eventually becoming treasurer-general. He served in that post for many years until, in 1791, his political enemies forced him out of office. As a consolation, Pope Pius VI made him a cardinal, even though he was not in orders and had never even been a priest.

When the royal family fled Naples, Ruffo came with them. A month or so later, he proposed that he be sent back to his home province of Calabria, where his family still had estates, to "...with God's help, raise an army to scourge the French out of Naples." His only qualification as a military leader was that the Vatican Ministry of War had once been under his control when he was treasurer-general; but, if that's what he wanted to do, the King had no objection. No one actually expected him to succeed.

Try as he might, Nelson could not imagine what possible news there could be from Ruffo that would cause an emergency meeting to be held.

The answer was not long in coming. As he and Sir William entered the enormous book-lined palace library, he saw the King seated behind a large, highly polished oak table. Standing next to him was the officer Nelson had seen speaking with the King earlier.

"Sir William... Admiral... thank you for coming," the King began. "There is some news from our friend Cardinal Ruffo. It seems he's about to retake Naples."

Nelson and Sir William could not have been more astonished if the King had said that the Cardinal had flapped his arms, flown across the Strait of Messina, and was on his way over for tea.

"But perhaps I should let the captain fill you in on the details."

"Thank you, your highness.

"As I am sure you are both aware, the cardinal was recently sent to Calabria to organize a counter-revolution against the French. On February 8th he landed at La Cortona and began raising what he called the *Armate della Santa Fede*—the Army of Holy Faith in our Lord Jesus Christ.

"This was the document he had posted on every church door in the province."

The captain slid a printed piece of paper across the table, which Sir William picked up and translated for Nelson's benefit:

> Brave and courageous Calabrians, unite now under the standard of the Holy Cross and of our beloved sovereign. Do not wait for the enemy to come and contaminate our home neighborhoods. Let us march to confront him, to repel him, to hunt him out of our kingdom and out of Italy and to break the barbarous chains of our holy Pontiff. May the banner of the Holy Cross secure you total victory.

"Are you saying that thing worked? He got a bunch of farmers to fight against a professional, well-disciplined French army?" Nelson asked.

"Within a month he had recruited 17,000 men."

"Seventeen thou..." Sir William involuntarily blurted in astonishment.

"Yes, sir. 17,000 men. They call themselves the Sanfedisti. To be sure, they're a mixed bag of bandits, untrained ecclesiastics, impoverished mercenaries, thieves and murderers; and they spend as much time plundering and raping as they do fighting the French. But they're now approaching Naples, and they just might take it."

Sir William was still trying to grasp the situation, let alone it's implications. He asked, "You're saying Ruffo moved an army from Calabria, in the toe of Italy, all the way to

Naples—defeating the French along the way—and this is the first you've heard of it?"

The captain began to look more than a little uncomfortable. "No, sir. We've had other reports from him, asking for weapons, naval support, announcing various supposed victories, that sort of thing."

"And..."

"And we didn't take the reports seriously."

Sir William looked shocked. The King looked disgusted. But Nelson knew there would be time for repercussions later, and he cut to the heart of the matter.

"Where are they now, and what do they need?"

"They are setting up a siege around Naples. The cardinal is requesting gunfire support from the seaward side."

Nelson looked briefly over at Sir William, then at the king. He thought for a moment, nodded his head, and walked out of the room.

* * * * *

Acre was a city that had been crumbling for centuries. The walls, once proud and strong, had grown old and tired in the service of everyone from ancient Canaanites and Greeks, to Christian Crusaders and Muslim Mujahideen. Even worse, the same thing could be said of the people.

It had been inhabited for longer than humans had been keeping records. The Egyptians called it Aak, and later Akka. The *Bible* refers to it as Akko. The Greeks called it Ake, and later Ptolemais.

Acre was one of the few places from which the Israelites could not drive out the Canaanites. Alexander the Great had a small palace there, Herod built a spa, and St. Paul visited it on at least one occasion.

Then a period of warfare began that lasted for over 500 years.

With the rise of Roman Christianity, it became a Christian city. In 638, it was conquered by the Muslims. In 1104, it was retaken by the Christians. In 1187, it was re-retaken by the Muslims under Saladin; and soon re-re-retaken by the Christians under Richard I of England—Richard the Lionhearted. It was at that point that it was named Saint-Jean d'Acre, or simply Acre.

In 1517, the Ottomans under Sultan Selim I captured the city, and it began a long process of decay. After this, as one historian put it, "...a mournful and solitary silence prevailed along the coast which had so long resounded with the world's debate." By 1700 it had degenerated into a ruin, consisting of nothing but a caravansary, a mosque, and a few hovels.

In the mid-18th century, however, efforts were made to rebuild it. Much of this was done by Daher el-Omar, the Arab-Bedouin ruler of the Galilee district. But, to Smith's surprise, much of that work had been continued by Ahmed al-Jezzar—Ahmed the Butcher—the current occupant of the throne.

Acre sat on a peninsula at the top of a fishhook shaped bay that ran, approximately, north and south. At the opposite end, at the barb of the fishhook some 15 miles away, was the newly rebuilt city of Haifa.

At first glance, the city seemed impregnable. The Acre peninsula extended in a northeast-southwest direction, and was surrounded on three sides by water. A thick crenellated wall, over a mile in circumference, ran all the way around the city, including on the seaward sides. On the land side, the wall was fronted by a deep dry-moat.

Roughly mid way along the northern wall, al-Jezzar's palace rose amid the narrow winding streets, and towered over the surrounding low dilapidated rooftops. To the east of this was an extensive garden, highlighted by fountains and tall dark-green cypress trees. To the west was the Burj el Hazana, the treasury tower, and to the west of that was the Citadel, where al-Jezzar both housed his troops and imprisoned his enemies.

To the south, however, was Jezzar's pride and joy, the Masjid al-Anwar—the great mosque of lights. He had started work on it 18 years earlier, and had it completed in less than a year. It was also known as the white mosque because its silvery-white dome and thin minaret could be seen glittering for miles around.

Smith was found where he normally was in the heat of the noonday sun. Rather than retire to some shady spot within the city, he would climb to the Burj el Commander—the Commander's Tower—at the far northeast corner of the city walls. There in the shade of the tower roof he would savor the breezes coming in off the Mediterranean, look out at Bonaparte's troops—and think.

Smith's reveries, however, were ended by the sound of footsteps coming up the circular stairwell leading to the top of the tower. Lucas Walker soon appeared around the corner.

"A runner said you wanted to see me." Walker gasped.

Smith looked at his wheezing friend, and smiled. "You know you really should see a doctor about your physical conditioning."

Walker was now leaning over the tower wall, breathing heavily. "I AM the doctor, Sidney. The only one within 500 miles, not counting Jean Larrey and his friends across the way."

"Well, then, if your heart and lungs can bear the strain, could you brief me on how we stand regarding the medical side of things."

Walker paused for a moment to collect himself. "If Bonaparte can find it in his heart to not attack us for the next few days, I think we'll be in reasonably good shape.

"I am assuming the action will all be on the land side of the city. That simplifies matters a bit. I've put aid stations at the foot of each of the major towers along the wall—Burj Kapu, Burj Nebi Zalah, this tower, Burj Mahmat, and so forth. Casualties from the wall will be taken to the closest aid station. There they'll undergo the triage process I learned from Larrey. Those for whom there is no hope will be treated with laudanum to kill the pain and left to die. Those whose injuries are minor will be treated on the spot. Those who might be saved through surgical intervention will be sent to me. I am setting up a surgery in the Burj el Hazana."

"How will they get to you?"

"I have every woodworker and blacksmith I can beg, borrow, or steal working on converting wagons to something that Larrey calls *ambulance volantes*—flying ambulances. Each will only have a single horse, but they will be lightweight enough to travel the streets very quickly."

"You seem to have become something of a disciple of Larrey."

"Well, I only knew him for a few weeks, and even then, technically, I was a prisoner; but yes, I admire him greatly. I often wonder what things he and I might have accomplished together if there wasn't this damn war in the way."

Smith gave a small chuckle and thought to himself, *Yeah, I sometimes wonder the same thing about Bonaparte.*

"All right, but it seems to me that your whole plan rests on these aid stations. Who's going to man them?"

"Yes, that's potentially the weak link; but I've got the all the surgeon's mates from the *Theseus* and the *Tigre* rounded up. They will supervise each of the stations. Assisting them, I've given Susan the task of recruiting and training some... ah... auxiliaries."

"Where on earth is she going to get..."

"I am going to get them from a place you never thought of." Susan had come up the stairs so quietly that neither man had heard her. Walker looked at her with wonderment, trying to figure out why she was not breathing hard.

"I am glad I found you two in the same place," she continued. "I've got your medical auxiliaries all lined up."

"You found them? Where?" Sidney inquired.

"In al-Jezzar's harem."

The two men looked at each other, then back at Susan. Walker was the first to speak.

"You found them in the Jezzar Pasha's harem? Susan, you could have been killed if anyone had caught you in there."

"No, *you* could have been killed if anyone had caught you in there. You're a man. I am a woman, in case you haven't noticed."

"Trust me when I tell you... he's noticed." Smith quipped.

Walker cast an annoyed glance over at Smith, but Susan just continued, ignoring Smith's comment, "From what Wright tells me, Jezzar Pasha agreed to place all his 'troops and other assets' under Sidney's command. Well, I need people to help out in those aid stations—people who have nothing else to do during the battle. His harem is the very definition of people who have nothing else to do, so I recruited from there."

"Susan, when Wright made that agreement, he was talking about troops and other assets like cannons, cannon balls, gunpowder, and so forth," Smith pointed out.

"An asset is an asset," Susan simply said. "I start training them this afternoon."

"Does al-Jezzar know about this?" Walker asked.

"Oh yes," Susan replied while blowing upward to get a stray lock of frizzled brown hair out of her eyes. "I think he views them as expendable—easily replaced should they become... 'contaminated,' I think was the word he used.

"But Sidney, I have to tell you about something that rather disturbed me."

"That'll be a first."

"I am serious. I am not sure how to put this... but... they're all *white!*"

"Who's white?"

"The harem. Every one of them. There isn't an Arab, a Syrian, or Palestinian among them. They're all white girls from Bosnia, or the Caucuses, or Greece. There's even a

French girl in there, Maria Corriveau. I've met her. In fact, she's my translator."

"All right. Jezzar has a taste for white girls from Bosnia. What am I supposed to do about it?"

"You have to do *something*! This is a harem, for God's sake. Those girls are nothing more than... well, they're *sex slaves*."

"Susan, I don't know how to break this to you, but the North African Muslims have been taking white slaves out of Europe for centuries. Hell, they've even raided Ireland from time to time."

"But you have to do something about *these* girls!"

"I am."

"What?"

Smith turned to Susan and said, with a bit of an edge to his voice, "I am doing my level best to make sure they are not serially raped by the entire French army."

* * * * *

It started with a single shot—a ranging shot from one of Bonaparte's batteries about a quarter-mile away. It hit a berm, well short of the wall. The cannon was tilted upward slightly and fired again. A direct hit. It was only an 8-pound ball and did little damage, but the Battle of Acre was on.

Outside the walls of Acre lies a broad, rolling plain, dotted with olive groves and small, once prosperous farms. Beyond that are a series of hills, upon which Bonaparte made his various camps—Reyniers Division on one hill, Lames Division on another, provisions on a third, and so forth.

The landward walls of the Acre peninsula were in the shape of the letter "L" placed on it's side. The long side ran west to east for about a half-mile, then made a 90-degree turn to the south for about a quarter-mile. Both ends of the walls were anchored by the Mediterranean Sea—which is where Sir Sidney's ships were positioned.

Smith began the expedition with two warships, the 74-gun *Theseus* and the 80-gun *Tigre*, along with the *Alliance*, a store-ship with 22-guns, the sloop *Marianne* (4-guns), and Smith's "attack canoe" the *Torride* with 2-guns. But he had also captured Bonaparte's supply ships, and these he pressed into action as well.

On the west side of the peninsula, he placed the *Theseus* so she could fire straight down the east-west line of the wall. In addition, he placed the *Dangereux*, the *Deux Freres*, and the *Torride* on the west side to harass any French batteries they might be able to reach with their smaller guns. To fire down the short end of the letter "L", the north-south wall, he placed his flagship, the *Tigre*, and the *Alliance*. To harass the French cannons, he positioned the *Dame de Grace, Negresse, Marianne*, and several smaller gun boats.

The easiest and most vulnerable place to attack almost any fortress is at its main gate; but at Acre, that was located where the north-south wall met the harbor. Bonaparte made a few probes in that area, but his troops were quickly scattered by gunfire from Sir Sidney's ships. The next most vulnerable place was at the angle where the north-south and east-west walls met. Spies had informed him that on the other side was the Pasha's extensive garden, and the only thing that separated the garden from the city was a small, largely decorative, wall.

That's where Bonaparte decided to strike.

Attacking there, however, presented him with two problems. First, he had lost his supply ships to Sir Sidney and aboard those ships were the large caliber heavy siege guns. He had ordered more from Alexandria, to be landed at Jaffa and brought overland, but that would take time. Still, he had succeeded in opening a breach in the walls of Jaffa with the guns he currently had, so they would have to do.

The second problem, however, was more serious. Bonaparte could not just march his troops up to the walls and pour them through a breach. Smith's ships would cut them to pieces. The only solution was to dig... and dig... and dig. Bonaparte needed trenches to protect his troops all the way to the wall, as well as protect at least some of his fire-bases so his artillery could operate free from Smith's harassment.

The first few trenches were parallel to the wall and designed to provide initial staging areas for the troops. The second series, more numerous, were in zigzag patterns running toward it. Soon the artillery began pounding at one particular spot on the wall.

Despite heavy answering fire from the walls and from Sir Sidney's ships, on March 28th the French succeeded in opening a breach. This was made even wider by a mine that had been placed the previous night by sappers.

Commands were shouted and French troops began filling the trenches leading to the walls, with more pouring in every minute from behind. Seeing that the number of men was threatening to overflow the channels, General Kléber began pushing and cursing his way through the mass of humanity to get to Bonaparte's side. He needed to find out what was happening. Why was he hesitating?

He found Bonaparte in one of the connecting trenches, but was shocked by the look on his face. It was the first time he had ever seen indecision there. Bonaparte's face was white, as if he had seen his own ghost before these walls. He kept stepping up on a short ladder to briefly look at the breach, and then he would step back down and look wildly at the people around him—people who were, in turn, looking at him, waiting for an order that only he could give.

"Général! Général, the men are ready." Kléber began. "What are your orders?"

Bonaparte stared at Kléber, his eyes wide.

"What are your orders, sir? The men are ready; and I am not sure if we can hold them back much longer."

A look of resignation finally passed over Bonaparte's face. He glanced at the ground for a moment to pull himself together, looked up at Kléber and softly said: "Attack."

It was all Kléber needed to hear. He was a giant of a man, well over six feet tall, with a stentorian voice to match. He began bellowing the command "Attack!" This call was taken up by others, and soon the drummers and buglers began sounding the *pas de charge*.

The plan was simple and straightforward. The lead elements would rise out of the trenches, carrying ladders. They would cross the shallow dry-moat, and put the ladders up against the wall. This would allow them to get out of the moat and into the breach. Their job then was to hold the breach open against all comers until the supporting troops could come up, climb those same ladders, and rush into the city.

The red-coated grenadiers of Kléber's 75th Demi-Brigade had the honor of leading the attack. They rushed, screaming, from the trenches and ran toward the wall. When they got to the dry-moat, however, their charge abruptly stopped. The moat was not a shallow one—Picard Phélippeaux had seen to that in the days of preparation leading up to the battle. It was now 15 feet deep and 20 feet wide. The French, in their over-confidence, had not bothered to check it.

The grenadiers, undaunted, lowered their ladders into the moat, climbed down, and raced the ladders to the other side so they could climb up again. They were not long enough to reach the breach, so they had to scramble up the remaining wall rubble as best they could. The problem was that their support was left on the other side of the moat with no way to get down—no way to come to their aid. Nevertheless, the grenadiers pressed on.

The Turks, seeing the determination of the grenadiers, panicked and fled from the wall. As they scrambled down the steps, however, they were met by none other than Jezzar Pasha. He was in a rage, beating men with the flat of his sword, screaming, and shooting at them as fast as his pistols could be reloaded. Slowly, the still terrified men returned to their positions.

Once they got back, they reassessed the situation and realized that the initial charge of the French redcoats was a failure. They were trapped with no hope of reinforcements from the other side. The British marines and sailors on the wall had been pouring a murderous fire into the grenadiers. Men were being shot in the face and chest from nearly point-blank range. The Turks soon joined in and, along with their musket fire, started pouring boiling oil, flaming pieces of tarred wood, and large rocks on to the hapless French soldiers. Sidney Smith's ships were streaming fire down the length of the north-south wall, gouging long grooves in the Frenchmen milling about for their chance to go up.

Eventually the French, realizing the hopelessness of their attack, gave up. They scrambled down the ladders, across to the other side, and back to their trenches. It was then that the real barbarity began.

Turkish men started pouring through the breach and into the moat. Their mission was to cut off the head of every Frenchman they could find. It didn't matter whether they were dead, or very much alive and pleading with them. Their heads were sawed off.

Back in the courtyard, Jezzar Pasha had set up a large, almost throne-like chair. Surrounding him were the heads of the Frenchmen. As each man came up, he accepted the head, briefly examined it, threw it on the growing pile, gave the man a coin, and smiled triumphantly.

The first attack was over.

* * * * *

There was no further fighting that day, but the silence that had descended on the battlefield was almost as nerve-wracking as the battle itself. As the sun grew higher in the sky, feral dogs began to appear. At first, there were only one or two, then larger and larger packs. Initially they were attracted by the smell of blood; but after tentatively licking at some of the reddish-brown pools, they began approaching the bodies. They were hesitant, as if such a wealth of food just lying on the ground had to be some kind of trick. It wasn't, and they soon began gorging themselves.

Cecil Durbin leaned out through one of the crenellated openings at the top of the wall. He knew he was not supposed to be there. In fact, he had been expressly forbidden by Sir Sidney to leave the ship. He was "too old for that kind of thing"; and besides, he was the commodore's personal servant. That made him exempt from most of the regular shipboard duties, and certainly kept him out of any kind of land fighting.

He pulled himself back in and turned toward his friend, Isaac Pulley. Technically Pulley wasn't supposed to be there either; but at least as the commodore's coxswain he was charged with going ashore from time to time. He was sitting on the hard stone walkway with his back leaning against the wall, and his head in his hands. He was a worried man.

"Cecil, wen 'e finds out, Sir Sidney is gonna have our hides. Just wen I were gettin' used to this here cock-son duty, you talk me into this craziness. We're both gonna be broken to common seamen, if he doesn't have us flogged. In fact, he'll probably do both."

"You know, you're such a damn worrier," Durbin replied. "'Have a look... if he asks, I'll just say I had to go ashore to get some more coffee for him—you know how 'e loves his coffee—and the battle started, and well, one thing led to another and I found meself up here on the wall. You were good enough to run me ashore, and got caught up in the same tangle. That's all we have to say."

Pulley nervously glanced to his right. "Cecil, the man's not a hundred yards away from us right now. Wot if he comes over here?"

"He won't. He's goin' down to the courtyard. Probably wants a talk with The Butcher. We'll be all right."

Pulley was not persuaded and continued to stew. Durbin continued to look out at the moat.

"Isaac, wot's that down there?"

"Are they buildin' a gallows for us already?"

"No, I'am serious. Come have a look."

Pulley sighed and hauled his body upright. "Wot am I supposed to be lookin' at?"

"Over there, on the left, near that broken ladder, ain't that a general's uniform on that body?"

Pulley glanced over. "Yeah, it prob'ly is. So wot?"

"Well, it don't seem right, him just layin' there like that."

"Cecil, he's dead. He's missin' his head, which might account, in large part, for why he's layin' there. But, you keep an eye on him, ya hear. If he gets up and starts dancin' around, let me know." With that, Pulley sat back down.

"I don't know. Some bloke ought to do somethin'. Bury him or somethin'."

"Well, why don't you do it?"

As Pulley slid back into his funk, a light came on in Durbin's eyes. He left the wall only to return a few minutes later with a pickaxe, a shovel, a rope tied around his waist, and several burly sailors. He went to the wall and started waving at the French soldiers in the nearest trench, all of whom had drawn a bead on Durbin's head the moment it appeared.

"Mounseers, a-hoy! Avast heaving there a bit, will ye? And belay over all with your poppers."

With that, he hoisted the pickaxe and shovel over his shoulder, and was lowered down into the moat. The French had no idea what this lunatic was doing; but miraculously they withheld their fire.

Durbin proceeded over to the headless general, the muzzles of the enemy muskets following his every move. He looked over the corpse's length for a moment, and started digging a grave next to the body. When it was completed, he put down his shovel, took off his cap, placed the general's hand in his, and formally shook it. Ceremony completed, he reverently slid the body into the grave, filled it in, and smoothed the surface.

As he was about to leave, he had another thought. He set up a slab of stone at the head of the grave, and took a piece of chalk from his pocket. Kneeling over the stone, he wrote: *Here you lie...* but then stopped when he realized he didn't know the man's name. After a moment, he shrugged his shoulders and decided to use the slang phrase for a decapitated man: *Here you lie, old Crop.*

Just as he arrived at his lift rope, he looked up and for the first time realized the number of French muskets that were trained on him. Without missing a beat, he executed his best imitation of a courtly bow and foot-scrape to the French soldiers—and both sides erupted in cheers as he was hauled up the wall.

* * * * *

"He did what?" Sir Sidney blurted out. "Indeed, General, I'll get him in here right away.

"Durb-i-i-i-n! Where the hell are you? Durb-i-i-i-n!"

"I am right here, sir," Durbin replied as he shuffled in from the pantry. "No need to carry on. I hear yeh."

"Durbin, General Devereaux and I were discussing some prisoner exchange issues, when he told me about your little *unauthorized...*" Smith emphasized the word "*...foray* onto the walls yesterday. It seems he has some words for you."

"Ah, yes. It is my honor to meet you, sir. While our two nations are at war, it is good to know that even in this land of barbarity we can still be civilized. Your actions yesterday in burying our fallen comrade..."

The general went on for some time in a formal language that was going completely over Durbin's head, even though Sir Sidney was expertly translating.

"And so, for your gallant deed we wish to offer you this token of our gratitude." The general reached into a coat pocket and held out a small leather bag, obviously filled with coins.

Durbin looked at it for a moment, and then shook his head. "I'm mighty grateful, yer generalship, but they's no need. Back in '96 me and the commodore here were captured by frog... ah... by French forces, and imprisoned fer a spell. I have ta say, ye treated us right; and if one of us died, you always gave us a proper burial. It were the least I could do now."

"Nevertheless, we French are very serious about our honor, and that honor demands that you receive this token."

Durbin looked at the bag again, knowing that it probably contained a year's salary. His resolve started to waiver. Finally, some little piece of logic fell into place in his head, and he took the bag.

"I'll take it this time, sir. But I pledge to you that if we're ever on a battlefield, and I spot ya dead, I'll bury ya—for nothin'."

Sidney Smith's eyes closed, his shoulders slumped, and his head dropped toward his chest in complete resignation.

Chapter Four

Rarely had a city seen as much horror, in as short a period of time, as had Naples. In the span of six months it had suffered two popular uprisings, two invasions, two sacks, and two rounds of fierce hand-to-hand fighting in it's streets.

The Army of Santa Fede—Ruffo's army—had reached Castello del Carmine at the southeast corner of Naples, overlooking the harbor. As a fortress, the castle wasn't much. Indeed, it was nearly indefensible; so the defenders quickly surrendered. They laid down their arms, were marched out of the stronghold—and were immediately massacred. It was a scene that was being played out repeatedly throughout the city—engagement, honest surrender, followed by massacre.

A few hundred yards away from the castle a man, dressed as a monk, was hurrying across the plaza known as the Mercato, the main marketplace of Naples. His name was Giuseppe De Lorenzo. He had been a mid-level functionary within Ferdinand's government before the city's occupation by the French, and had stayed around to continue those duties under the French. Many years earlier he had briefly known Cardinal Ruffo when he was the treasurer-general of the Vatican. His hope—his only hope—was that Ruffo would remember him.

He kept to the side streets and alleyways, trying to look as inconspicuous as possible, until he got to the Strada de Tribunali and the great Naples Cathedral. There he knew Ruffo would be holding court.

The outside of the cathedral was not that impressive, but the inside was simply stunning. There were frescos by Domenichino and Giovanni Lanfranco, altarpieces by Stanzione and Ribera, canvasses by Perugino and Giordano, and a superb soaring altar, designed and built by Francesco Solimena.

But the highlight was a simple silver reliquary. There, between glass plates, were two cylindrical ampoules containing drops of blood from St. Januarius, the city's principal patron. Twice a year, on the first Saturday in May and on September 19th, the Saint's feast day, the ampoules were taken in procession from the Cathedral to the Monastery of Santa Chiara. There a priest would hold up the vials to show that the contents were solid, and place them on the altar next to the Saint's other relics. After much praying by the faithful, the priest would hold up the vials to show that they had liquefied. If the blood of St. Januarius should fail to liquefy, it means that it will be a very bad year for Naples. Earlier that spring, it had done exactly that.

Ruffo, with his guards and senior officers around him, was standing in the nave, with a line of petitioners running all the way back to the main door. People were falling on their knees before the Cardinal, pleading their circumstances, setting forth their passionate embrace of Catholicism, and above all, begging for mercy. The Cardinal would briefly hear their appeals, smile benevolently, make the sign of the cross over them, and forgive their transgressions. The now relieved petitioners would then be lead out a side door into the rear courtyard, and killed.

De Lorenzo eventually made it to the front of the line; but instead of falling to his knees he straightened his monks habit, opened his arms and said: "Your Eminence! Do you not recognize your old friend from Vatican days?" And with that he moved forward to embrace the Cardinal. Ruffo slammed a fist into his chest, knocking him backwards.

"Yes, I remember you De Lorenzo. I seem to recall you as someone who specialized in selling the Vatican barrels of tainted wine. But, you've obviously reformed. Taken orders have you? I don't recall having heard that."

De Lorenzo tried not to look embarrassed. "In these troubling days, your Eminence, it is sometimes necessary to dress according to your heart, even if that dress is not consistent with certain legalities."

"Yes, I can imagine. What is it you wish, Giuseppe?"

"Your Eminence, I just want to assure you of my undying loyalty to the King, the church, and to you. This city has undergone a kind of madness in the past few months, beginning with the arrival of the French. And it is true that many of it's citizens have been traitorously disloyal to the crown; but I was not among them. You know me. You know I would never do that. Although I am nothing but a simple clerk, I have never wavered in my allegiance."

Ruffo, thought for a moment. "You know something... I actually believe you. I don't think you have enough intelligence or imagination to be political." He sighed deeply and began making the sign of the cross. "Go then. You will not be harmed." And he looked up to see who was next in line.

De Lorenzo was ushered out the same side door as all the others. When he got outside, however, he was horrified to see the body of the person who had preceded him being swung onto a growing pile of corpses. He turned to look at the two guards who had brought him out of the cathedral, and saw one of them raising his sword. Before it could be lowered, a voice called out.

"Stop! Don't execute this one. It seems the Cardinal really did know him. Send him to the group that is going to the Ponte della Maddalena."

"De Lorenzo a small group of five other prisoners were tied, two by two, and marched to the Strada Carbonara, where they were integrated with a group of about 35 others. Soon they set off on a journey of less than a half-mile; but it was one that would live in De Lorenzo's memory forever.

The streets were littered with scattered bodies, stripped of all possessions including their clothing. He saw men and women being pulled out of their houses, bound, and dragged along by howling mobs, or pricked and pushed along by bayonets. All were maltreated and bloodied, most had no clothing but a shirt, many were completely naked. De Lorenzo had no idea where these wretches were being taken, but had a good idea of what was going to happen when they got there.

Their march took them to the Largo Mercatello where they were forced to halt. It was in this plaza that the French had erected a Tree of Liberty, which had been recently pulled down. As the prisoner file walked by, several royalists were in the process of urinating on it.

At about the same time another column of prisoners arrived at the other end of the plaza. This group was marched, five at a time, to the fallen Tree of Liberty and shot. The problem was that the soldiers were too drunk to shoot straight; thus some victims were killed outright as was intended, but many others were only slightly wounded. It made no difference. After the "executions," all—the living and the dead—had their heads cut off with bayonets and mounted on poles around the plaza.

The group continued and De Lorenzo noted that an almost a festive air had developed around the rapine. He could hear groups of royalists walking around, drunk, and singing:

> *Chi tiene pan' e vino*
> *Ha da esser giacobbino!*

> [He who has got bread and wine
> He must be a Jacobine!]

On each street, when the mobs saw the line of prisoners, their screams and howls reached inhuman levels. They started spitting and throwing rocks at the miserable file and threatened to tear them apart. The guards did nothing to stop them.

Eventually they reached a plaza that they had to cross to get to their assigned prison. To do that they had to run a gauntlet of frenzied royalists wielding stones, tree limbs, clubs, and in some cases even horsewhips and knives. Not all the prisoners made it to the other side alive.

The initial group of forty was thrown into a large cell, but those numbers were increased by several hundred within an hour and a half. De Lorenzo looked about him and saw many people he recognized—priests, artisans, public officials, professors, and military officers of every rank from cornet to general. Included with them were their families. All were battered and bruised and many were severely wounded. Those who had clothes, wore them as tattered remnants. Most, however, wore only shirts and were either naked from the waist down, or completely naked.

De Lorenzo asked a fellow prisoner about all the nakedness. He was informed the mob believed that all Jacobins had a picture of the Tree of Liberty imprinted on their thighs. Thus, to find out who was a traitor, all you had to do was look; and to do that the person had to be stripped. It made no difference that no Tree of Liberty imprints were ever found. The people were arrested, stripped, and indecently inspected. De Lorenzo was not surprised to observe that most of the men retained their shirts, many of the older women retained at least some clothing, but every young woman and girl—no matter how young—was completely naked.

The following morning they were roused by their jailers, and slowly, painfully, got up. None had been given any food or water since before their arrest, and were feeling that torment along with their other miseries.

They were told that they were being taken to another prison and were lead off in the direction of Portici by a column of solders under the command of a priest who was armed with a sword and two pistols. As they went, the guards invited the citizens along the way to insult, throw stones, and beat them. After a few miles they stopped and the priest directed everyone with shoes to take them off.

"Why?" someone asked.

"Because this is the place where you will be executed."

This threw the prisoners into pandemonium. After the initial shock wore off, some dropped to their knees in prayer. Families huddled together to make tearful expressions of love for each other. Men made agonized pleas for mercy, at least for their children if not for themselves. Women were torn between letting tears flow, and staying calm so as not to panic the children. The children had no such restraints. They were openly wailing and calling for their mommies and daddies to make everything right again—something they could not do.

The first group of people were lined up with a firing squad placed not ten feet away.

"Present!" called the priest, and muskets swung up to shoulders.

"Aim!" and the line of soldiers steadied their muzzles.

There was a lengthy pause in which the victims expected to feel the shattering punch of a musket ball in their chests, and their families thought to see their loved ones die in agony. Finally the priest said.

"Ground weapons!"

"This is no good," he continued. "If we kill them here it'll be too difficult to get the wagons in to haul away their bodies. We'll go a little way further up the road." And the march continued.

The "execution" was repeated three or four times, each time it was delayed at the last second for one reason or another, until finally it lost it's effect. Eventually the prisoners were begging to be shot so as to be put out of the misery of apprehension. At that point the game was no fun any more, and they were marched back to town.

The pillaging of Naples continued for over a week—along with the rape, murders, and executions.

Several days into it, Cardinal Ruffo received a letter from Queen Maria Carolina that said, in part: "I hope, from the prudence of your Eminence, that you will punish no one, who has punished an enemy of the State."

The Queen knew what was going on in her former capitol city; and if she knew, the King knew. If the King knew, the Hamiltons knew. And, if the Hamiltons knew—Nelson knew. Indeed, he had sent in ships to monitor things.

* * * * *

During the following days—every day—the Ottomans maintained an unremitting barrage of cannon fire from the walls of Acre. This did the French little harm, but the defenders had an almost unlimited supply of cannon balls and powder, compliments of the British, so why not indulge?

For their part, the French encouraged this display of pyrotechnics. Because of the loss of their siege equipment, they were short of almost everything, especially the cannon balls needed to pound the city wall. Bonaparte solved the problem by posting the following notice throughout his encampment:

All soldiers who during today and tomorrow find cannon balls
on the plain and bring them to headquarters
will be paid accordingly:
36 and 33 pounders - 20 sous each
12 pounders - 15 sous each
8 pounders - 10 sous each

The program was almost too successful. A 33-pound cannon ball represented a days wage for most of them—more than enough to get drunk even at the inflated prices being charged for spirits. In many cases men were going after the shot before the defenders had finished firing, which proved to be hazardous to the health of several of them.

However, there was another reason why the French were content to maintain a standoff, at least for a while. The first major attack was a disaster, and Bonaparte wanted "that damn wall" completely down; but the only sure way to do that was to mine it. Accordingly, a team of engineers and miners began working on a tunnel that was designed to go under the wall. Once there, they would hollow out a large area, and support it with timbers. Before their next attack, they would set fire to the supporting timbers. When those timbers fell, the hollowed out area would collapse, and bring down the wall above.

That procedure took time, but time was on Bonaparte's side. He had sent to Alexandria for more siege guns and equipment; but it would take a while for them to arrive. The shipment would have to be sent by sea to Jaffa, then overland to Acre to avoid Smith intercepting them again. He was hoping the mine would be ready about the same time that the new equipment came. At that point, Acre would be his.

In the meantime, Sir Sidney and Bonaparte began a game of cat and mouse. In a later age it would be called psychological warfare; and, like the modern equivalent, it had a very serious purpose behind it.

Camped out on top of the hills overlooking Acre were scores of Christian, Muslim, and Druze tribes. They were not participating in the battle; they were there as spectators, waiting to see who won, and would align themselves with the victor. Bonaparte badly needed the support of those tribes, not so much to take Acre, but to continue his campaign beyond. If they were to align with him, it would be like a snowball rolling downhill as he moved further up the coast. More and more tribes would join until his combined army would truly become invincible.

Accordingly, he put together two proclamations, one to be sent to the Christian tribes, and one to the Muslim and Druze. Both were designed to play on the fear and hatred they had for the heavy hand of the local Ottoman rulers, especially Jezzar Pasha.

The proclamation to the Muslim and Druze tribes read as follows:

> For a long time, your rulers have insulted the French nation and its traders. The hour of their punishment has come.
>
> For too long, rulers from Georgia and the Caucasus, people such as the butcher Jezzar Pasha, have tyrannized this most beautiful part of the world; but God, on Whom all depends, has ordained that their empire is finished.
>
> You will be told that I have come to destroy your religion; do not believe it! Reply that I have come to restore your rights, to punish the usurpers, and that I respect more than your rulers do, your God, His Prophet, and the Quran.
>
> I believe that all men are equal before God; that wisdom, talents, and virtue alone make them different from one another.
>
> But, what wisdom, what talents, what virtues distinguish your rulers, that they should possess exclusively that which makes life pleasant and sweet?
>
> Is there a good piece of farmland? It belongs to your rulers. Is there a beautiful slave girl, a fine horse, a beautiful house? They belong to your rulers.
>
> If this land is their farm, let them show the lease which God has granted them.
>
> Let all men know that we are the friends of the true Muslims.
>
> Did we not we French destroy the Pope, who said that war should be waged against the Muslims? Did we not destroy the Knights of Malta, because those insane people thought that God wanted them to wage war against the Muslims? Have we not been for centu-

ries the friends of the Ottoman Sultan (may God fulfill his wishes!); but have not rulers like Jezzar Pasha, on the contrary, always revolted against the authority of the Sultan? They do nothing but satisfy their own whims.

Thrice happy are those who join us! They shall prosper in wealth and rank. Happy are those who remain neutral! They will have time to know us and they will take our side.

But unhappiness, threefold unhappiness, to those who are themselves for the rulers and fight against us! There shall be no hope for them; they shall perish.

The proclamation that was prepared for the Christian tribes was similar, but with a completely different twist. It pointed out that his army represented the Christian West and that, although France no longer had an official religion, it was an army whose men had been born and raised in the Christian tradition. Most significantly, he painted himself and his officers as knights, like the crusaders of old, come to free all Christians in the Holy Land from their bondage and oppression.

Sir Sidney Smith obtained copies of both proclamations; and, in an attempt to be helpful, had the documents reprinted exactly as written. To be even more helpful, he had them distributed to the tribes. Unfortunately, there was a slight mix-up, and the Christian tribes received the Muslim document, and the Muslim tribes received the Christian. Accidents happen.

For his part, Sir Sidney was trying to think of ways to undermine French morale, and remembered a tactic he had used in the early days of his assignment to the western Mediterranean. He had asked the Sultan for permission to distribute a leaflet to Bonaparte's troops in Egypt that promised them safe passage back to France, or anywhere else they wanted to go. All they had to do was present themselves to any allied or British unit, and their safety would be assured.

He had large quantities of these guarantees printed and dropped into the French trenches at Acre.

Bonaparte was furious, not so much because Smith had done it—it was a common practice in warfare—but because it was having an effect. He sent orders that no soldier was to have any communication whatsoever with any Muslim defender or British sailor. Then he went further. He published accusations that Sir Sidney Smith had deliberately sent earlier French prisoners back on a plague-infested ship—leaving aside the question of why he would intentionally expose his own officers and men to the disease. Then he claimed that Sir Sidney Smith was, in fact, mad.

Now, Sir Sidney was furious. Under a flag of truce, he sent a message to Bonaparte challenging him to a duel on a neutral beach southeast of the city. Bonaparte replied:

I am in receipt of your demand for satisfaction. Unfortunately, I have too many weighty affairs on my hands at the moment to trouble myself with so trifling a matter. If the demand had come from the great Marlborough, it might be different; but not from you.

Still, if you are absolutely bent on fighting, I would be happy to send a grenadier from my army to the neutral ground. There you may satisfy your humor to the full.

But the most serious propaganda offensive was launched by Bonaparte. It was not directed at the Christians, or the Muslims; it was directed at the Jews, and it was a shocker. He offered them their own nation.

General Headquarters, Jerusalem 1st Floreal, April 20th, 1799, in the year of 7 of the French Republic

BONAPARTE, COMMANDER-IN-CHIEF OF THE ARMIES OF THE FRENCH REPUBLIC IN AFRICA AND ASIA, TO THE RIGHTFUL HEIRS OF PALESTINE.

Israelites, unique nation, whom, in thousands of years, lust of conquest and tyranny have been able to be deprived of their ancestral lands, but not of name and national existence!

Attentive and impartial observers of the destinies of nations, even though not endowed with the gifts of seers like Isaiah and Joel, have long since also felt what these, with beautiful and uplifting faith, have foretold when they saw the approaching destruction of their kingdom and fatherland: And the ransomed of the Lord shall return, and come to Zion with songs and everlasting joy upon their heads; they shall obtain joy and gladness and sorrow and sighing shall flee away. (Isaiah 35:10)

Arise then, with gladness, ye exiled! A war unexampled In the annals of history, waged in self-defense by a nation whose hereditary lands were regarded by its enemies as plunder to be divided, arbitrarily and at their convenience, by a stroke of the pen of Cabinets, avenges its own shame and the shame of the remotest nations, long forgotten under the yoke of slavery, and also, the almost two-thousand-year-old ignominy put upon you; and, while time and circumstances would seem to be least favorable to a restatement of your claims or even to their expression, and indeed to be compelling their complete abandonment, it offers to you at this very time, and contrary to all expectations, Israel's patrimony!

The young army with which Providence has sent me hither, led by justice and accompanied by victory, has made Jerusalem my headquarters and will, within a few days, transfer them to Damascus, a proximity which is no longer terrifying to David's city.

Rightful heirs of Palestine!

The great nation which does not trade in men and countries as did those which sold your ancestors unto all people (Joel 4:6) herewith calls on you not indeed to conquer your patrimony; nay, only to take over that which has been conquered and, with that nation's warranty and support, to remain master of it to maintain it against all comers.

Arise! Show that the former overwhelming might of your oppressors has but repressed the courage of the descendants of those heroes who alliance of brothers would have done honor even to Sparta and Rome (Maccabees 12:15) but that the two thousand years of treatment as slaves have not succeeded in stifling it.

Hasten! Now is the moment, which may not return for thousands of years, to claim the restoration of civic rights among the population of the universe which has been shamefully withheld from you for thousands of years, your political existence as a nation among the nations, and the unlimited natural right to worship Jehovah in accordance with your faith, publicly and most probably forever (Joel 4:20).

This was serious indeed. In the more than 1700 years since the fall of Jerusalem, no significant leader had ever offered the Jews their land back, and the Jews were important players both within Acre, and throughout the region. The proclamation landed on the city like a lightning bolt.

While Haim Farhi was Jezzar Pasha's chief advisor, he was also the acknowledged leader of the Jewish community. He read the proclamation at first with disbelief, then with wonderment, then with excitement.

"Our own state," he muttered to himself. "A place where we can come together as a people again. A place called..." he hesitated, as if afraid to speak the words. "A place called Israel."

* * * * *

The defenders called it the Commander's Tower; and, in the days leading up to the battle, it was Sir Sidney's refuge, the place where he could be alone with his thoughts—and his fears. But once the fighting started it acquired a different kind of significance. It stood at the corner of the north-south and the east-west walls, and from it you could fire guns down the length of either. The French called it *La Tour du Démon*, the Devil's Tower, and if they were to take the city of Acre, it had to fall. Bonaparte knew that. Smith knew that. Everyone within 100 miles knew that.

Sir Sidney Smith put his hand on the stone wall for the hundredth time and looked over at John Wesley Wright.

"You can feel it, John Wesley. Right here. Put your hand right here. You can feel them digging. Every time a pick strikes, or a shovel hits a rock, it radiates up through the stone."

Neither Wright nor Picard Phélippeaux said a thing. What was there to say? The French had driven their trenches to within a pistol shot of the wall, then started work on a mine running underneath the tower.

After a long moment, Wright asked, "Picard, can we countermine? Can we drive a shaft from our side of the wall, break through into theirs, and destroy their work?"

Phélippeaux, the engineer, was near exhaustion. From his first day at Acre, he had worked around the clock to shore up the city's defenses. He did a magnificent job in the time he had available, but it had taken a terrible toll. With a voice that sounded as tired as he looked, he replied, "No. The current city is built on the ruins of an old Crusader fort. To get underneath the wall from our side, you would have to bore through a solid granite foundation, the remains of the old fortress. We could never do it in time, if it could be done at all."

The three men fell silent again, and the sounds of the French mining effort became magnified by their imaginations. Then Wright spoke, "Then there's nothing for it. We have to take out that mine from the surface."

"What do you have in mind?" Smith asked.

"Do you have any Ottoman soldiers you can depend on?"

"Some. Not many, but some."

"Then I propose this afternoon you assemble them at the main gate. When they're in place, we send a signal from this tower; they sortie out, and attack the trenches from the flank. While the French are reacting to that, we lower a small group down the wall, attack the mine entrance, destroy their operation, and return the way we came."

"Who's the 'we'?"

"Myself, of course, and maybe Major Oldfield, the Marine commander from the *Theseus*. I know he'd want a piece of this. We'll each pick three additional men to accompany us. Eight people in all. That should do it."

Smith looked at Wright for a long moment, and then said, "I don't see that we have a choice. Get ahold of Oldfield and get your people together; but, for God's sake, be careful, John Wesley."

* * * * *

The plan went wrong from the very beginning. The Turks, who were supposed to remain completely silent until they fell upon the French, began screaming war cries as soon as they were through the gate. Thus alerted, the French began a deadly fire into the Ottomans, and started looking around to see what else was amiss. It didn't take long for them to spot the eight men that had come down the wall.

It was too late to turn back. The group rushed for the mine entrance through a shower of musket fire. Wright and Oldfield arrived first along with two heavily armed sailors and a pikeman. Not expecting an attack, the entrance was not guarded and provided a measure of protection from the deadly fire.

Wright turned to the pikeman, "Where are the demolition men, and the gunpowder?"

In a shaky voice he replied, "Ded, sir. They was the last down the rope ladder, and didn't make it."

Wright shot a quick look of alarm at Oldfield, then recovered. "All right. You two men stay here and guard the entrance. We'll go back a bit further and see how far they've gotten."

The three didn't have far to go. There was no way that Wright could get an exact fix, but it was clear that the miners were close to the wall. The two officers lit a nearby lantern and began inspecting their surroundings.

"Those supports are huge," Wright said as he pounded a beam in frustration. "If we only had that damn gunpowder..."

"Or, if the French hadn't built this tunnel so well," Oldfield added.

A long stony silence descended on the group. Not only had the mission apparently failed, but they had no clear way to get back to the wall.

Finally, the pikeman said, "No, sir."

"No, sir... what?" Wright asked.

"I don't mean to be talkin' out'a me turn, sir; but them frogs didn't build this tunnel right at all."

"What do you mean?"

"Well, sir, I am from Gulval, and me family's been workin' the tin mines as far back as maybe. In fact, I meself worked in both the Wheal Malkin and Hard Shafts Bounds mines, 'til that recruiter feller came by."

"So what's wrong with this mine?"

"Everthin' sir, startin' with those supports. Look at this." He walked over to the last support in the line. "They used a mortise and tenon ta marry the overhead beams with the pillars; and that's fine. But they didn't peg 'em in; and that's crazy, sir. The slightest horizontal movement and that support is gonna come down. And if this one goes, all that extra weight is goin' ta be transferred ta the next one. When that goes, it will all be transferred to the one after that, and on down the line." He looked again at the beam and sniffed, "No proper Cornishman would ever build it that way, I can tell ya."

A gleam came into Wright's eyes. "Give me your pike."

Wright poked a space above the last overhead beam in the series, ran a rope through it, and tied it around the beam. He cleared a similar space over the next overhead beam, and looped the rope around it as well. He then lead the rope end back to the mine entrance, where the sailors were keeping the French soldiers at bay with sporadic musket fire.

"All right, everyone lay on this line. Every time I say, 'Heave!', pull as hard as you can."

It took several tries, but eventually the first two overheads came out, taking their supporting pillars with them. Suddenly the weight of untold tons of dirt and rock shifted to the third overhead. The beam and pillars shattered, which transferred even more weight to the fourth one, and so on down the line. In all, 20 yards of tunnel collapsed before a length of rock strata in the mine's ceiling stopped the chain reaction.

The five men dropped to the ground until the mineshaft ceased belching dust and dirt.

Wright was the first up. He looked down the length of the mineshaft, but couldn't see much through the lingering dust; so, he turned his attention to the mine entrance.

After briefly looking out, he said, "We don't have much choice. We have to make a break for the wall. If we stay here, the French will eventually force this opening and we'll be killed." Left unspoken was the statement that was on everyone's mind ...*and if we make a break for the wall, we'll also be killed.*

"Maybe," he continued as if reading their thoughts, "we'll find some debris we can hide behind until we can be rescued." Wright paused for a moment. "Everyone ready? All right... let's GO!"

Wright shot out of the mine entrance, followed closely by Major Oldfield and the others. Two of the sailors didn't get ten yards before they were cut down. The pikeman got to the edge of the moat before he fell. Wright and Oldfield made it into the moat and started scrambling up the other side.

Just as they reached the top, Wright heard a squishy "thump" sound, like a rock being thrown hard into a pool of mud. He turned and saw Oldfield with a look of complete astonishment on his face as he fell back. Wright started to scream "Tom!" when a musket ball found him as well. He tumbled into the moat behind Oldfield where they contributed their bodies to the lake of human corruption that was forming under the blistering Levantine sun.

* * * * *

Word of the mine tragedy spread rapidly through the British community, and an almost palpable melancholia descended. This was in contrast to the high spirits of the Ottoman soldiers. Even though their failure to follow the plan caused it to fail, they came back elated—with stories to tell, and fresh heads to sell to the Pasha. This exuberance did not go over well with the sailors, and several fights had to be broken up both on the wall and in the city.

Sir Sidney did not leave the wall for even a moment; and was soon joined by Lucas and Susan in a silent vigil. They took turns looking over the parapet at odd intervals, hoping to see some sign of life in the moat, some sign that their friend was still alive. As the shadows started to lengthen, Sir Sidney came to a decision, and sent for Durbin and Pulley.

The two showed up with Pulley looking nervous and furtive, twisting his cap in his hands, wondering what they had done now. Durbin had the same look he always wore—outwardly sober and serious, but with a hint of wry amusement in his eyes that you couldn't quite define.

"Durbin, you seem to have an affinity for rummaging around in the moat. How much would you dare to do?"

"What darn't we do, yer honor?"

Pulley's head shot around. "We?"

Smith pointed to the carnage that lay sweltering in the ditch below. "I dare you to go down there and bring us the body of poor Mr. Wright."

"Now, sir?"

"Yes, now. I don't want Wright down there overnight where the dogs can get at him. Take Pulley with you, and try to get Major Oldfield as well."

"Aye, sir. We'll be back in a jiffy. You kin count on us!"

A few minutes later, the two met at the main gate. Durbin was wearing his usual canvas trousers, neckerchief, a shirt that rumor has it was once white, and a dark blue vest. Pulley had much the same attire; only he had added a sash. In the sash were three pistols, a ship's cutlass, and he was carrying a musket.

"Isaac, wot on earth are you doin'?"

"Wot am I doin'? I'm goin' out to fight the entire damn French Army, thanks to you."

"And you think you're gonna cut your way though a demi-brigade of Bonaparte's Invincibles with three pistols, a sword and a musket?"

"No, I'm gonna do it with two pistols, a sword and a musket. The third pistol I'm savin' for you for getting us into this!"

"Now Isaac, there ya go again—always the pessimist."

"Pessimist, eh, mate? You spot somethin' cheery about all this? Soon as we go out there, they're gonna start shootin'... at us, mind you! Damn! Here I am, overflowin' with human kindness, never hurt a fly in me life; and now that tender, innocent life is about to be snuffed out way before its time."

"Well, they most certainly *will* start shootin' if you go out there like that."

"It's the best I could do. The cannon was too heavy for me to get off the wall."

"No, I mean..." Durbin started removing the weapons from Pulley one by one. "we're goin' out there unarmed. Trust me. It's the only way."

"Trust you?" Pulley grumbled. "Trusting you were 'ow I got 'ere."

Durbin emerged first through the wooden sally port, held out his hands, and said, "Ahoy, mounseers. It's me again. We got no poppers, so belay whatever ya got in mind."

He turned back to the open doorway. "Come on, Isaac. Come on."

Pulley tentatively poked his head around the corner, and then emerged.

"This is me mate," Durbin continued to the confused French. "Don't shoot 'im neither. We're just gonna take a little stroll down this 'ere moat. Gotta find one of our killed men—don't mean no harm—then we'll be outta your hair. So, you can all just relax a bit."

The two men traversed the length of the ditch, slipping in pools of blood, and tripping over scattered limbs and bloated bodies. The sights, and especially the odors, were so overpowering that the two men eventually became numbed—their senses simply stopped registering the carnage that was all around them.

Finding John Wesley Wright and Major Oldfield was not that hard. They were on top of a small pile of corpses not far from the Commander's Tower. Durbin grabbed Wright's legs and pulled him off the pile so Pulley could get to his arms. As he did so Wright's head bumped on the ground.

A low moan issued from Wright. His eyes partly opened and a voice, barely above a whisper, murmured, "Damn you, Durbin! That hurt."

Durbin looked at Pulley to see if he had heard what he thought he had heard. The look on Pulley's face was all the verification he needed.

Kneeling, Durbin took off his neckerchief and began fumbling with Wright's jacket, seeking the source of the wound. "Mr. Wright, sir. Are ya alive, sir?"

Wright responded with a stifled yelp, which indicated both that he was alive and Durbin had found the entrance to the wound on his back. As he stuffed the sweaty neckerchief into the gaping hole, he said, "Isaac, we 'ave to get both'a these blokes back to the city."

"You might get zat one back, but not zis one."

Durbin looked up to see a squad of three French soldiers, armed to the teeth, and led by a sergeant. He stood up cautiously.

"And 'oo might you be?" He said to the sergeant.

"Who I am doesn't matter. What matters is zat I have been told to recover zes body," and he kicked Major Oldfield in the side.

"You want him, is it? Ain't there enough French bodies 'round?"

"Not like zis one. This is Colonel Phélippeaux, your chief engineer, and the Général himself has ordered his body be collected. It seems they know... knew each other. They went to school together before the war."

"And Bonaparte wants 'is body?"

"Do you have a hearing problem?"

"No, mounseer, it's just that he's goin' to be disappointed. That's not Colonel Phélippeaux; that's Major Oldfield, a marine officer from off the *Theseus*."

"And you wish me to believe you would send a party to destroy our mine, without including an engineering officer to direct it?"

I trust you'll believe me when I say, I weren't consulted on the matter; but, yes, that's obviously wot happened."

"Well, I am not that naive, monsieur. So, if you will excuse me, please get out of my way."

"No!" Pulley suddenly exclaimed. "You're not gonna have 'im."

Durbin looked over at his friend in surprise at his uncharacteristic aggressiveness. "Isaac, it's no big deal. Wen they cop him back to their camp, Bonaparte'll know he's not Phélippeaux, and they'll send him back or bury him themselves."

"But it's not right, Cecil. Even if it were Phélippeaux, it's not right that they should have the body. He deserves to be buried by 'is own kind, not a bunch of..."

"Enough of zis nonsense." The sergeant gestured to one of his men, who went over and grabbed Oldfield's legs.

"I said, no!" Pulley ran over and grabbed the neckerchief that was around Oldfield's neck, and a bizarre tug-of-war ensued. Both of Oldfield's legs had been badly broken, so the Frenchman was working with what amounted to two thick pieces of rubber; and Pulley's grip on Oldfield's neckerchief was tenuous at best. It was a standoff. Oldfield's stretched-out body was pulled back and forth, first one side with the advantage, than the other.

Durbin looked on with horror for a moment, and then joined Pulley at the neckerchief end. "You talk about me, do ya? You're the one 'oo's gonna get us killed," he mumbled under his breath.

"It's wrong, Cecil, and that's all there is to it."

With Durbin helping, the British side began winning. Seeing this, the French sergeant grabbed a halberd—a long spear with an ax head at the end—from one of his men. With a mighty swing, he sunk it deep into the side of Oldfield's body, and began tugging.

Eventually the neckerchief broke, and Oldfield shot over to the French side. With a smile of satisfaction, the French sergeant led his squad off, carrying Major Oldfield with them.

* * * * *

Three knocks sounded at the door of the Admiral's cabin. Nelson was inside finishing off some letters, and the knocks pounded in his head like the blows of a sledgehammer. Ever since receiving his head wound at the Battle of the Nile, Nelson had been a changed man. He was having constant headaches, he couldn't sleep, and he was displaying a degree of callousness that no one had seen before.

"Come!" He snapped.

In through the door came the midshipman of the watch, George Parsons. "Sir, the Captain sends his respects, and would like to see you on the quarterdeck at your earliest convenience."

"Very well. I'll be there shortly."

Nelson gave a deep sigh and looked at the letter he had just composed. Only a week ago he had written Emma Hamilton, "It gave me great pain to hear both Sir William and yourself were so very unwell. I wrote to Sir William yesterday that if you both thought the sea air would do you good, I have plenty of room. I can make for you private apartments, and I give you my honor the sea is so smooth that no glass was smoother." Emma jumped at the chance to be with Nelson again, and to be in the thick of important events. As a result, both she and her husband were onboard the *Foudroyant* with Nelson, on their way to Naples with seventeen other warships, to "settle matters there and take off (if necessary the head of) the Cardinal."

Shortly after that, he received a letter from his wife, Fanny, who suggested that she join him in the Mediterranean. He had just finished writing his reply: "You would by February have seen how unpleasant it would have been had you followed any advice which carried you from England to a wandering sailor. I could, if you had come, only have struck my flag, and carried you back again, for it would have been impossible to have set up an establishment at either Naples or Palermo."

He thought about what he had just written and felt a twinge of guilt. Then he thought about Emma Hamilton.

Arriving on deck he could see his flag captain, Thomas Hardy, peering intently through his telescope.

"What is it, Hardy?" Nelson asked, slightly irritated that he had been called on deck.

"Sir, we have Naples in sight, but... well look for yourself." He handed the glass to Nelson.

"You have Fort Oro on the peninsula there, and then move northeast to Fort Nuovo. Up there in the hills is the Castle of St. Elmo. They're all flying flags of truce."

Astonishment flashed across Nelson's face as he quickly lifted the glass to his eye and confirmed Hardy's observation.

"Where is Foote? Where's the *Seahorse*?"

Hardy silently pointed to a corner of the bay, where Captain Edward Foote, Nelson's onsite commander, and his frigate were anchored. His ship was also flying a flag of truce.

"Anchor near the *Seahorse*, and fly signal flags for "Captain repair on board."

An hour later Edward Foote was standing before the Admiral, in his cabin, looking pleased. Foote was considered a rising young star in the Royal Navy. He had commanded one of the scout ships under Jervis at the Battle of Cape St. Vincent, and was assigned to Nelson for the Battle of the Nile. Unfortunately, he did not arrive in Alexandria in time for the battle, but the *Seahorse* still managed to distinguish herself by capturing one of the fleeing French ships. Rising star or not—his career would not survive this meeting.

Nelson was seated behind a massive, highly polished, jet-black mahogany table, the kind of heavy wooden item you would never see aboard a ship-of-the-line, unless it was the prized possession of an admiral. Behind him stood the equally massive Thomas Masterman Hardy, one of Nelson's closest friends and captain of his flagship. Between the size of the table in front of him, and the size of Hardy behind him, Nelson looked diminutive—almost petite—but the look on Nelson's face belied any weakness. It was a look that Hardy knew well, and tried to avoid at all costs. Foote had no way of recognizing it.

Foote was wrapping up his report. "So, you see Admiral, things have gone surprisingly well. We've avoided any further bloodshed, and we've settled things before any help can come from France to relieve the rebels."

Nelson peered at the 32-year-old captain. "And you've done this by negotiating a truce—an armistice?"

"Well, I didn't do it personally, of course. That was in the hands of Cardinal Ruffo; but I wholeheartedly support his action. The rebels in the forts, and the remaining French troops at Castle St. Elmo, have agreed to lay down their arms within 21 days. The French troops will be shipped back to France, and the rebels may choose either to go with them, or return to their homes under a general amnesty."

"And you did this without my approval, or the King's?" This was said in a low, ominous, almost indiscernible voice.

"Yes, sir." Foote was now becoming alarmed at Nelson's tone. "I didn't know when you would be arriving; and, as I am your representative in these waters, I thought..."

"You thought?" Nelson's voice was now rising. "You don't have a thought anywhere in your head! You're going to turn loose over 500 French soldiers, and God-knows how many rebels, to do what? The soldiers will go home to fight us again at another time. The rebels will go home to undermine his Sicilian Majesty at another time. And all of this is supposed to happen under the shield of the British crown?"

Foote's face had now gone white. "I am sorry sir, but..."

"But nothing! This truce will not stand. I am annulling it as of this moment."

"But... But sir, you can't do that. I signed the document. I gave my word. The Cardinal, he..."

"I can't do that?" Nelson's head was pounding again. The pain was to the point that he didn't even realize he was now almost shrieking. "I've got 18 warships and 1700 troops that say I can. You and that jumped-up priest of yours have made a complete mess of things. You had no authority—no right—to negotiate that treaty.

"Now be damned, sir, and get off my ship. Tell the Cardinal I want him on my quarterdeck at nine o'clock tomorrow morning."

* * * * *

Cardinal Ruffo hated ships. He hated boats. He hated barges. He hated anything having to do with water. Even the frequency of his bathing was... moderate. But, as he was being rowed out to Nelson's flagship, he had to admit the British fleet made an impressive sight.

Nelson had anchored his ships before the city, bow to stern, in a line of battle. Remembering how his forces had slipped between the French vessels at the Battle of the Nile, he ordered his ships to be no more than 130 yards apart—about two-thirds of a cable—and linked with chain, not rope. Neapolitan gunboats, manned by tested, loyal crews, guarded his flanks. If the French fleet arrived, they would have to take the British head-on. There was no way they could get around or through his line.

The ships represented hundreds of guns; half of them were directed out to sea, and half of them were pointed toward Naples. There were no guns run out, but Nelson had ordered every gun port to be opened. The message was not lost on Ruffo.

The deck crew of the *Foudroyant* had fitted a "bosun's chair" to get the Cardinal aboard. As he was being slowly swung over the side, Nelson had a chance to study the man.

Fabrizio Ruffo struck Nelson as looking more like a small-town mayor than a Cardinal. Of medium height and weight, he had the heavy dark eyebrows and prominent nose that Nelson associated with Italian peasantry; but he also had the easy smile and confident carriage of a politician.

To think of Ruffo as being a mere peasant, however, would be a mistake. He was a shrewd, tough, political infighter, who was capable of utter ruthlessness, if need be.

Nelson greeted him with the usual shipboard honors due his rank, and the two men disappeared into the Admiral's quarters.

After the servant had poured glasses of wine, Nelson dismissed him. The two men maintained a tense but cordial light conversation for some time before they finally got down to business. Nelson started it off.

"Cardinal, I understand from Captain Foote that you have negotiated a cease fire and a truce with the rebel forces."

"Indeed, that is so," he replied. "And Captain Foote informs me that you are somewhat distressed by that action." Ruffo displayed his best gentle-shepherd smile.

"Distressed?" Nelson fumbled for the right words. "Cardinal, do you realize what your foolishness has done? You have hundreds of French troops, and perhaps thousands of traitorous rebels pinned down in three fortresses; and you want to turn them loose? That is unconscionable, sir. Absurd and unconscionable!"

"My son..."

"And let's get that straight, right away." Nelson interjected. "I am not your son. I am not your grandson. I am not even of your faith. So may we dispense with the rubbish?"

Ruffo's eyes flashed. Gone was all pretense of being a cardinal—a prince of the church. His clerical garments were now nothing more than irrelevant stage props, and his voice acquired a sudden sharp edge.

"Fine, and pray tell what you would do with them, Admiral?"

"Kill them."

"Kill them?" The Cardinal's eyebrows lifted as if he wasn't sure he had heard him right.

"Yes. What could be more obvious? The rebels must lay down their arms, unconditionally surrender, and await the pleasure of their King. Then, in my opinion, they should be rounded up and executed."

"And what of the women? You know, there are many women in those forts."

"Any woman who has collaborated in this rebellion will be treated the same way—and without pity.

"Cardinal, there are only two kinds of people in those forts. They're either French soldiers, or they're traitors. Either way, they must be put to death."

Cardinal Ruffo, stopped and gave Nelson a questioning look, like he just had a major insight.

"You're mad." He said quietly, with a tone of wonder in his voice.

"Mad? You think I am mad?" Nelson's voice was rising, as if to give credence to Ruffo's statement. "It's you who are mad, sir.

"I am not doing this because it gives me pleasure. It is absolutely necessary. If we don't do it, within six months the King would not be able to govern his people." Nelson was now up and pacing the room, becoming more agitated as he continued.

"The leaders must be killed, sir. Second-level people should be sent off to Africa, or to the Crimea—we'll be better off without them. The others... the others deserve to be branded. Yes, that's it. Brand them on the face so others will not be deceived by them."

Ruffo had had enough; his tone now became as forceful as Nelson's. "Tell me, Admiral. How in God's name did you conclude that Naples was nothing more than some Irish town in rebellion?

"You say that if we don't do this monstrous thing, within six months the King would not be able to govern his people. I say to you, if we do it, the King will have no people to govern. Naples has been decimated, sir! Between the excesses of the republicans when they had power, and... yes, unfortunately, the excesses of my own army... between the two, our leading families, our merchant class, our artisans, our skilled laborers, our military—all have been nearly destroyed. Now you want to kill some more, or ship them off to Africa, or mutilate them? Tell me sir, how is the King going to rebuild his kingdom with no building blocks?

"You come in here and make all these pronouncements; but in a month or two you'll be floating around a thousand miles from here. You don't have to live with the consequences of your actions. We do!"

The pounding in Nelson's head had now reached epic proportions. The two men were almost shouting at each other.

"I don't care what your speculations might be, you had no authority to sign that truce."

"Really? And what is your authority to annul it?"

That stopped Nelson in his tracks. It had never occurred to him that he might not have the authority.

Ruffo continued, "I am the commander of the *Armate della Santa Fede*—the Army of the Holy Faith. I was placed in my position by the King. For months I've waged a campaign to rid our country of the French and the Republicans. I have retaken Naples in the name of the Lord Our God, and the King. By what right do you now overrule me? Show me the document that gives you that authority!"

"I have the confidence of the King to..."

"Show me the document, Admiral!

"I signed a treaty of armistice. So did your Captain Foote. We both gave our word—backed by our honor—and the rebels have laid down their arms on the basis of that word and that honor. And you now want to annul it as if we were errant schoolboys playing a prank. Does the word 'honor' have any meaning to you at all?"

Nelson leaned aggressively on the table, and glared at Ruffo. "You will revoke that armistice agreement!"

Ruffo vaulted to his feet. "I will not!"

"I have several hundred guns that say you will."

"And I have an army that I will pull out of Naples; and you can capture the city on your own, Admiral!"

Word spread rapidly in the city that Nelson was about to annul the treaty, and panic ensued. Families, who had only recently moved back into town, clogged the major roadways, trying to get out before the fighting started again. Muskets that had been given to the monarchists by Nelson were broken out of their boxes. People were again being hunted down because they were Jacobins, or suspected Jacobins, or simply because they were someone's personal enemy.

As Nelson lay in his bunk, he could hear the crackle of sporadic musket fire all night long. His head was killing him.

* * * * *

"This is the spookiest place I've ever been in," remarked Susan Whitney. "Maria, are you sure you know where you're going?"

Maria Corriveau, Susan's translator and new-found friend, was leading the way through a rough stone tunnel with a torch. "Of course I do. I wasn't supposed to, but I've been down here many times. It's wonderful. You'll see."

The tunnel had the musty smell of a place that did not want to be visited. The air was uncomfortably cool, and the darkness outside the arc of torchlight seemed absolute and final. Just as Susan was starting to feel a bit claustrophobic, the tunnel opened out into a huge room.

"This is it," Maria said holding the torch up. "This is the

knight's hall." Susan was suitably impressed.

Some 25 feet underneath the City of Acre was a second city, the remains of the crusader fortress built by the Hospitallers—the order of the Knights of the Hospital of Saint John.

As Maria walked toward the center of the room, she became a tour guide.

"This is what they call the Great Hall." She again raised her torch so Susan could see better. "It's about 50 yards by 30 yards in size. The ceiling is thirty feet high and there are 20 vaults supported by 15 columns." Although she was not a native of Acre, and was only there because she was a harem girl, there was a touch of pride in her voice.

"Amazing!" Susan declared. "What was this place used for?"

"We're not sure, but we think it was a hospital. There are other rooms as well. Down that passage," she said pointing with her torch, "is what was probably a dormitory and the cloister of the Knights. Off of that is what appears to be a dining room, with some wonderful *fleur-de-lis* carved into the stones."

They walked toward the fireplace on the other side of the room, the sound of their footsteps seemingly absorbed by the darkness all around them. In the middle of the room there was an opening in the floor, a stairwell, which they stepped around.

"What's down there?" Susan asked.

"That's the dungeon—or it was once a dungeon. Later on it was turned into a burial chamber for the knights. It has some fascinating tombstones, and..."

Suddenly, the women could hear an eerie whistling noise. In the semi-darkness the sound seemed to be coming from everywhere and nowhere, bouncing off the hard stone walls and amplified by the vaulted ceilings overhead. It had the timbre of the living about it, but also the resonance of the dead.

The two women looked at each other—Susan with an expression of growing concern, and Maria with an appearance of confusion.

"That's it. I appreciate the tour, Maria, but I think it's time for us to go."

"This is very strange. I've never..."

"Let me rephrase that. It's time for *me* to go; you can stay if you want."

With that Susan turned to leave as did Maria; but Maria chanced a glance backward.

"Wait a minute," she said. "There's a light coming up the stairwell."

A moment later, a lantern appeared followed by the whistling man who was holding it.

"Picard!" Susan exclaimed. "You scared us to death. What on earth are you doing here."

"Ah, Susan," Picard Phélippeaux replied in surprise. "I might ask you the same thing."

"Maria was showing me the old crusader fortress. You know Maria Corriveau, don't you?"

"I have seen you about, but I fear I have not had the honor. Mademoiselle Corriveau, may I introduce myself. I am Colonel Louis-Edmond Antoine Le Picard Phélippeaux—at your service." With that, Maria gracefully held out her hand, and Phélippeaux kissed it. The exchange between the French colonel, and the former French debutante was as natural as could be, even 25 feet underground, standing over a burial chamber, in a pitch black 12th Century ruin. Old cultural habits, it seems, die hard.

"But I still don't know what you're doing here," Susan continued.

"Ah, that. I heard a rumor there was a tunnel leading out of the city down there," he said, nodding toward the stairwell. Supposedly, it runs under the wall just about where Bonaparte is trying to knock it down."

"Is there?"

"Well, there's a tunnel, but it doesn't run out of the city. It's on the right just after you go down these stairs. It goes for about 30 yards, and then opens up into a room. I think the room was once a hidden cache where the crusaders could store arms."

"Too bad you didn't find what you were looking for."

"Oh, but I did; or at least I might have. By my initial calculations, that hidden room is right underneath the breach in the wall. I was just going outside to take some more measurements to confirm it."

With that, the three headed out of the underground ruins. While Susan loved looking at historic old sites, she was quite glad to be leaving this one.

Horatio Nelson

Napoleon Bonaparte

Sir Sidney Smith on the Wall at Acre

Jezzar Pasha Administering Justice
(Haim Farhi is shown third from left)

John Wesley Wright

Admiral John Jervis

Queen Maria Carolina

Sultan Selim III

Lady Emma Hamilton - One of the most beautiful
women of her day, and Nelson's mistress.

Sir William Hamilton

Captain Ralph Willett Miller
of the *Theseus*

An 1819 print of Daniel Bryan burying the French General at Acre.
(Thus proving there were Cecil Durbin wannabes even then.)

Eleonora Fonseca Pimentel
Hung for writing a series of pamphlets
implying that Emma Hamilton and
Queen Maria Carolina were in
a lesbian relationship.

Love-à-la-mode, or *Two dear friends*, a caricature by James Gillray, depicting
the rumor about a relationship between Lady Emma Hamilton and Queen Maria
Carolina of Naples. Text in image: One lady to the other "Little does he imagine
that he has a female rival" Gentleman in nautical uniform (Nelson?) "What is to
be done to put a stop to this disgraceful business?" Other gentleman "Take her
from Warwick" (one of her lovers prior to Nelson)

MAP OF
LOWER EGYPT
and Part of
SYRIA.
TO ILLUSTRATE THE EXPEDITION TO EGYPT,
and the
CAMPAIGN OF 1798 – 1801.
A.K.JOHNSTON, F.R.S.
Scale of English Miles

Routes followed by Bonaparte

BATTLE OF
ABOUKIR
25 July 1799.

BATTLE OF THE
PYRAMIDS
21 July 1798.
Scale 1 English Mile

French ■ Turks
Cavalry ■ Infantry
■ Artillery

PYRAMIDS
of Gizeh

Bonaparte's Syrian Campaign

125

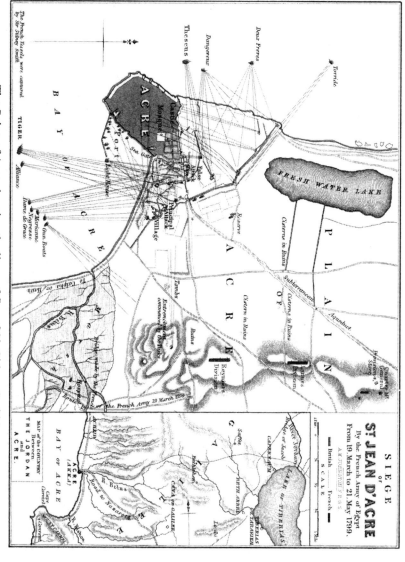

The Seige of Acre showing the lines of fire of Sir Sidney Smith's guns.

Chapter Five

Susan was at the aid station at Burj Kapu. She was list-
lessly inspecting the supply room when a runner breathlessly
appeared, seemingly out of nowhere, to announce something
exciting to her interpreter, Maria Corriveau. Maria looked at
the runner questioningly, asked him a quick return question,
got an answer, then turned to Susan and simply said, "John
Wesley is alive."

"Alive?" She asked. "How could he be alive? We saw his
body."

Corriveau shrugged, "I don't know, but that's what he
said. He's at the..."

"He's at the Burj el Hanza," she interrupted. That's where
Lucas has set up his operating theater."

The two dashed out of the aid station and into the bright
sunlight. They set off across a large courtyard that was once
open and expansive. It was now cluttered with needed supplies for the people manning the walls, as well as pushcarts
and ramshackle vending stands of people who were selling
"desirable supplies" to those same soldiers.

The two could not travel very fast in their ample, western-
style dresses. Initially Susan came into the city dressed in ba-

sic sailor's attire, which is what she normally wore aboard ship. The Muslim leaders were scandalized and begged Sir Sidney to order her to wear proper clothes. Sir Sidney knew that "ordering" Susan to do anything was not the wisest course, but he did make the request. She grumbled, but complied.

Maria Carolina Corriveau was another matter. She was French, but she was also a member of Jezzar Pasha's harem. When she was a teenager, she had accompanied her father, a wealthy fur trader, to southern Russia on a trade mission. He fell ill and died, suddenly leaving her alone in an utterly alien land. Word of her presence, and vulnerability, soon got out and attracted the attention of a slave party from Constantinople, which was in the area looking to buy young boys to be trained as Mameluke warriors. Maria was an unexpected prize, and they knew the Sultan would be most pleased.

He was indeed pleased and she remained in his harem until she was "too old"—over twenty—whereupon she was given to Ahmed al-Jezzar for his diligence in tax collecting. He too was pleased, and she had been a part of his harem ever since.

For Maria, Susan's arrival was a Godsend. Because she spoke French, Turkish, and a bit of English, and Susan spoke French quite well, she was assigned to be the medical interpreter. It wasn't so much that she liked being free of the harem environment, or that she could speak her native tongue with someone—although those things were important. It was the dresses. She could wear western clothes again, compliments of Susan's somewhat limited wardrobe, and she reveled in it.

After several near-death experiences with two vendor carts and a stack of gunpowder barrels, they arrived at Burj el Hanza, burst through the doors, and quickly found Lucas Walker bent over the prostrate form of John Wesley Wright. Without even looking up, he said, "It's about time you got here, Whitney. Now both of you get ready; I am going to need some help."

Susan led Maria over to a chest where she pulled out two aprons. "Here put this on, then go rinse your hands in that basin over there."

"I understand the need for the apron, but why wash my hands? They're not bloody yet," Maria asked Susan in French.

"Well, you're not washing your hands, exactly; you're dipping them in acid."

Maria instantly drew her hands back and looked shocked.

"Oh, don't worry, it's just a little carbolic acid, diluted with water. If he doesn't have any carbolic acid, he'll make me dip my hands in vinegar, or sometimes even wine."

"But why?" Maria asked, genuinely astonished.

"I don't know, exactly; but he insists on it. He says, it reduces infection."

"Susan, that makes no sense. How could that possibly be?"

"I have no idea—and neither does he. Frankly, I think it's just a superstition. You know, like dipping everyone's hands in acid before an operation brings him some kind of good luck."

This was something Maria could understand. Having spent time in two harems, she was well aware of the peculiarities of men.

John Wesley was laying face-down on a table, naked except for a sheet across his buttocks. When Susan came up to the table, Wright turned his head, and softly said, "Yeah, Susan, it's about time you got here. This barber here was about to give me a shave from the inside out without you to supervise."

"Don't you worry," she replied, patting him on his good shoulder. "I've been supervising him for years, and I am not about to stop now."

"If I could trouble you two comedians to pipe down... Susan, I need two grains of opium."

Susan was now all business. "How do you want it?"

"Forty drops of laudanum."

"Sydenham's?"

"Yes."

As she went to the cabinet to measure the laudanum into a small cup, Walker pulled several instruments from his prized engraved oak "tool chest" as he called it, and placed them into a shallow dish of carbolic acid.

"Ah, zis is your goode luck charm?" Maria asked in broken English, indicating the dish.

Walker looked up. "I see you've been talking to Susan."

Before Maria could reply, Susan returned with the laudanum. Walker and Maria helped to raise Wright slightly, so he could drink the potion.

While they were waiting for the laudanum to take effect, Susan asked, "So, how is he?"

"I don't know for sure. The ball entered his back here," he said pointing, "but it didn't exit. I fear it hit his scapula. If so, it would have been deflected, but I would have no idea where it might have been deflected. If it missed the scapula, then maybe I can pull it out."

After a few more minutes, Walker inserted his finger in the hole. Wright, whose sense of pain was only somewhat deadened by the laudanum, grunted.

"Damnation!" Walker exclaimed. "It hit the bone. Not by much, just grazed it, but it deflected. It could be anywhere."

Both Susan and Lucas knew this was a death sentence. The ball and any pieces of clothing it carried in with it, had to be removed. If it weren't, he would die from infection. If Walker tried to find it by opening him up without anesthesia, he would die of shock. Either way, he was dead.

Walker looked down at his friend for a long moment and, sadly, started to put his instruments back into the chest. Suddenly Maria asked, "If it could be anywhere, how do you know it's not on the other side, close to the surface."

Both Lucas and Susan looked quickly at each other. The chances of that happening were probably one in a million, but still...

Walker slid his hand underneath Wright's chest and started feeling around. After nearly a minute, his eyes widened. "There it is. I can just barely feel it, but it's there. It deflected down about two inches. It's in his right breast."

Walker placed a linen pad over the entrance wound and the three of them turned Wright over.

"Now, John Wesley, this might be a bit painful; but I've got to go in from this side to get that ball out."

Wright slowly lifted his groggy eyelids. "May I assume you're going to use something more subtle than your finger this time?"

"Yes, actually, this won't hurt nearly as much as you might think."

Wright mumbled something that sounded vaguely like "Bullshit!", and closed his eyes.

Walker took out a scalpel and made a three-inch cut through Walker's skin, and lifted the blade. Susan sopped up the blood with a small damp towel. The scalpel went in again, cutting through muscle. Wright gritted his teeth. Susan again soaked up the blood. Again the scalpel, cutting even deeper, through more muscle. Wright made a sort of strangled urgent sound. Walker went in one more time, and hit the ball. It was nestled in a little package of cloth left over from his shirt, but it was there.

He cut around it, and picked up a small set of forceps. In a moment, Walker was holding a gooey red glob of iron and cotton aloft like a championship trophy.

Maria Corriveau was handing Susan Whitney a steady stream of white cotton squares, wetted with water, to stanch any additional bleeding; but there wasn't much to be seen.

"He's not out of the woods yet," Walker observed, "but his chances are a whole lot better than they were a few minutes ago."

Susan looked at Walker and gave a long drawn out sigh of relief.

At the same time, a nearby flea, no more than 1/10th of an inch long, did an astonishing thing. From that sigh, he smelled carbon dioxide. The carbon dioxide itself didn't interest him so much as the organism that was exhaling it. His last home had died—for some reason they always seemed to die on him—and he was looking for a friendly new host. From a nearby shelf, he snapped open his multi-jointed legs, which exploded him into the air. He made a leap of over 20 inches, 200 times his body length, in the direction of that inviting cloud. It was a prodigious jump in human terms, but quite ordinary for the flea—nothing remarkable at all.

The flea landed on the corner of Susan's collar, crawled inside, and found himself a nice, warm new home.

* * * * *

Sidney Smith had retired to his ship after Bonaparte's latest assault on the walls. It was a half-hearted attempt, more for show than anything, and Smith knew why he had done it. It was to let the defenders of Acre know that he was still around—still around and waiting for proper siege guns to arrive from Egypt. When they arrived, it would be all over.

But Sir Sidney had not been idle either. He had dispatched messengers to Sultan Selim III in Constantinople asking, begging, for reinforcements. He thought the Sultan would provide them, but the issue was when. The Ottoman bureaucracy was not known for its swift reaction time; and it was by no means certain how long he could hold out.

No, his best hope lay with British arms and, to that end, he had been drafting a message to both Admiral Jervis, and Admiral Nelson.

And so you can see, my Lords, that we have a unique opportunity.

I am asking for five ships, loaded with soldiers, to

be dispatched to the eastern Mediterranean. Two would join our forces here at Acre; and three would be tasked with an amphibious landing at Joppa. Bonaparte would then be trapped. He could not move further north, because we are blocking him at Acre. He could not move east because of the numerous hostile tribes living there. He could not board his men onto ships and go west, because we own the sea lanes; and he could not move south to Egypt because of the forces at Joppa.

In short, he would be utterly trapped; and if he didn't surrender his entire army, we could destroy him at leisure.

I look forward to your approval of these measures, and your assistance; but I must emphasize that time is of the essence. If Bonaparte gets reenforced with heavy cannon, I don't know how long we can last.

As Always,

Your Obedient Servant

Sir Sidney Smith

Several days later, Nelson received Smith's appeal for help. He thought about it for a moment, and dropped it into the bottom drawer of his desk. A thousand miles away, Admiral John Jervis paced his study in Gibraltar while reading the same message. He too thought about it for a moment, and dropped the letter into the fire.

Sir Sidney Smith was on his own.

* * * * *

On the other side of the wall, Bonaparte was having his own problems. Spies in Damascus had reported that a large number of Janissaries and Mamelukes had crossed the Jordan River. This was confirmed by his picket outposts at Safed and Nazareth. The pickets had reported that two large columns of Arabs had passed by, both headed in the direction of Mount Tabor.

Not having his siege guns at Acre was an inconvenience; but this was a danger. If a substantial army were allowed to assemble at Mount Tabor, they could come right up the Jezreel Valley and attack him from behind—pinning him against the walls of Acre with no where to go.

His first move was to dispatch General Junot with 300 infantry and 160 cavalry to reconnoiter the area. He needed verification of the enemy force, their number, composition, and exactly where they were located. Junot found them without a great deal of difficulty. As his troops rounded Mt. Loubi, they were attacked by 4000 screaming horsemen.

Junot miraculously fended them off and retreated to Nazareth, but Bonaparte still had no idea of the size of the army that was massing against him. So, the next day, he sent General Kléber with a larger force to the area.

He was within a mile of where Junot was located, when a huge force of Arab infantry and cavalry came pouring out of the hills. Before they could form up on the plain, Kléber attacked and scattered them. Later, however, he wrote Bonaparte a frantic message saying that there were 15,000 to 18,000 enemy troops near Mt. Tabor, and possibly as many as another 30,000 Turkish, Syrian, and Mameluke troops that captured soldiers said were on the way.

Bonaparte was now truly alarmed. Kléber was an old warhorse, a veteran of a dozen campaigns, and not given to exaggeration. He had to coax him out of retirement to accompany him on the Egyptian Campaign, and he trusted him completely.

Time was now a critical factor. He had to attack before the enemy could get organized. He sent General Murat to the northeast with 1000 infantry and a brigade of horse to hook around to the enemy's rear and cut them off from retreat across the Jordan River.

Leaving two divisions to keep the Turks and the English

pinned down at Acre, he took the rest of his army, along with eight cannon, to Mt. Tabor. But instead of coming down the Jezreel Valley, the route that would have been expected, he took a more difficult path.

Following bridle trails, he scaled the backside of the hills on which Nazareth is located. This allowed his army to reach the heights overlooking Mt. Tabor without the enemy knowing he was coming. More to the point, Kléber didn't know he was coming either.

Kléber had moved his troops several miles to the southwest of Mt. Tabor, near a range of hills by a little village called Fouli. With the hills at his back, he decided to make his stand.

He formed his troops into a huge hollow square. This tactic had been originally invented by a British general, Marlborough, and had been used to perfection by Bonaparte at the Battle of the Pyramids a year earlier.

The one thing that all infantrymen feared was enemy cavalry. Horsemen could easily burst into an infantry formation, running down or hacking to death everyone in sight, and there was nothing they could do about it. Nothing, until Marlborough came along.

What the Duke figured out was that no horse, no matter how well trained, will intentionally run into a wall of bayonets—and there is nothing you can do that will make him change his mind. You can yank on the reins, kick him in the flanks, curse at him, beat him with a whip, but he will *not* run into a wall of sharp steel.

The problem for the Arab army was that it consisted mostly of cavalry.

The horsemen would ride at the French troops, screaming blood-curdling cries, waving scimitars over their heads, rush up to the bayonet-studded French square, and almost be tossed off their mounts when their horses came to a screeching halt. That left them with two options. Option A was to ride in a big circle around the square and get shot like ducks; or Option B, retreat. They did both, numerous times, and the only thing they had to show for it was a mound of dead cavalrymen.

However, Kléber had problems of his own. His squares were holding—but he was running out of ammunition. He looked desperately down the Jezreel Valley, saw that there was no relief in sight, and resigned himself to his fate. He would fight on to the last man, but this was clearly to be his last battle, and he knew it.

In the quiet between two of the Arab attacks, however, he heard a cannon fire. Strangely, it didn't come from the west, but from the north, from the Nazareth Hills.

Bonaparte crested the hill at about noon. He looked into the valley below and saw Kléber's 2000 troops being invested by some 20,000 cavalry. The sun was blazing hot and there wasn't a breath of breeze to be found anywhere. The dust kicked up by the circling horsemen rose straight up in the air and spread out like a horrible mushroom.

What puzzled Bonaparte the most was the rate of fire coming from his forces. He could see the blue-coated soldiers had gotten the best of things so far, but why weren't they firing faster? Then it dawned on him. They were low on ammunition and trying to conserve it as much as possible.

Bonaparte swung immediately into action.

The first thing he did was to order a cannon to be fired to let Kléber know he was here. He was rewarded a few moments later by a lusty cheer coming from Kléber's troops.

Next, he sent a large contingent of cavalry to attack the Arab camp, some two miles away. This cut off the enemy from both supplies and safety.

Finally, he sent Generals Vial and Rampon out with his ground forces. They quickly covered the few miles of intervening ground and positioned themselves into two hollow squares. The three defensive formations, Kléber, Vial, and Rampon formed an equilateral triangle with the Arab cavalry in the middle. Now the cavalry were not being shot like slow moving ducks, they were being shot like fish in a barrel.

The Arab forces scattered in all directions; and the battle was over.

In all, 30,000 Arab troops took part in the battle, and were destroyed by 4,500 disciplined French soldiers. The threat from the east having been dealt with, Bonaparte could turn his attention again to Acre.

* * * * *

Cardinal Ruffo was looking out the window of his office in the Church of the Carmina, just off the south end of the Piazza del Mercato. He looked down on the plaza with sadness, thinking about all the executions that had taken place there in recent months, and prayed there would be no more. Then, almost in answer to his prayer, there was a knock on his door.

A young British naval lieutenant walked in, bowed slightly, and handed a message to the Cardinal. "This is from Sir William Hamilton, your Eminence. I was instructed to deliver it only into your hands, and wait in case there should be a reply."

He opened it up with a mixture of dread and anticipation. The note read:

> Lord Nelson begs me to assure your eminence that he is resolved to do nothing which can break the armistice, which your eminence has accorded to the castles of Naples.

Ruffo was surprised, and more than a little suspicious. He dashed off a note to Hamilton expressing his delight at the news, but asking that it be confirmed by Nelson himself.

That afternoon he received two more unexpected visitors, Captain Thomas Troubridge of the *Culloden*, and Captain Alexander Ball of the *Alexander*. He welcomed them, led them over to a corner of his office where there were three overstuffed chairs and a small table. He ordered tea and asked whether they had any news from the Admiral. Troubridge smiled and handed over a note that came directly from Nelson himself.

I am just honored with Your Eminency's letter; and as His Excellency Sir William Hamilton has wrote you this morning, that I will not on any consideration break the Armistice entered into by you, I hope Your Eminency will be satisfied that I am supporting your ideas. I send once more Captains Troubridge and Ball...

Ruffo leaned back in his chair.

"So it's true? Nelson is going to honor the truce?"

"He is indeed, your Eminence," Troubridge said. "Captain Ball and I are both thoroughly informed of the sentiments of Lord Nelson, and we can say with complete confidence that he will not interfere with the execution of the capitulation."

Ruffo could hardly believe it, especially after their last meeting. "But, why would he change his mind like that?" He asked. "Only yesterday he sent me a note saying he would not permit the rebels to embark, that the plan ought not be carried into execution, and so forth. Why the sudden change of heart?"

"That we cannot say," Bell answered. We were called to the flagship late this morning and were briefed by Lord Nelson himself. I can say, therefore, that the Admiral is completely sincere. He will not oppose in any way the surrender of the forts or the embarkation of the rebel troops. Indeed, to that end, he said he would provide 14 polaccas to transport them, and 500 marines to assist in their embarkation."

"Polacca? What might that be?"

"It's similar to a xebec," Ball replied in an off-hand manner.

Ruffo look blank until Troubridge cut in. "It's a small ship, quite solid, and quite capable of getting the rebels to France, or just about anywhere else in the Mediterranean, as long as they stay fairly close to the shore."

Ruffo had his elbows resting on the arms of the chair, his fingers steepled. He thought for a bit, then said: "Excuse me for just a moment, gentlemen."

He sat down at his desk, wrote something on a piece of paper and returned to the officers. Placing the paper down on the table before them he said, "Would you be willing to sign this?" The paper read:

Captains Troubridge and Ball have authority on the part of Lord Nelson to declare that his lordship will not oppose the embarkation of the rebels and of the people who compose the garrisons of the Castles Nuovo and dell' Ovo.

Ball looked surprised, and Troubridge looked offended. Troubridge spoke first.

"Your Eminence, I hardly think such a document is necessary. We have told you what we *know* to be the case; and we are, after all, gentlemen. Our word is as good, if not better, than any document we could sign."

Troubridge continued to offer assurances; but, all the while, Ruffo was wondering if they had been ordered not to sign anything, and whether he was getting the whole story. Still, everything seemed to be correct. Nelson himself wrote that he would not break the armistice—he had the note in his possession—and both of these officers seemed sincere when they said that Nelson would not oppose in any way the surrender or the embarkation. Perhaps he was getting too cynical and jaded.

Ball was now talking about the mechanics of getting the Jacobins down to the docks and aboard the ships, when Ruffo interrupted.

"Gentlemen, you have convinced me. This is truly a remarkable day, and I thank God I have lived to see it.

"There is much to be done, however. First, I must write Lord Nelson and Sir William Hamilton and tell them what a relief it is to know that things were being so happily concluded.

"But more importantly... could I prevail on you two gen-tlemen to accompany my assistant, Micheroux, to the castles to announce the good news?"

* * * * *

By two o'clock that afternoon the castles had been in-formed, and by four o'clock the French troops and their Ja-cobin supporters were streaming out of their fortresses—for-tresses that they had once vowed to defend to the last man. They marched with the full honors of war, flags flying, and bands playing, which was their right, for they had not been defeated. In one case, the literal keys to the fort were handed over by the commandant, with some ceremony, to his Nea-politan counterpart.

The defenders marched down to the dock area near the old arsenal, grounded their weapons, saluted the naval and marine officers standing there, and boarded the waiting ships.

At first they were a bit confused because the ships did not seem to have the supplies of food and water necessary to make a voyage, but they assumed they would be provisioned the following day before departure. After all, how could the British know exactly how many people to expect in each ship?

The following day the weather was perfect for sailing, with a generous off-shore wind being provided by mother nature. Right on schedule, small British gunboats arrived to escort the polaccas to sea—only they never quite got into open water. The ships got underway, traveled as far as the line of British warships, and dropped anchor. Immediately, several hundred ports opened and guns of all sizes were rolled out.

Thousands of republican supporters were now, officially, prisoners. Nelson had approved the embarkation of over 2000 rebels, but no one noticed that he had not said anything about allowing them to sail. He had drawn the rebels out of their strongholds and tricked them into delivering themselves into captivity—including those who might otherwise have fled and those who had not previously been identified as rebels.

The situation can perhaps best be summarized by a letter written a few days later by Sir William Hamilton to Lord Acton:

> Lord Nelson kept the promise he had given to the cardinal. He did not oppose the embarkation of the garrisons, but once the garrisons were embarked, it became patent what he had done with them.

* * * * *

The ancient Greeks called it an "Etesian." The Turks called it a "Meltemi." Either way, it was a strong, dry wind that periodically came roaring out of the Aegean Sea and down the coastline of the Levant. Normally, for sailors, it was a welcome sight as it signaled clear weather and cooler temperatures. Not so this time, however.

The wind speed was at a constant 35 to 40 miles per hour, with spikes of over 45. The sea was up, and waves of 18 to 20 feet were tossing Smith's ships around like corks in a maddened washbasin. The crests of the waves were being broken off by the high winds, flinging spindrift into the faces of the sailors, making even routine deck tasks difficult, if not impossible.

It was not that the ships were in serious peril—all of them had survived worse storms than this—but they did need to seek shelter. Fortunately, shelter was near at hand. A few miles to the south of the Bay of Acre is the Carmel Range, a series of limestone and flint hills several miles wide that jutted into the Mediterranean. The ships could take refuge behind those hills and wait out the storm. To do that, however, Sir Sidney had to leave Acre under the sole command of Jezzar Pasha, and that would prove to be a mistake.

From Jezzar Pasha's standpoint, it was a golden opportunity to show that he was a brilliant commander and a true leader. It was also a golden opportunity for the French. Without the British ships firing shot down the length of the walls, they could work in the open. Swarms of French soldiers now emerged to extend their trench lines and mines ever closer to the walls.

Jezzar mounted the wall with his entire retinue; and he was dressed as he thought a proper warrior should. On his head, he wore a bright red *zamt* surrounded by a white turban, so that just the peak of the hat stuck up in the center. His coat was red with wide yellow trim down the front and on the cuffs of the sleeves. Around his middle was a large yellow silk belt studded with gold, silver, and precious jewels of all sorts. In that belt was a magnificent scimitar, whose grip and scabbard were even more gem-encrusted than his belt. Around his neck, he wore a huge blood-red ruby called the "Eye of Allah," something that was never brought out in public except for special occasions.

Along with him was an entourage of several dozen people. In addition to his chief advisors and officials were his *silahdar* (armor bearer), *saqi* (cupbearer), *jamdar* (master of robes), his *bunduqdar* (keeper of his bows and arrows), and even his *jukandar* (polo master) who was in the back of the crowd, incongruously holding Jezzar's polo sticks. Off to the side his personal secretary was at a portable table, furiously recording events for posterity.

And it was to posterity that Jezzar Pasha was aiming this moment. After a minute of thoughtfully gazing out over the battlefield, Jezzar ordered one of his slaves to kneel on all fours in front of the wall; but his back was too high.

"Lower, you fool!" He ordered, and the slave scrunched down halfway between being on all fours and flat on the ground. The Pasha then placed a foot on his back and continued his thoughtful battlefield gaze. From the ground level, the summoned crowd could not see the prostrate slave. They only saw the Pasha standing on the wall in an extremely dramatic posture. Jezzar Pasha, however, was not thinking deeply about the coming battle, as his pose might indicate. He was thinking about what artist he would choose to capture this moment in a painting, or a work of sculpture, or both. At a minimum, he knew he would have a suitable inscription carved in stone at this very location.

He looked down at the French soldiers working on their trenches far below. At about that same moment, the soldiers noticed him. This began an interval of the soldiers shouting jeers and catcalls at the Pasha, supplemented with gestures that could only be interpreted as obscene in any language.

The Pasha was beside himself with fury.

"Farhi! Where's Farhi?"

Jezzar's chief advisor, Haim Farhi, shuffled over. "Yes, sire?"

Jezzar Pasha could hardly form the words. Spittle flew out of his mouth as his spoke. "Those men down there," he said pointing. "They're mocking me. Do you hear me? Mocking! I want them killed immediately."

Farhi briefly looked over the wall and laconically replied, "Sire, we've been trying to kill them for the past four weeks."

It was as though Jezzar suddenly remembered where he was. Outwardly, he calmed down; but his fury, now contained inside, was building. He walked over and said something to the captain of his guards, who ran off; and Jezzar Pasha started slowly walking to the south end of the city wall—the part that faces the ocean.

Shortly after arriving at his destination, the captain and a squad of soldiers materialized with every French prisoner they had captured since Bonaparte had arrived. Chief among them was a young officer who Bonaparte had sent to the city with an initial surrender demand—a routine part of the protocol of besieging a city. Normally this emissary would have a protected status, but Jezzar Pasha had thrown him into his dungeon.

The young officer was now standing before the group of

prisoners. All were looking more than a little nervous, and all had their hands tied behind their backs. Jezzar had the officer brought over and placed next to him in front of the French troops who were still jeering below. He ordered two men to hold the officer, grabbed him by the hair, and slowly started to cut his head off. To make matters worse, he did it in such a way that the last thing to be cut would be his carotid arteries. The man was therefore conscious throughout, screaming at first, but settling into a gurgle as Jezzar's knife slowly sawed through his windpipe.

The French jeering stopped immediately when they realized what they were seeing.

Next, Jezzar Pasha ordered the remaining prisoners to be brought forward two at a time. Jezzar ordered that each man have his legs bound in addition to his hands, and then each pair of prisoners were tied together, back-to-back. A large cloth sack was placed over each and tied at the bottom. Finally, to the horror of all the onlookers—French and Turk— each sack was thrown over the wall into the sea.

The sacks quickly bobbed to the surface, where the frantic struggles of the men inside could clearly be seen—but to no avail. The sacks soon filled and sank beneath the waves.

For several hours, there was utter silence on the wall, among the French troops, and even in the city.

When the storm was over and the British ships rounded the Mt. Carmel cape, Sir Sidney was on the quarterdeck of the *Tigre*, watching the city of Acre hove into view, and idly wondering how the Pasha was doing.

* * * * *

While Sir Sidney's ships took refuge behind Mt. Carmel, Lucas Walker, Susan Whitney, and Maria Corriveau remained ashore. True, there was a lull in the fighting, but that did not mean that their workload had ceased.

To begin with, there were people in recovery from

wounds sustained in previous fighting, for in this war there was no such thing as a "minor" wound.

Generally speaking, treatment protocols were relatively straight-forward. If a person was badly hit in an arm or leg, the treatment was to remove the limb. If he were hit anywhere in the central part of the torso, the treatment was to call a clerical person, for the man was as good as dead. Flesh wounds in either location could be initially treated, but Walker knew that the real danger wasn't from the wound; it was from infection. That was the wildcard.

It was widely known that infection was contagious in a hospital; and this was especially true if the hospital were crowded, or located on low marshy ground in the hot season of the year. However, if this were true, how did one account for people getting infected wounds, who had been nowhere near a hospital or any other infected person? In addition, even if you were in a hospital, how was it transmitted from patient to patient?

Walker knew that if you applied the discharge of an infected patient to an abraded or ulcerated surface in another person, that second person's wounds would also become infected. This would happen most often when hospitals re-used dressings; but Walker didn't do that, yet he still got infections in his patients. In fact, he insisted that dressings not be re-used which, along with dipping his instruments and hands in a mild acidic solution, was another thing about him that people thought strange; but he also took all the other standard precautions. He tried to keep his wards well ventilated, and the linen, bedding, and floor of his wards were sprinkled or washed with a solution of the chloride of lime or soda on a weekly basis.

However, fighting infection, once the patient had it, was another matter. He refused to bleed his patients, so that was out. He had tried various emetics and purgatives to see if the patient could expel the disease by causing him to throw up or via bowel movements, but that didn't seem to help either. Some physicians reported success by dowsing the wound with either citric or diluted sulphuric acid, but that made no sense to Walker. How could pain cause infection to go away? Indeed, about the only treatment he had was to give a severely infected patient liberal doses of the pain-killer, laudanum, and hope for the best. If the patient did not recover on his own, perhaps the laudanum would ease his path through what would be a long, slow, painful death.

But his patient list did not end with soldiers. Almost every day there would be a line of people outside the Burj el Hanza, wanting him to examine them or a loved one. There would be mothers with children, old people, young people, he even looked out one day and saw a man standing in line with a donkey.

He carefully inspected the donkey and solemnly advised the owner that he needed to change the animal's feed. He had absolutely no idea what was wrong with the animal, but then he had no effective idea what was wrong with most of the people that were in line either, and that advice seemed as good as any. He was astonished when the man came back several days later bearing two chickens. It was his payment to the wonderful *farangi* doctor for curing his animal.

* * * * *

In that things were so quiet, he was surprised one day when he noticed that he had not seen Susan all morning. This, in itself, was not astonishing. Susan was apt to go off to do God knows what, with who knows who, at any time. But usually she would let him know beforehand.

Maria was walking down the corridor carrying a load of towels and linen. "Maria, have you seen Susan anywhere?"

"Yes, sir. She's... she's resting."

"Resting?" Walker pulled out his pocket watch and glanced at it. "It's almost noon. This is the time of day when she's usually just getting going."

He gave Maria a skeptical look. "What is she resting from?"

Maria looked uneasy. Finally, she said, "Doctor, I think she's sick."

"Sick? As in... what kind of sick?"

"I don't know. She's been complaining lately about not having any energy. Then, during the day, her hands would be cold as ice, but at night, when it's cooler, she would be burning up. Now she's burning up all the time, complaining of headaches, muscle aches..."

Walker was now alarmed. "Why didn't you tell me this sooner?"

"I am sorry, doctor, but she made me promise to..."

"Where is she now?" Walker snapped.

She nodded down the corridor. "The small room, at the end, on the right."

Walker quietly entered a former office that had been converted into a hospital room, one of the few private areas available. It was darkened because the light hurt Susan's eyes so badly. She was lying on a makeshift bed with a wetted cloth folded over her forehead, undoubtedly put there by Maria Corriveau. He sat down next to her and held her hand.

"Susan, this is a hell of a time for you to get a cold," he said softly.

She smiled, "Yes, that's all it is, a cold—maybe the flu. Just let me lie here for a bit and I'll be fine."

Walker reached up, removed the cloth, and felt her forehead. At the same time, he shifted the way he was holding her hand and started taking her pulse. Her pulse was weak and rapid, and her head was blazing.

He reached down, raised her dress, and opened her legs slightly.

"Really, Lucas. Now is hardly the time..." she mumbled.

High on the inside of her right thigh were three buboes, one very large, and two somewhat smaller. They looked like huge blisters, pasty white on the raised surface, with an angry red ring circling it.

Susan Whitney had the plague.

* * * * *

It was a beautiful day in Naples. The sun was glinting off the iridescent blue waters of Naples Bay, gulls were wheeling and soaring over the British ships in their never-ending quest for human scraps, and Nelson's flag snapped in the warm breeze that was sweeping over the *Foudroyant* from the southwest.

In many ways, the *Foudroyant* was still recovering. Several days before, it was announced that the King and Queen would be arriving soon, along with their Prime Minister, Sir John Acton, and a coterie of foreign ambassadors. There were plusses and minuses to this news. On the negative side, there were so many dignitaries to be housed that the *Foudroyant* officers would be bumped, and would find themselves sleeping in rather unaccustomed places. Even Nelson would have to bed down in his first lieutenant's tiny compartment. Offsetting this inconvenience, however, the officers—and especially the midshipmen—had never eaten so well. Among the advance men was His Majesty's personal chef who, half-paralyzed with horror at having to prepare meals in a ship's galley, nevertheless conjured up dishes the like of which had never been seen aboard ship.

The previous day's dinner had been served about noon to the ship's officers. It was a leisurely affair, lasting several hours. Following this, Lady Emma Hamilton was coaxed into playing her harp and singing. Later, as the sun went down, a large decked galley came alongside filled with opera singers from the city to serenade the company well into the evening.

Life was good again for some people—but not for everyone.

That night a small group of fleeing Jacobins was discovered by banditti, hiding in a cave in the mountains of Calabria. Given the original richness of their now haggard clothing, the bandits surmised that these men might bring a reward of some sort. They were right, for among them was Admiral Francesco Caracciolo.

Caracciolo was born a nobleman, and chose to serve his King in the Neapolitan Navy. He learned his craft under the British Admiral George Brydges Rodney, and served with distinction in the War of American Independence, as well as against the Barbary pirates and the French. In short, he was very highly regarded by King Ferdinand and his Queen; and, when Nelson engineered their escape from Naples, the royal family sailed on his ship, the frigate *Sannita*.

But Caracciolo was dismayed by the King's flight. How could he just leave his people like that? How could he abandon them to the French? So, shortly after the royal court was settled in Palermo, he asked for permission to go back to Naples to take care of some family business concerning his ancestral lands. It was granted, and he never came back.

It must be said that he never intended to switch sides in the conflict, but contact with his old friends, who had become infatuated with the French revolution, soon weakened his resolve. Even more to the point, if he had not subscribed to the revolution, his property would have been confiscated by the state, and his family left penniless. He was appointed the commander of the new republic's naval forces, and fought with the same effectiveness that he had shown when he was with the Royalists. That fact was to come back to haunt him.

Nelson was on the quarterdeck of the *Foudroyant* when the boat carrying Caracciolo came alongside. He was brought before Nelson looking haggard from misery, his clothing dirty and torn; but he still had a glint of pride and resolution in his eyes. Whatever happened, he would endure it like a man.

Nelson looked at him for a long moment. "Caracciolo..." Nelson started to say something, then stopped as if he had changed his mind. "Caracciolo, you have a board of inquiry waiting for you in the wardroom."

"Admiral, am I to be given no time to prepare a defense?"

Nelson thought about that for several seconds. "There is a board of inquiry waiting for you in the wardroom," he finally repeated. Then waving to the marine guards, "Take him away."

The marines led him off the quarterdeck, down the starboard ladder, through the ornate doors and into the wardroom. There his worst fears were realized.

Behind a table, covered in green cloth, were six Neapolitan naval officers. In the middle was Admiral di Thurin, Caracciolo's worst personal enemy and the president of the board of inquiry. He was seated before the panel.

Without preamble, Di Thurn began, "Sir, this board has been convened by Admiral Nelson to examine your recent actions on behalf of the rebel forces lately occupying Naples.

"I must begin with this question: Are you indeed Admiral Francesco Caracciolo, Duke of Brienza?"

"I am."

"Is there any member of this panel who does not recognize this man as Admiral Francesco Caracciolo, Duke of Brienza?" Di Thurn looked to his left and right. Seeing no dissent, he continued, "The orders I received are as follows:

> Whereas Francisco Caracciolo, a commodore in the service of His Sicilian Majesty, has been taken and stands accused of rebellion against his lawful sovereign, and for firing at his colors hoisted on board his Majesty's frigate, *La Minerva*, under your command. You are, therefore, hereby required and directed to assemble five of the senior officers under your command, yourself presiding, and proceed to inquire whether the crime with which the said Francisco Caracciolo stands charged, can be proved against him, and if the charge is proved, you are to report to me what punishment he ought to suffer.

"Do you have any questions?" He said to Caracciolo.

"Yes, I have several.

"I was captured last night, and brought aboard this vessel not a half-hour ago. I demand the right to prepare a defense—something I have obviously not had the time to do."

"Denied," Thurn replied. "Your activities are manifest, no further witnesses are needed."

"Then that brings me to my next question. "Your orders say I '...stand accused of rebellion...' Who accuses me?"

Di Thurin did not expect this question, but quickly deflected it. "The orders do not say."

"Then by what right is this board being held?"

"I read you the orders authorizing this inquiry."

"Orders issued by Admiral Nelson?"

"Yes."

"And by what right does he issue them? For that matter, this inquiry is being held aboard the *Foudroyant,* a British man-of-war. It is, in effect, a piece of sovereign British soil, sitting here in Naples harbor. But I am not a British citizen, nor are you. So by what right does Nelson issue these orders, and why am I being tried on British soil?"

This was not going at all as di Thurn had anticipated, and he had to regain control.

"Your arguments are specious. If you require an accuser, I shall be that person. As for who issued the order for these proceedings and where they are held, it's irrelevant. You stand accused of rebellion against His Majesty, and we are all lawful officers in His Majesty's Navy. That's all that matters.

"So, you are both my accuser and my judge, is that it?"

Di Thurn ignored the jibe. Instead, he said, "I have some questions of my own.

"Admiral, have you ever taken up arms against His Majesty?"

"Yes, I was forced to."

"We'll get to your defense shortly, if you have one; but first I must establish some facts for the record.

"You have admitted taking up arms against His Majesty. Did you also command the gunboats that, on several occasions, prevented His Majesty's troops from landing to stage a counter-offensive against the rebels?"

"Yes, I did."

"Have you ever given written orders tending to oppose the arms of His Majesty?"

"Yes, I did."

"Did you ever cause your ship, or any ship, to fire upon His Majesty's frigate, *La Minerva*."

"Yes, I did."

Di Thurn sighed and sat back in his chair. He was silent for a long moment, and then said, "Admiral, from your own lips you have condemned yourself as a traitor—as a man who abandoned his King in a time of need. Do you have anything to say for yourself?"

Caracciolo looked down, gathering his thoughts.

"You accuse me of deserting my King in a time of need. I would submit to you, gentlemen, that to the contrary, the King deserted me and all his other faithful subjects.

"Do you recall the time before the French moved down to take our city? General Mack had our army in the hills, with superior numbers to the French, and was prepared to fight those troops. But then our King took flight, and worse, *he took the treasury with him!* He took all the money, and everything that could be converted into money, loaded it aboard British ships, and fled to Palermo to live in riotous luxury.

"Now, all of you know that the sinews of war is money. Without it, Mack could not hold the army together. He couldn't pay their wages, or buy their food, or provide shelter, or gunpowder, or bullets. Mack's army dissolved and the French wound up occupying Naples. After such uncalled for, and I must say, cowardly desertion, who then was the traitor, gentlemen—the King or myself?"

Caracciolo paused again.

"I feared, and rightly so, what would happen once the French occupation began. As I believe all of you know, my possessions lay in the city, and that my family is quite large. If I had not succumbed to the ruling power, my children..." Here Caracciolo had trouble speaking. "...my children would have been vagabonds in the land of their fathers.

"Gentlemen, some of you are parents. Place yourselves in my situation. How would you have acted? What would you have done?"

There was an eerie silence in the room. No one spoke. The only sounds that could be heard were the calls of the gulls sweeping past the aft windows of the room. Caracciolo continued.

"But I think my destruction has been predetermined," he looked pointedly at di Thurn, "and this court is anything but a court of justice. If I am right, my blood will be upon your head, and on the heads of your children!"

Again, there was a long silence, finally interrupted by di Thurn. "I think we've heard enough. The prisoner will leave the room while we confer."

The marine guards took Caracciolo away, but soon found themselves escorting the prisoner back.

Standing before the court, he heard di Thurn say: "Admiral Prince Caracciolo, you have been found guilty of the charges brought against you. You have repaid the high rank and honors conferred on you by a mild and confiding sovereign, with the blackest ingratitude. We will make our sentencing recommendations, and call you at Admiral Nelson's pleasure."

The marine guards took Caracciolo away again, and di Thurn met with Nelson on the poop deck of the *Foudroyant*. No one could hear what they were saying, but they seemed to be arguing. Soon Sir William Hamilton came up and joined in the discussion. Because the vote was a divided one—four to two—the board recommended to Admiral Nelson that Caracciolo be sentenced to life imprisonment; but Nelson would have none of it. He wanted the death penalty—and more.

The board reconvened, looking very somber. Caracciolo was standing before the green-clad table. Di Thurn sat rigidly, with his bicorne hat firmly on his head.

"Admiral Caracciolo, it is my duty to read to you the following orders from Lord Nelson.

To Commodore Count Thurn

Commander of his Sicilian Majesty's frigate *La Minerva*.

Whereas a board of Naval Officers of his Sicilian Majesty, has been assembled to try Francisco Caracciolo for rebellion against his lawful sovereign, and for firing at his Sicilian Majesty's frigate *La Minerva*;

And whereas the said board of naval officers have found the charge of rebellion fully proved against him, and have sentenced the said Caracciolo to suffer death, you are hereby required and directed to cause the said sentence of death to be carried into execution upon the said Francisco Caracciolo accordingly, by hanging him at the foreyard-arm of his Sicilian Majesty's frigate *La Minerva*, under your command, at five o'clock this evening, and to cause him to hang there till sunset, when you will have his body cut down, and thrown into the sea."

Caracciolo was not surprised by the verdict or even the sentence. But he was shocked by the way it was to be carried out.

Di Thurn continued, "Do you have anything to say?"

Caracciolo quickly recovered. "Admiral, I have not been tried at the order of my country, or even in my country; but I do not challenge this verdict. I've lived a full life and, under the circumstances, I am not eager to prolong it; but the disgrace of being hung like a common seaman is dreadful to me. I appeal to you... please, sirs... let me at least be shot by a firing squad instead of hung."

"We recommended that to Lord Nelson. He denied it."

"But... five o'clock is only a few hours away. Is it not the law that a condemned man be given twenty-four hours to seek peace with his maker?"

Di Thurn was uncomfortably searching for the right words. He and Caracciolo had been enemies for years, but even he was not comfortable with the way things had turned out. Finally he replied, "That is Neapolitan law, but... it's unclear whether Neapolitan law strictly applies here."

Caracciolo stood in stunned silence. Di Thurn finally broke it. "Francisco, for what it's worth, both Sir William Hamilton and I argued for more time; but Nelson, he..."

"I understand. Thank you." Caracciolo turned and left the room without the assistance of the guards.

* * * * *

At precisely five o'clock that afternoon, a gun was fired from *La Minerva* signaling that the hanging had been carried out. Nelson was in the wardroom of the *Foudroyant* having dinner with Sir William and Lady Hamilton. The sound reverberated across the bay, just as Nelson was finishing his soup course.

Chapter Six

It was an experiment; but it was one in which Captain Ralph Miller was eager to participate.

Both the French and the British navies had been using grapeshot for as long as ships have had guns. In its simplest form, it consisted of a mass of lead balls loaded into a sack, and shoved down the barrel of a naval gun in lieu of the normal round shot. When the gun was fired, the balls spread out like a shotgun blast causing extensive personnel injuries, as well as damage to enemy rigging. It was similar to the canister shot used by the army, but the lead balls were much larger in the naval version, so they could punch through the sides of ships.

The problem with grape or canister shot, however, was that the lead balls tended to spread out too much. The individual balls could kill a person at 300 yards; but by then the pattern was so spread that, if you did hit someone, it was pure luck.

They tried using hollow iron shot, filled with black powder, and sporting a burning fuse. While this made an impressive thunderclap when it detonated, and probably deafened a few people, it didn't otherwise do all that much damage, because its "punch" was limited to the amount of metal that was contained in the shell's outer wall.

What was needed was a true exploding shell—a combination of these two approaches—one that would travel to the enemy, explode in the air, and release the deadly lead balls, which would hit the enemy in a tight pattern.

Several years ago Captain Miller had run into a young man by the name of Henry Shrapnel, who was a lieutenant in the Royal Artillery. The young man would go on and on about an idea he had for just such a shell, something he called a "spherical case shot." It would not rely on a lit fuse; instead, it would have an internal timing mechanism that would be made active when the shot was fired. Inside the shot was a mixture of lead balls and black powder.

Miller knew that the Admiralty was considering Shrapnel's ideas; but he also knew that the new shells had a problem. It seems that occasionally the heat produced by a ball traveling down the barrel of a gun would ignite the powder within the ball, leading to premature explosion and a dud.

It was a problem the French were having as well, and now was the time to see if they had solved it. When Sir Sidney captured the French ships that were attempting to resupply Bonaparte's Army, onboard one of them was a quantity of their new exploding shells. Captain Miller had ordered twenty of them brought to the gun deck, along with fifty British 20-pound shells, and a large assortment of various sized powder cartridges to be used in the test. If you were going to try out these newfangled shells, what better target than Bonaparte's own troops?

Near the after hatch on the gundeck two midshipmen were sitting on the floor, doing what 12 and 13 year old boys usually do when they're bored. They were playing. The shells, flannel powder bags, and fuses had been brought up from the forward magazine, and were stacked near the main mast. Their job was to "watch them" until they were ready to be used.

"Watching things," however, can be an onerous job for a boy, especially when confronted with the "hurry-up and wait" mindset that has been a part of military life since military organizations first began. It was a perfect time for Jimmy Webb, the older of the two midshipmen, to show his friend, James Bigges Forbes, a trick he had learned on a previous ship.

"James, me boy, have I ever showed you the mystery of the dancing twig?"

"The dancing twig?" he asked.

"Yes. You've heard of the dancing twig, haven't you?" This was said with the kind of worldly-wise authority that can only be generated by a 13 year old when talking to a 12 year old.

"Why, no. I don't believe I have. What are you talking about?"

"Well, actually, I don't know if I should be showing you this. You're awfully young, you know."

James Forbes was now hooked. "Young? I am 12 and a half. In a few months I'll be as old as you."

"Yes, but by then I'll be 14."

"So what? Come on, Jimmy. What's the dancing twig?"

Jimmy Webb sighed. "All right, if you insist."

Jimmy got up and went over to the stack of gunnery supplies that were only a few feet away, and grabbed a handful of quill fuses. Crossing over to the other side of the ship, he picked up a mallet and several nails left by the ship's carpenter, and returned to his friend.

Settling back down, he laid one of the fuses on the deck, positioned a nail at one end, and picked up the hammer. "Watch this," he said and then brought the hammer down, driving the nail into the fuse.

Suddenly the fuse erupted with a substantial "bang," and the quill flew up in the air, turning over and over before landing a few feet away.

Forbes thought that was one the neatest things he had ever seen. Truth be known, Jimmy Webb thought so too, so he repeated it with a second fuse.

Now Forbes wanted to try it, and he replicated Jimmy's feat with three additional fuses. Then Jimmy had an idea.

"Let's try one where you drive a nail into one end and, at the same time, I'll drive one in the other. Let's see if we can get two pops."

This miraculous feat was, in fact, quite possible. The fuses in question were hollowed out quills that were filled with a special mixture of gunpowder kneaded in spirits of wine. When a gun was loaded with powder and shot, one of these quill fuses would be shoved through a vent hole, breaking open the powder bag. A flame from a slow match, or a spark from a flintlock, would ignite one end of the quill, which would rapidly burn to the other end, igniting the powder bag, and firing the gun. The thing is, it didn't matter which end of the quill you shoved down the vent hole. Both ends were equally explosive.

Jimmy obtained a second hammer. "All right, now. At the count of three, we'll both hit our nails.

"One... Two... THREE!

Both boys hit their targets at about the same time. There were indeed two pops; but the quill did not fly up into the air. Two flames rushed down the inside of the quill, meeting in the middle. This, in turn, disintegrated the quill sending tiny hot splinters in all directions. Against impossible odds, one of those splinters traveled to a powder bag, at just the right angle, with just enough force to penetrate the flannel, and with just enough heat to ignite the powder within.

The official Report was written by the First Lieutenant of the *Theseus*, Mr. England, and sent to Sir Sidney Smith. It read as follows:

Tom Grundner

Theseus, at Sea
off Mount Carmel in Syria
15th of May, 1799

It is with extreme concern I have to acquaint you that yesterday morning, at half past nine o'clock, twenty 36-pounder shells, and fifty 18-pounder shells, had been got up and prepared ready for service by Captain Miller's order, the Ship then close off Caesaria, when in an instant, owing to an accident that we have not been able to discover, the whole was on fire, and a most dreadful explosion took place. The Ship was immediately in flames in the main-rigging and mizen-top, in the cockpit, in the tiers, in several places about the main-deck, and in various other parts of the Ship. The danger was very imminent, and required an uncommon exertion of every one to get under so collected a body of fire as made its appearance, and I have the happiness to add, that our exertions were crowned with success, the fire got under, and the Ship most miraculously preserved. I here feel myself called upon to declare how much obliged I am to all the officers and ship's company, but more particularly to Lieutenant Summers, Mr. Atkinson, master, and the officers and men, whose assistance on this occasion was truly great, and enabled us to get the better of so great a calamity.

Our loss from the explosion, I here lament, has been very great; and Captain Miller, I am sorry to add, is of the number killed, which amount to 26; 10 drowned; and 45 wounded. The whole of the poop and after-part of the quarter-deck is entirely blown to pieces, and all the beams destroyed; eight of the main-deck beams also broke, which fell down and jammed the tiller; all the wardrobe, bulkheads and windows entirely blown to pieces, and the Ship left a perfect wreck. In short, a greater scene of horror or devastation could not be produced; and we are all truly grateful to God Almighty for His most signal preservation, in saving us from a danger so very great and alarming.

In transmitting this Report to Earl St. Vincent, Sir Sidney Smith alluded to Captain Miller as follows:

The service suffers from this loss at this conjuncture, in the proportion by which it gained advantage from his gallant example, his indefatigable zeal, and consummate skill, in conducting the operations for the defense of the north side of this Town, committed to his management. He had long been in the practice of collecting such of the Enemy's shells as fell in the Town without bursting, and of sending them back to the Enemy better prepared, and with evident effect. He had a deposit on board the *Theseus* ready for service, and more were preparing, when, by an accident, for which nobody can account, the whole took fire, and exploded at short intervals.

Sidney took Lieutenant England from the *Theseus* and made him First Lieutenant of the *Tigre*. He then took Lieutenant Canes from the *Tigre* and made him acting captain of the *Theseus*. But in Captain Miller the Royal Navy had lost an excellent officer, and Sidney Smith had lost one of the few fellow naval officers he could call a friend.

* * * * *

There was no formal announcement that Bonaparte's siege guns had arrived. There was no need—the guns announced themselves. From early morning until dusk, an unending stream of 24-pound fists banged on the walls, demanding entrance; and their tireless insistence could be felt throughout the town.

However, the shots were not random. They were concentrated on one particular place—the breach that had been begun weeks earlier by the lighter 8- and 12-pound cannons. That was what had Sir Sidney concerned. If the French could force an opening at that point, it would give them admittance to the Pasha's extensive, wide-open, garden area on the other side of the wall. From there, they could branch-out to every corner of the city, and all would be lost.

Sir Sidney was aboard the *Tigre,* sitting at the long table in his stateroom pretending to do paperwork, but with little success. His face was hollow-cheeked and pale. His eyes had lost the infectious luster they once radiated. His body, not large to begin with, had lost considerable weight in the past two months; making his clothes look like a blue and gold parody of a uniform. He wasn't physically sick. He was a man who was simply exhausted from worry.

Three sharp raps sounded at the cabin door. The door opened, a marine guard materialized and snapped to attention. "Sir. Dr. Walker to see you."

"Very well, send him in." Sir Sidney's voice sounded tired; but, in truth, he was glad to see his old friend—glad, that is, until he saw the look on Walker's face.

Walker sat down at the table and a servant quickly came in bearing a glass of wine and a glass of lemon-water. Sir Sidney took the full glass of wine; Walker took the lemonade. Walker was an ex-alcoholic, and this was the strongest drink he allowed himself.

The two men said nothing for a long time, and Smith took the opportunity to study Walker over. He looked as bad as Smith felt. He too was haggard. He too had lost weight; but the lines in Walker's face were not from worry, they were from frustration.

Smith thought about a reoccurring nightmare Walker once related to him. He was in a situation where a group of innocent people was being attacked by a tiger. He was the only one with a chance of stopping the animal, but all he had was a bow and arrow. Sometimes the bow and arrow worked and the tiger was slain. Other nights—most nights—the arrow did not work. He would wake up in a sweat, still able to see the faces of the people who were dying because of his inadequacy.

The silence was broken by Sir Sidney. "She's dead, isn't she?"

Walker looked up. "Dead?"

"Yes, I know that look in your eyes, Lucas. Someone is dead. It's Susan, isn't it?"

"No, she's not dead—at least not yet."

"John Wesley? I thought he was on the mend."

"No, he's doing fine. I don't think you *can* kill him."

"Then who?"

"Phélippeaux. He died today about 1:00."

Sidney slumped back in his chair. Picard Phélippeaux was not only his friend, as a military engineer, he was vital to the defense of the city. Suddenly a cloud passed over Smith's face.

"Damn it! How many times did I tell him not to go out into that moat? The French snipers were just waiting to pick him off, and the fool..."

"He wasn't shot. He just dropped over. His workers say it was from overwork, and they're probably right; but I wrote sunstroke on his death certificate, which could also be correct."

Again, there was silence as Sidney thought about the terrible loss of his friend. Then he looked up and asked, "What about Susan? Are we going to lose her too?"

"I don't know, Sidney. I just don't know. I mean there's nothing..." Walker's voice caught for a moment. "There is nothing I can do about it. I can give her cold compresses. I can give her painkillers and try to make her comfortable. Maria Corriveau is with her night and day; but there's not a damn thing I can DO that will make her better. I can do nothing about Susan. I can do nothing about the kid I saw this morning with the gangrenous infection. I can do nothing about bullet wounds to the stomach. I can do nothing about..."

Walker swung his hand to make his point, and knocked over the glass containing his lemonade.

"I am sorry, Sidney," Walker said; but Smith had already grabbed a cloth and was sopping up the spill. "It's just I am so frustrated."

Smith tried to lighten his friend's burden a bit. "Susan, will do all right, Lucas. You said yourself that not everyone dies of the plague; and if anyone can beat it, it's Susan."

"Well, you're certainly right about that," Walker agreed.

"Remember when we were making our escape with Prince William out of Yorktown?" Smith continued. "The road to Gloucester? Where I supposedly 'sold' Susan to that blagger so we could steal his horse and wagon?"

Walker started laughing. "Yes. Yes, indeed. That whole plan was her idea. Then remember how mad she was when Bill Parish and I went off into Alexandria without her, and got captured. But, you know, she ran that ship's medical department like she was the doctor and I was a junior assistant off on a holiday."

Smith smiled and countered with another recollection. "Remember the time she conned us out of that money so she could go off and buy books to start a library for the men on the *Diamond*, and teach them how to read and write? Who ever heard of anything so crazy? Yet, I understand there are a dozen ships now that have books for the sailors and not just the officers. They call them 'Whitney Libraries'."

Both men smiled, thinking about this extraordinary woman—a woman who was like a sister to Sir Sidney, and to Walker... perhaps something more, if he would ever allow himself to admit the obvious.

But the nostalgic relief was brief. Susan was dying a horrible death, and the words kept pounding in Walkers head like hammer blows: *She's dying and there's nothing I can do. There's nothing I can do. There's nothing...*

More silence, this time broken by Walker.

"When's it going to end, Sidney? This siege, I mean."

"It will end when either Bonaparte defeats us and takes Acre, or we defeat him and send him packing. Not a moment sooner."

"But *when* will that happen? It's been almost two months now. How much longer can it go on?"

It was Sir Sidney's turn to look uncomfortable. "That's what has me scared, Lucas. I think it will be ending soon; and I can't guarantee you, in all honesty, that we'll be on the winning side.

"Bonaparte has his siege guns now, so it's only a matter of time before he knocks a hole in the wall large enough to drive his entire army through; and I don't think we can stop him. We've sent for reinforcements to Rhodes and Constantinople, but... nothing so far, and I am afraid they won't arrive in time."

Walker had gotten up and was now pacing, animated, relieved to be able to turn his attention to this new topic. "What about British troops?" Walker shot back. "Didn't you ask for British troops? Men, ships, guns, supplies? I can understand the bloody Turks not showing up, but what about our own people? For God's sake, the last time I checked this was a Royal Navy ship, and we were here in the name of King George."

Smith bit his lower lip for a moment then said, "I haven't heard back."

Walker was looking out the windows in the stern gallery of Smith's cabin, debating whether to ask the next question or not; but he had to ask it. He had to get it off his chest.

"Sidney, have you considered the possibility that this lack of support from Nelson and Jervis is intentional?"

"Lucas, be careful. You are a warranted officer in His Majesty's Navy. You are dancing around the edges of insubordination, if not outright treason."

Walker came around, sat directly across from Smith, and looked at him hard. "Insubordination be damned. I'll ask you again. Have you ever considered that your lack of support from Nelson and Jervis is intentional?"

Smith would not meet Walker's gaze, and he turned in his chair so as not to have to deal with it. "I have no idea what you're talking about."

"Like hell you don't. You've got Bonaparte checked, something none of those blockhead generals in Europe have been able to do. If Nelson, or Jervis, or even the Admiralty in London would send some troops to reinforce you, and provide another force to cut Bonaparte off from retreating south, he wouldn't just be checked—he'd be trapped. They've certainly had enough time to do so."

"What are you saying, Lucas? That my superiors are trying to kill me?

"Yes!" Walker's hand slammed down on the table.

"Lucas, I am warning you, your statements are bordering on..."

"Then let me rephrase my answer. I am not saying that they have sent a team of assassins out to do you in; but think about it. They know you are engaging Bonaparte; you send them both constant reports. They know you don't have enough of anything, and in the past five days, Bonaparte has made three assaults. But, most importantly, they know *you*, Sidney. They know it's only a matter of time before you do something insane and eat a musket ball.

"I can see the report to London now. 'It is with the deepest regret that we must inform your lordships of the heroic death of Captain Sir Sidney Smith.' But, heroic or not, you'll be dead. The last remaining rival to Horatio Nelson will be gone. Out of the way."

It was Smith's turn to get out of his chair. He paced to the stern windows to look out, his hands behind his back, rocking back and forth on the balls of his feet. "You're talking nonsense," he finally murmured.

"Really? Admiral Jervis became the Earl of St. Vincent, because Nelson disobeyed his orders and won a battle for him. You think he's not grateful for that? Since then Nelson has been his fair-haired boy—his personal protégé.

"You, on the other hand, merely burned ten French ships of the line at Toulon—which made Nelson's victory at the Nile possible. Have you heard anyone mention that little fact in conjunction with Nelson's victory? But the biggest mistake you made was escaping from the Temple. Did you have to do it in such a breathtaking, hair-raising, way? When you got back, you were the toast of England. Hell, I can still hear Jervis' and Nelson's teeth grinding at that.

"But the Temple escape would be a mere childhood prank compared to beating Bonaparte, head-to-head, here at Acre. You would be a god in the mind's of the British public. Unfortunately, in the minds of Jervis and Nelson, there can be only one God in heaven, and one in the Royal Navy—and that's Nelson!

"Don't you get it, Sidney?"

Sir Sidney Smith *did* get it. He just couldn't say it—not even to his closest friend.

* * * * *

Midshipman George Parsons had never seen anything quite like it, nor had anyone else on the *Foudroyant*. They were celebrating the first anniversary of Nelson's victory at the Nile a bit early, but that did not dampen anyone's enthusiasm.

Parsons and several other midshipmen had secured places in the starboard mainmast ratlines, along with as many other sailors as could be accommodated. People were standing on yardarm foot-ropes, crowded along the gangway, perched anywhere that would afford them a view of the amazing sight. The only place that was not overrun with sailors was the quarterdeck and the poop. That was reserved for the King and Queen, Nelson, Sir William and Lady Hamilton, Lord Acton, and a host of other dignitaries that Parsons could not identify.

Earlier that afternoon a grand feast was held. The King and Queen, of course, dined with Nelson and the Hamiltons; but there was so much good food laying about that even perpetually hungry midshipmen and ship's boys were satiated. At dusk, a twenty-one gun salute was fired in Nelson's honor by every Sicilian ship in the harbor, and all the forts overlooking it.

But the main event—the one that everyone was anticipating—was yet to come.

Across the darkened water, a vessel could be seen approaching the *Foudroyant*. It was a barge that was fitted out like a Roman galley, with a red lamp on each oar. Closer and closer it came, like an unearthly water bug, until at last it pulled along side. Suddenly lights started to come on all over the ship. In a surprisingly brief time, some 2000 lamps of all different colors were lit. In the center of the vessel was a Greek column bearing a pedestal with Nelson's name emblazoned on it. In the stern were two golden angels holding an oversized picture of Nelson. Then, as the gasps of the audience were reaching a crescendo, a small boat that was towed behind the galley started launching small fireworks.

The dignitaries were applauding vigorously, and the men were cheering wildly. One of the sailors got so carried away that he lost his footing on the main yard and fell into the bay, taking a second sailor with him, thus mixing laughter with the applause and cheers. It was a glorious sight.

After the fireworks died down, a master of ceremonies appeared on the bow of the galley. Behind him, on deck, was an orchestra. The master of ceremonies called for silence.

"Your Majesty, Admiral Nelson, esteemed guests, it is my extreme honor to bring you the trifling entertainment we have for you this evening. Behind me is an orchestra and a choir consisting of the very best musicians and singers in all of Naples—which means they are the finest in the world." At this, the members of the royal court started applauding, which was taken up by the British officers, and then by the sailors. The host continued.

"But our best musical effort, on our best day, would be wholly inadequate to express our gratitude to Admiral Nelson for his courage and brilliance in defeating the French in Egypt." More applause.

Each piece of music we perform tonight, Admiral, will be dedicated to you. We were once in distress; but Nelson came—the invincible Nelson. We were preserved and again made happy."

Amidst the wild cheers this statement engendered, Nelson stood to wave to the performers, his face aglow with satisfaction.

As the applause began to die down, the man called the orchestra and choir to attention and began the first song. It was a little ditty taken from a play first performed in 1740 and rapidly gaining popularity in London. It was called "Rule Britannia."

Following the musical, there was a pause as preparations were made for a massive fireworks display. George Parsons and his friend Midshipman George Antram were still perched on the ratlines, and adjusting their positions while awaiting "the good part" to begin.

"Is this not the most remarkable thing you've ever seen?" Parson's commented.

"It's all right, but it's not as good as the fireworks'll be, I'll wager. But either way, it won't be the most remarkable thing you'll ever see. That will come in another day or two."

"What do you mean?"

Antram paused for a moment, looked around, and lowered his voice. "Remember the fisherman that came along side this morning?"

"Yes."

"Well, I was in charge of the party to off load his catch and got to talking with him. He says Caracciolo has risen from the bottom of the sea, and is coming as fast as he can to Naples, swimming half out of the water."

Parsons looked at his friend with a mixture of skepticism and pity.

"You are so gullible."

"I am not. He says he saw it with his own eyes."

"George... Caracciolo was hung. Hung—as in the total separation of body from soul. Then he was placed in a canvas bag, with three double-headed shot tied to his legs. That has to be at least 250 pounds of weight. He was then taken out of the bay, and dropped overboard; and you're telling me that he is now merrily making his way back to Naples, by swimming no less, and we should expect him for tea any day now."

"I am just telling you what the fisherman told me."

"And you believe him?"

Antrum thought for a moment. "Yes. Yes, I do. There are stranger things in this world than you can imagine, George Parsons. A long shot stranger than you can imagine."

* * * * *

It seemed like he had dropped off to sleep only a few minutes earlier, when Parsons felt someone shaking his shoulder. He looked up to see Lieutenant Septimus Arabin. "Get up Georgie-boy. The King is up early this morning; and it's your turn to attend him."

"Attend him? How?"

"Just hover in the background. Anything he needs—anything you even think he needs—you go do it or fetch it. Understand?"

Parsons quietly grumbled, but rolled out of his warm hammock and quickly got dressed. Emerging on deck, he found the new day to be quite different from the celebrations of the night before. A chilly fog had rolled, in casting a once colorful world into a million shades of gray. Visibility was at best only 30 or 40 yards, and there was the kind of eerie silence that can only be found in the padded embrace of a thick mist.

King Ferdinand was standing at the aft rail of the poop, the highest deck on the ship. When Parsons arrived, he turned to see who it was, nodded, and resumed his contemplation. Parsons took his place at the breastwork, as far away from the King as he could get, yet still keep him in view.

After several minutes, the King started to stroll along the larboard rail when he suddenly stopped and looked hard into the fog. He turned to Parsons, "You there, boy. Fetch me a telescope!"

Parsons ran down to the quarterdeck and got the telescope that he knew would be in the drawer under the binnacle, and ran back.

The King snatched it from his hands and began studying the fog. Suddenly the telescope fell to the deck and he started making frantic but inarticulate sounds. Parsons rushed to his side, alarmed, and looked to where he was pointing. There was no need for a telescope. Slowly emerging from the fog was the bloated body of Francisco Caracciolo, still manacled, floating upright, and facing the ship as if making an accusation. His face was swollen and discolored from the water, and his eyes were popping from their sockets by the strangulation of the hanging; but it was clearly him.

George Parsons was now as terrified as the King; but he could not simply remain frozen in place. He ran down the ladder to the quarterdeck, grateful to be out of sight of that...

that thing. He dashed into the wardroom where he knew the duty officer, Lieutenant Arabin, would probably be taking his breakfast.

"Lieutenant! Please, come quick."

"What's happened?"

"There's a... There's a..." Parsons didn't know how to describe it. "Just, please, come quick."

The two ran up on deck, followed by several other officers who had just sat down with Arabin. The King was at the same place by the rail, but now he was kneeling in prayer and shaking with fear. When he saw the British officers arrive, he stood, pointed to the hideous body, and made some gurgling sounds.

The ship was now in alarm and people were emerging from all corners to see what the disturbance was about. Arriving on the poop half dressed, Nelson saw the body and immediately turned pale. The King whirled on him.

"Do you see? Do you see what you've done? I knew it! I knew God was going to punish us. He has cursed us." Then suddenly realizing that other people were listening, he grew silent.

Nelson was not a big believer in the supernatural; but he was completely unable to explain what was so clearly before him.

"Your highness, this is... That is... sometimes when bodies are cast into the sea..."

"Sire, I believe what is happening here is quite clear." The authoritative voice was coming from one of the King's numerous religious advisors, and one of the quicker minds. "Obviously the spirit of Admiral Caracciolo cannot find rest until you personally forgive him; and he has risen from the sea to implore that forgiveness."

The King's eyes were still wide with fright; but this was something he could cling to—something that might restore some sanity to his world. "Yes. That must be it. That *must* be it!"

He turned to the sightless body of Caracciolo, which was still patiently bobbing in the early morning chop. There was a note of desperation in his voice. "I forgive you, Francisco. Do you hear me? I forgive you. We are friends again. Just like the old days. Just like before... before all this..." The King broke down for a moment, gathered himself, and continued in a similar vein.

Nelson eventually turned away from the King's babbling, and quietly ordered a boat to pick up the damn body and tow it ashore for burial.

* * * * *

Smith could hardly see anymore because of the constant exposure of his eyes to gun-smoke and the effects of peering into a blazing sun. He was becoming exhausted by constantly having to be on-duty, and so were his men. Yet, despite this, for days on end Sir Sidney Smith seemed to be everywhere.

Aboard ship, he was directing the naval units, large and small, in their unremitting harassment of the French troops. There was a small island in the Bay of Acre, called the Tower of Flies. He moved guns from the crippled *Theseus* to the island to provide yet another gunfire angle into the enemy lines.

When he wasn't aboard ship, he was in the city examining their supplies of food, water, and ammunition, and looking in on Lucas Walker to see how the sick and wounded were doing. He was especially concerned about Susan, of course; but the prospects of the plague sweeping away what few fighting men he had left literally kept him awake at night.

If he thought an attack was imminent, he was on the walls. When all was quiet, he would go outside the walls on what he called "intelligence expeditions." Indeed, one such expedition was almost the end of him.

The French knew that Sir Sidney had a penchant for making these excursions, and had a number of sharpshooters moved forward to try to pick him off. They also knew that if Smith could be killed, Acre would fall. On one such occasion, a group of marksmen had moved in front of their trenches to get a better shot. Midshipman Richard Janverin spotted them.

"I see them lying down under the ridges of sand in front," he whispered to Sir Sidney, "and they'll put a ball through you before you can say Jack Robinson."

Smith surveyed the situation and knew they were essentially trapped. If they moved in any direction, they would be immediately shot. If they stayed where they were, they would be shot a little later. Their only hope was to surprise the riflemen by sprinting for the breach in the wall that had been created by Bonaparte's guns.

Smith outlined the idea and said, "Now, boys, the devil take the hindmost," and they all made a break for it. The 34-year-old Smith stumbled over the rubble of the demolished wall before some of the men, who were half his age, could get halfway there.

In between all the above, he was writing to everyone he could think of—Constantinople, Naples, Gibraltar, and London. Eventually, when the Turkish troops had still not arrived, he decided to pull rank.

Before leaving Constantinople, he had received a firman from the Sultan, giving him command of all Ottoman naval and land forces. He now decided to use it. He wrote a letter to the Turkish commander in Rhodes *demanding*—not asking—that he send ships and troop reinforcements immediately. Unfortunately, he had no similar power over British assets.

Bonaparte had received his siege guns from Alexandria. This was made possible because HMS *Lion*, a 64-gun third rate, had to go off station to replenish her water supply. This allowed three French frigates and two brigs to sail out of Alexandria with Bonaparte's much needed supplies. When the *Lion*, under Captain Sir Manley Dixon, got back on station and saw the French ships were gone, he headed to Palermo to report the fact to Admiral Nelson and get further orders. Instead of being sent to help out at Acre, the *Lion* and her 64-guns was sent to patrol off Leghorn in northern Italy.

Sir Sidney could expect no help from Nelson.

The defenders were running short of everything. On the land side of Acre was a long sandy plain that radiated heat and midday sunlight with equal viciousness. To the north, glimmering like a mirage, was a freshwater lake about a mile long and a quarter-mile wide. It was the only body of water that Bonaparte controlled, but it was an important one. The city had several wells but they were not enough to completely meet the needs of the population. With access to the freshwater lake cut off, the shortfall had to be met by British ships bringing water in from the outside. The same was true of food. There was enough of both to sustain life, but only just barely. The whole town had been on rationing for weeks and that fact added to Sidney Smith's concerns, but not as much as what he was now looking at.

To the northeast and east were a series of low hills. On some of them were hordes of Druze tribesmen, waiting to see who was going to win the fight. The winner would get their support, and if the winner were Bonaparte, it would mean the addition of some 15,000 fresh troops to his army.

Other hills contained the French unit headquarters. The most prominent was called Richard Coeur de Lion's Mount, and it was there that Smith, through a telescope, could see Bonaparte gesturing wildly to his staff. He knew what that meant. Another attack would be coming soon.

As if on cue, a half-hour later, the siege guns began their deep-throated thunder, and even more of the wall began to crumble. A half-hour after that, Smith could see a huge column of troops forming up and beginning their slow, inexorable march to the wall; but this time there would be a surprise waiting for them. It was Picard Phélippeaux's last gift to Sir Sidney.

* * * * *

In the makeshift hospital, Susan Whitney had an existence that was altogether different from that of her friends. There was no day or night. Indeed, there was no time, as she formerly understood it. It was an endless cycle of pain and misery, broken only by brief periods of euphoria and delusional sleep.

The plague had spread, and her body was in the process of literally decomposing while she was still alive. Black dots appeared all over. Her lymph nodes were swollen and hemorrhaging, her limbs were aching, and she was more tired than she had ever thought possible. Her temperature was consistently over 102 degrees, and yet she still felt cold.

Her world consisted of a two-hour cycle. It began with something that was more than mere pain. She had, of course, experienced pain before, when some portion of her body hurt and it could be felt in contrast to other parts that did not. This, however, was something different. It was like pain was the natural state, and her task was to find anomalous islands in her body in which it was *not* felt. Making matters worse, she was vomiting blood on a regular basis, and each retch caused her to be enveloped in a searing cloud of pain that she could not even begin to describe.

To counter this, Walker had prescribed laudanum, the only effective painkiller that he had; but he couldn't use it in the dosage that he would have liked. Susan was vomiting blood, and he was afraid that if she were completely insensible she would take the vomitus into her lungs and suffocate.

Throughout it all, Maria Corriveau hovered over her like a guardian angel for as many hours of the day and night as she could. Whenever she would see signs of pain in Susan's face, she would give her the laudanum that Walker prescribed, then wait patiently until the pain lines eased somewhat.

This gave Susan the only approximation of relief that she could experience. The drug did not kill the pain, it only dulled it somewhat; but because it was opium-based it gave her the euphoric feeling that, while the pain was there, somehow it didn't matter. This reliably lasted for about ten minutes—sometimes as long as twenty—before she would move into the third stage of her cycle, sleep.

Here again, it was sleep but not as she had previously known it. It was a gray, hazy area, somewhere between consciousness and sleep. It was her fantasyland, a playground for impossible images and situations that would sometimes enlighten, sometimes amuse, and sometimes terrify her. Sooner or later, however, it would end and pain would reenter her world with the force of a cymbal crash, and the cycle would start all over.

Susan was dying. Walker knew it. Smith knew it; and she knew it.

* * * * *

Things were not going well for Bonaparte either.

Losses had been heavy on both sides, but there was no time or inclination for polite burial details. The ground was covered with dead and rotting bodies, radiating an odor that was horrendous. Morale in the French Army was at an all-time low, and the troops were becoming reluctant to form-up for additional advances against the wall. There had simply been too many rash attacks, and criticism was growing both around the campfires and in the officer's tents.

Bonaparte had just finished a meeting with his generals where he stood overlooking the battlefield and indicated what he wanted done in the next attack. He could sense their growing reluctance as well. To help stem the tide of this disaffection, he decided to walk out among the troops—to let them see him, to talk to them, to let them draw upon his confidence. It had always worked in the past, but this time it was different.

He was surrounded by the brown coats of the 85th Demi-

Brigade. There was nothing happening that could rise to the level of insubordination, or even disrespect, but there was a sullenness that Bonaparte had never seen before, at least not this bad. He was complementing the men, telling them what great soldiers they were, what glory they were bringing to France, when a young officer broke away from the others.

"And what about André Gilles, general? Where is his glory?

"André Gilles? Who might he be?"

"He was my friend, General, and an officer of yours. We had known each other since childhood. He and my sister... Well, he's dead General. Dead! He died two attacks ago against that accursed city. Shot through the head. Why?"

Bonaparte turned and moved away to study something off in the distance, ignoring the man; but he followed him.

"Why did he have to die, General? That city should have fallen weeks ago, yet we keep on making attack, after attack, after attack. It's as though we're planning to scale the walls on a pile of our own corpses. How many men have to die, sir? How many people like André who..." and the officer broke down in tears.

Bonaparte kept walking, showing no emotion, but signaled General Crozier over to him. "That is exactly how some artist should depict Niobe weeping for her children." Then he paused, thought for a moment, and said, "If he starts again, have him shot."

* * * * *

Captain Joseph Moiret was beyond being tired. He was at a point where his mind no longer registered the complaints it was receiving from his body. His mind would send commands to his arms and legs, then break-off communication, making his world leaden and unreal.

Suddenly the camp was assaulted by the sound of blaring trumpets and beating drums. It was the call to form up for yet another assault. It was the 14th attack they had made, without any permanent success in any of them. He dragged himself upright with a soft groan. "Let's go sergeant. Get the men in formation."

Sergeant Duvalier cast a sidelong glance at Moiret, sighed once, then turned and began bellowing, "All right you miserable dogs. Let's go. Get up. You think this is some kind of party? Well, you're right. It is, and the Général has the girls all lined up for you, but they're on the other side of that wall."

The men were slow to react, and a great deal of grumbling could be heard, but they obeyed.

A bit before sunset a long, ragged, French column could be seen marching slowly toward the breach. Smith's ships, led by HMS *Tigre*, began slamming 24- and 36 pound balls into the French line. The smaller ships launched shells to explode over the French heads; but still the line came on.

The first to reach the breach was an element of the advance guard led by General Francois Rambeaud. Initially there was confusion, then elation. The breach was undefended! A shout went up from the advance men, which was picked up by the army as a whole, as the word quickly passed down the line.

These leading soldiers, known as the "forlorn hope," moved past the breach and into the Pasha's garden to make way for the rest of the advance guard. Soon there were about four hundred French troops inside the walls, preparing to spread out into the town.

"This is wrong," Captain Moiret muttered to himself.

"Sir?" Sergeant Duvalier asked.

"This is wrong, Sergeant," he said, looking anxiously around. "I can understand carrying the breach. I can understand fighting our way into town. I do not understand getting past the breach and into the town without firing a shot. It's not right. There's something…"

However, before he could complete the sentence, his world exploded.

Muskets appeared through every window of every building surrounding the garden and opened fire. Other men popped up from the rooftops and added their volleys. A cannon from the commander's tower and another one from the wall, showered grapeshot into the staggered French troops—but even that was not the worst.

After the initial blasts from the cannons, a thousand Turkish warriors poured into the plaza from the side streets, each one armed with a scimitar in one hand, and a dagger in the other. Next to the musketeers on the rooftops, there appeared hundreds of Turkish women, each making the traditional high-pitched lu-lu-lu-lu call that inspired their men, and caused French blood to run cold. Within moments, dozens of French heads were being trampled in the dirt as bayonet fought scimitar with the life of their owner at stake.

General Rambeaud tried to rally his men, to get them into some kind of order so they could retreat through the breach. He was waving his sword over his head and shouting orders as a musket ball entered his mouth and took off the back of his head. And the hand-to-hand combat continued.

Outside the wall, General Lannes, who commanded the main assault force, knew that something had gone terribly wrong. He commanded his troops forward, but the breach was no longer open. Turkish troops had circled around the trapped advance guard and sealed the breach. That left Lannes locked out of the battle. With his troops being pounded by gunfire from the British ships, plus cannon and musket fire from the walls, he and his men were sitting ducks.

He tried to force his men forward, but a musket ball caught him in the neck, and one of his aids had to drag him by one leg back to safety.

Inside the walls, the horror had risen to insane levels. French soldiers, whether fighting as individuals or in groups were being cut down like stubborn stalks of wheat.

A cry finally went up... *Sauve qui peut! Sauve qui peut!* Every man for himself! And whatever sense of military cohesion was left in the men disappeared. The rout was on; but there was nowhere for the French troops to go.

The Turks worked in pairs, cutting out French soldiers one at a time. One would engage the man; the other would work around to the side and stab the Frenchman through the ribcage with his dagger, or slash him across the kidneys with his scimitar. When the man reacted to the pain, the first Turk would sweep the man's head off. On and on it went, with the screams of the dying French, mingling with the battle cries of the Turks, mixing with the constant ululating of the women.

Captain Moiret and his sergeant worked their way to the edge of the melee, along with a seven-man squad—all that was left of their original unit.

"Over there, Duvalier," Moiret said while nodding his head in a direction. "On the corner there. That building is a mosque. If we can get to it, maybe we'll be safe for a while."

"You think they won't kill us if we're inside a mosque?" he asked hopefully.

"No. I am sure they will; but maybe we can barricade the place, or hide out. I don't know, but anyplace is better than here."

A moment later the nine men broke free from the killing field, and raced through the Pasha's carefully cultivated flower garden, over a hedge, and across the street to the door of the building. Two Turks took swings at them with their swords as they flew past, but decided not to pursue. There were much easier pickings right in front of them.

Although the door to the building had a heavy bar affixed to the inside, it was not locked—mosques in Acre never were. The men crowded through the door and immediately slid the bar into place. A quick sweep of the mosque's single floor revealed they were alone.

The only thing they could do now was wait.

* * * * *

Waiting was also very much a part of the lives of over 2000 Jacobins who were crammed into 14 small ships in the Bay of Naples. An equal number awaited their fate ashore.

For the commoners, the system worked with clockwork efficiency. They would be taken ashore, or called from their cells, given a "trial" in which many defendants didn't even bother to point out their innocence, and were immediately hung or beheaded. The whole process, start to finish, could be accomplished in as little as a half-hour.

For the elites, however, their chances could be improved by demanding a more complete hearing from a judge who was a peer or by appealing to the British; and there was no shortage of people from high society who had thrown in their lot with the democratic ideals of the Jacobins. Among these were some of the best military and civilian minds Naples had to offer—the philosopher Mario Pagano, scientist Cirillo Manthone, Massa, the defender of Castel dell Uovo, Ettore Caraffa, the defender of Pescara, and Domenico Cirillo, one of the leading physicians, botanists, and naturalists in Europe, and the man who had introduced smallpox inoculation into Naples.

Day after day, boats could be seen ferrying people ashore, or lined up before the *Foudroyant*, Nelson's flagship. They would not be seeing Nelson, however. He could not be bothered with listening to "excuses from rebels, Jacobins, and fools." Instead, the task was delegated to Lady Emma Hamilton.

Emma was seated on the quarterdeck, flanked by marine guards. She was in her finest dress, bedecked with jewelry, and carried herself like a queen. Indeed, because she was representing King Ferdinand and Queen Maria Carolina, in her mind, she *was* a queen—or as close as a blacksmith's daughter would ever come.

In front of her was a beautiful, graceful, aristocratic young woman, not more than a teenager. She was trying to retain the pride and dignity of her class, something that had been drilled into her since childhood. However, anguish had changed her clear olive complexion to a sickly gray, her face was a mask of misery, and tears were now running freely from her dark eyes. Suddenly, she dropped to her knees with her hands clasped and raised to the heavens, begging Emma Hamilton to intercede, to show mercy to her and her family.

"And how can I show you that mercy?" Emma coldly asked. "Would it be on the basis of the loyalty you showed your monarch?"

"My lady, we did nothing to support that rebel trash! It's true; we could have gone to Palermo with the court. We could have fled, but what would have happened to our lands? What would have happened to the family we left behind? What would have happened to..."

"Enough!" Emma snapped. "I've heard enough. You chose to stay, no doubt because you thought you would bene- fit in some way. You placed your lot with the rebels; now let the rebel lot be yours. You say your heart is breaking for your family. Fine, go back to your prison ship where your heart may break at leisure."

Emma waved her hand, and two guards roughly picked up the woman by her arms and lead her off the deck to join several others in a small boat that was waiting for her. Ham- ilton sat impatiently waiting for the next person to come up the short ladder to the deck where she held court.

Although she would never have admitted it openly, at first, all this had been fun. She had power beyond anything she could have imagined. With a few words from her, with even a simple gesture, people would live or die; but somehow it had all turned uncouth. It was nothing more than an end- less parade of destroyed old men and weeping ladies. Where was the stimulation in that?

The next person up the stairway, however, was different. It was a woman in her late 40s, dressed in a long black gown that ran to her ankles. Her short curly hair was pushed back, revealing a high forehead, and framing dark intelligent eyes. There was no look of supplication about her at all; rather her demeanor was one of defiance.

Emma sized her up and immediately realized that she was dealing with a sister—a kindred spirit. If she was in her place, this is exactly how she would look and act; but that realization did not stop the drama from taking its course.

Although she was intrigued by this person, Emma still tried to sound as bored as possible as she asked, "And why are *you* here?"

"I am here because your thugs brought me."

Emma was astonished. "Who *are* you?"

"I am Eleonora…"

A voice from behind Emma's throne cut in. "She is Eleonora Fonseca Pimentel." The speaker was a lawyer from the Neapolitan court system, who was attending as an observer. "She fancies herself as a poet and writer, but is one of the revolutionary ringleaders."

"Is this true, madam?" Emma asked.

"The judicial oaf behind you has it partially correct. My name is indeed Eleonora Pimentel."

"And are you… were you… a revolutionary leader?"

"Alas, in truth I cannot claim that honor. Do I subscribe to the ideals behind the Republic? Yes, most certainly. Did I work to bring liberty and equality to Naples? Yes, and I will do so to my dying breath."

"Which might be a few hours from now," the lawyer retorted.

Emma waved her hand to silence him.

"What precisely did you do?"

"I was simply the editor of a newspaper called the *Monitore Napoletano*."

Emma was becoming frustrated with this cat-and-mouse game. "I don't have all day. Will someone tell me what's going on here?"

The lawyer stepped out from the small group behind the throne. "If I may... She is correct when she says she is the editor of *Monitore Napoletano*. What she is not saying is that her paper was the voice of the Jacobins. She published 35 editions..."

"Thirty-seven," Pimemtel interjected.

"...thirty-seven editions, each more scurrilous than the last." He then reached into a coat pocket and drew out a tattered newspaper clipping.

"This is how she began the very first article, in her very first edition. 'We are free at last, and the time has come when we, too, can utter the sacred words 'Liberty' and 'Equality.'"

"Is this true?" Emma asked.

"Yes," she replied simply. "But there is more to it than that.

"I am a writer, and I own the *Monitore Napoletano*. Naples was under the control of French forces that were bringing a new way of life—a *better* way of life, I might add—to the people. I felt it was my job to explain it to them. I wanted to create a paper that would discuss the issues facing us in a language the common person could understand.

"Indeed, most of the time I agreed with the new regime; but there were times when I did not. For example, when the Republican government decided to confiscate the property of those who had resisted the revolution, I was there to protest. I was there to stand up for the people. I was there to point out injustice. No one else was doing that, because no one else had the courage to do it."

"Counselor, I am confused," Emma said, turning to the lawyer. "This woman doesn't seem like the dangerous revolutionary you portray. She has made some bad judgments in her political beliefs; but I don't see where it rises to the level of the death penalty."

"My lady, there is more to it than that, as Mrs. Pimentel is wont to say. In addition to her newspaper writing, several months ago..."

The lawyer was looking decidedly uncomfortable. He paused, played with the white cravat around his neck for a moment, and then pressed on. "...several months ago she published a pamphlet in which she stated her belief that you and Queen Maria Carolina were... ah... on very intimate terms."

"Well, of course we are. She is one of my..." Then it dawned on Emma what the lawyer was saying, and the blood drained from her face. Emma had to admit that it had crossed her mind... then there was that time in the rose garden...

"She did what?" Emma, the actress, put on a great show of outrage.

Swinging around to Pimentel, she asked, "Is this true?"

Eleonora gave her a half-smile in reply, and shrugged her shoulders. Within minutes, the salt spray from the small boat was drenching her black dress as she was being rowed ashore.

From there, the process was quite straightforward. She was taken to the Mercato, which was once the hub of nearly all business enterprise in Naples, but was now a squalid piazza with weeds growing between broken cobblestones. In the southeast corner was the Church of the Carmine, and in front of it were several gallows and a guillotine.

She was taken to the church through a back door, in case she had any last minute petitions she wanted to make to the Almighty. She passed on that, but instead asked for a cup of coffee as a last indulgence before she died. The request was granted.

She then asked to be beheaded rather than hung. She pointed out that she was of noble Neapolitan birth, as was her husband, and could thus claim that right. However, she was too well known. Several people knew that she had been born in Portugal and, although naturalized, was still a Portuguese citizen. The request was denied.

Several hours later, her hands were tied behind her and she was lead out into the square with her group. Included was Gennaro Serra, a cavalry officer who had joined the Republicans; Giuliano Colonna, a nobleman; Michele Natale, the Bishop of Vico Equense; the two bankers Domenico and Antonio Piatti, father and son; Nicola Pacifico, an old priest, and Filippo Marini, the only son of the Marchese Genzano. A lad of twenty, Marini's crime had been cutting off the head of a plaster statue of Carlo III. Later, another man would be hung for the same crime on the same statue; and still later, they would find out that the statue had been broken by a street mob.

When she emerged from the church, she was assaulted by a blast of stifling heat and the roar of thousands of voices. The sunlight stung her eyes, so it was a moment before her vision could adjust; but when it did, she was amazed at the size of the crowd before her. To keep order, the great square was surrounded by troops, both foot soldiers and cavalry. High on the walls of the church were cannons pointed at the crowd, and additional troops were stationed on side streets in case they were needed.

When the prisoners emerged, the crowd roared their approval. It was a deafening sound, the kind of thing that is felt in your bones more than heard by your ears. Eleonora edged over to the man next to her, and above the tumult asked why there were so many people.

"Because as soon as we are dead, they're going to hold a lotto," he shouted back.

"What?" She replied. She thought she had heard him correctly, but she couldn't quite process what she thought she heard.

"We all have to be hung by noon, because afterward there's going to be a drawing of the lotto. That's why they're here. It's a double diversion—gallows and then the lottery.

Her world was becoming more unreal with every step she took.

The first to die were Gennaro Serra and Giuliano Colonna. Because of their noble birth, they were led to the guillotine. Amid the crowd noise, as Serra was being strapped to the board, he said, "I have always desired their welfare, and now they're rejoicing at my death!" He was right. Gennaro Serra was a good man—but that didn't matter anymore.

The remainder of the executions would take place at the gallows, a device that consisted of a simple vertical pole, with a beam at the top hanging out at a right angle.

The first up was Michele Natale, the Bishop of Vico. He was led to the pole where a noose was placed around his neck and, because he was a priest, he was given a moment for a final prayer. Next to him was the hangman and his assistant, a dwarf. The dwarf was cavorting around the condemned man like some kind of demented clown.

When his moment of prayer was over, the bishop was lead up a ladder by the dwarf, and the end of the noose was tied around the horizontal beam. Without warning the priest was pushed off the ladder, the dwarf swung on to his shoulders, and the hangman set the two of them swinging back and forth.

The crowd broke into laughter as the dwarf grabbed the struggling bishop by the hair to stay on board and screamed, "Keep him swinging. I might never again have the good luck to ride a bishop!" This brought even more laughter.

And so it went, through each of the condemned men—the same procedure, the same dwarf riding on the man's shoulders. The only variation was that sometimes the hangman would grab on to the victim's legs and all three would swing.

Because she was a woman, however, Eleonora was given the "privilege" of going last. In truth, it had nothing to do with chivalry; Eleonora was the featured attraction. It wasn't every day that the crowd got to see a woman hanged, and they wanted to save the event for the grand finale.

Eleonora was led up the ladder, with the hangman trying to place his head under her dress with every step. The crowd loved it. Once at the top, the dwarf tied off the noose, and the hangman asked her if she had anything she wanted to say— any final words. She started to speak, but as soon as she did, the hangman pushed her off the ladder and the dwarf mounted her shoulders, his legs on either side of her head, holding a handful of her hair to maintain stability. The hangman started her swinging and was lifting up her dress every time she swung past, revealing two rather shapely kicking legs to the crowd. Eleonora struggled for her life as the dwarf urged the hangman to swing her some more. He found himself with an unaccustomed hardening between his legs, and he wanted to savor it.

As she was pushed from the ladder, the roar of the crowd could be heard as far away as the Monastery of the Santi Apostoli, about a mile away. It could also be heard on the *Foudroyant* where Nelson was penning a letter to his wife, and getting ready for an evening's entertainment... with Emma.

And so the executions continued, day after day.

* * * * *

As mosques go, this one was not very big. It was one of dozens that were scattered around the city of Acre, and dominated by the giant al-Jezzar Mosque that was only about a half-mile away. But it's walls were stout, and that's all that mattered to the nine Frenchmen who were trapped inside.

Discrete lookouts were posted at the front facing windows to monitor what was happening in the park across the street. Satisfied that all was done that could be done, Captain Moiret had a chance to look around.

The mosque consisted of a single room, with no furniture whatsoever. This made it easier to get as many people as possible into the room for prayers. On three of the walls were magnificently inlaid Arabic calligraphy of Koranic verses to remind worshippers to focus on the beauty of Islam and its holiest book, the Koran. But the focal point of the room was the Qibla Wall opposite the entrance and facing toward Mecca. In the center was a beautifully carved mihrab, a wooden panel with a semicircular niche in the center, eight feet high and six feet across, with delicate scrollwork around the edges and yet another Koranic verse inlayed at the top. To the left was a lectern where the imam or some other speaker could offer a sermon. The floor was of highly polished wood, maintained in a pristine condition by the fact that no Muslim was ever allowed to wear shoes inside the mosque. The floor was now scuffed and marred by hard French boots.

Within an hour the noise from the Pasha's garden started to die away. Moiret glanced out a window, but could not bring himself to look for long. He felt a leaden weight form in his stomach. The ground was littered with headless corpses, some of the men he had known, some he had loved as if they were brothers. A swarm of defenders had descended on the bodies like locust, squabbling over the heads that they knew would bring a reward from the Pasha al-Jezzar.

Moiret was walking back toward the central door, when he heard a shot ring out behind him. He turned to see one of his men holding a smoking musket.

"There was a man, captain" the soldier stuttered. "A man appeared in the window. I... I don't know where he came from, but he saw me. I had to... I had to..."

"It's all right, Poupard. They were going to find us eventually."

Within minutes, a crowd of Ottoman soldiers—little more than a mob, really—had formed around the door trying to force their way in. It was bad enough that some Frenchmen had escaped their wrath, but for the infidels to desecrate a mosque was too much to bear.

The French were firing from the windows as best they could; but the angle was a sharp one, so they weren't hitting much. It was enough, however, to give the invaders pause.

Suddenly, the shouting from outside stopped and an eerie silence descended. A conversation of some kind could be heard, followed by pounding at the door, along with a voice speaking perfect French.

"Inside, there! Let me in. I am Commodore Sir Sidney Smith. If you value your life, let me in."

Smith had seen the activity around the mosque from on top of the wall. He suspected what was happening, so he gathered a group of British seamen and headed down the stairs. They had formed a semicircle around the entrance to keep the Ottoman at bay. He knew the incensed Muslims could overwhelm his little party any time they wanted; but they were unsure what influence these *farangis* had with the Pasha, so they held back.

Moiret opened the door a crack, saw Smith standing there, and quickly let him in.

"Commodore. Please! For the love of God, you have to help us."

"I don't *have* to do anything, captain," Smith replied. "You are a Frenchman. You are our enemy. A couple of hours ago you would have happily killed me, or any of my men. In fact, you probably *have* killed some of my men. I can choose to do nothing, and you will get what you deserve."

"Yes, we are enemies. But... but it's not the same. We are men of honor, you and I. We understand the rules that surround that honor. These savages... they..."

"Was it men of honor who slaughtered the unarmed defenders at Jaffa? Or was that you who did it?"

"Admiral, we had to. There was no way we could have transported that number of prisoners. Besides..."

Moiret caught the look of steel behind Smith's angry eyes; and he knew his pleas would not be heard.

"All right, then." He paused for a moment and drew himself up. "If we are to die, we shall die as Frenchmen. Please leave."

"Yes, but you see, that's the problem. You will not die like Frenchmen. You won't even die like human beings. You might kill some of them, but eventually you'll be overwhelmed and captured. You will be taken from here to someplace where even I can't find you. If you're lucky, they might let you die after three or four days. In the meantime, you will be turned into howling imbeciles."

Silence filled the room. Every man in it knew Smith was right.

After a long minute, Smith came to a decision and said, "All right. Do nothing until I come back; and, whatever happens, do *not* shoot at them." Smith cracked open the door, slid out, and addressed the crowd.

"Comrades, I have spoken to the prisoners and they have agreed to lay down their arms and surrender. We will take custody of them."

This caused an up swell of angry murmuring. Finally, one of them spoke up.

"That is not acceptable, Commodore. They are infidels, and they have violated our mosque. We *must* have vengeance; our honor and the honor of the Prophet demand it."

Smith looked around the semicircle of British seamen, who now had their bayonets lowered, and said, "And our honor demands that we take custody of those men."

"Yes, but we are over a hundred men. You have but ten."

Smith strode over to the spokesman like a sergeant inspecting a raw recruit.

"Have you ever wondered why Jezzar Pasha obeys me so readily?"

The man looked confused by the question.

"It's not because I am a British naval officer. It's because I carry a fiat from Sultan Selim III, who has placed me in charge of all Ottoman land and sea forces. Do you dare to disregard the wishes of the *Sultan*?" Turning to the group, "Do any of you wish to displease the Sultan?"

This ended the argument. They feared Jezzar Pasha with every bone in their bodies. To risk displeasing the Sultan, whom Jezzar Pasha feared with every bone in his, was beyond comprehension.

Turning to one of his sailors, he quietly muttered, "Now get those frogs out of there before they realize that the Sultan would most certainly approve of killing them for desecrating a mosque."

* * * * *

Louis Antoine de Bourrienne was officially Bonaparte's secretary, but in many ways, he was more than that. He was his friend.

They had known each other since they were schoolmates at the military school at Brienne. After leaving school in 1787, and having developed a singular distaste for the army, Bourrienne proceeded to Vienna to pursue legal and diplomatic studies. Years later he returned to Paris and renewed his acquaintance with Bonaparte, who was then a rising young officer. Together, the two young men led a rather Bohemian life, and cut quite a wide swath through the salons, and the damsels, of Paris. In 1798, when Bonaparte left for Egypt, it was only natural that Bourrienne accompany him as his private secretary.

At Acre, the two of them fell into an almost nightly routine, and tonight was no exception. Bourrienne met Bonaparte at his tent and they went down the hill to walk the seashore together. There was something about the constant cool breeze and the repetitive whoosh of the breaking waves that seemed to calm Bonaparte, and allow him to open up to his secretary in ways that he could do with no other.

The two walked in silence for a long time. Finally, Bonaparte stopped, picked up a stone from the beach, and threw it out to sea. While watching it go he said, "Do you know what Kléber said to me today?"

"I have no idea."

"I called a meeting of the generals this afternoon, and asked them for their thoughts on ending this damnable siege. He said: 'General, I liken the town of Acre to a piece of cloth. When I go to a merchant to buy it, I ask to feel it; I look at it, I touch it, and if I find it too expensive, I leave it.'

"What do you think, Louis? Has the cloth become too expensive?"

Bourrienne thought for a moment. "It depends on what the cloth can be made into, General. If it is to remain in a closet, unused and useless, then almost any cost would be too high. If it can be made into a beautiful ball gown that greatly pleases your wife or mistress, than almost no price would be too high."

Bonaparte turned to Bourrienne with a smile on his face. "How well you know me, my friend. This wretched place has cost me a number of men, and wasted much time; but things are too far advanced not to attempt a last effort."

"And what sort of gown will you make if the bolt of cloth is eventually yours?"

"Ah, that is the question, Louis. That is the question.

"If I succeed, as I expect, I shall find in the town the pasha's treasures, and arms for at least 300,000 men. I will stir up and arm the people of Syria, who are disgusted at the cruelty of Jezzar, and who, as you know, pray for his destruction at every assault.

"I shall then march upon Damascus and Aleppo. On advancing into the country, the discontented will flock round my standard, and swell my army. I will announce to the people the abolition of servitude and of the tyrannical governments of the pashas. I shall arrive at Constantinople with large masses of soldiers. I shall overturn the Turkish Empire, and found in the East a new and grand empire, which will fix my place in the records of posterity."

Bourrienne laughed. "You have never been accused of modesty, my friend, even when we were children. So let's assume this happens. What will you do once you have conquered Constantinople?"

"I am not sure. I want to go back to Paris at some point. Perhaps I will return via Adrianople, or maybe by Vienna, after having annihilated the house of Austria. Many options will be open to me."

"But what will you do if these tribes you talk about do not flock to your standard? After all, to them you are a westerner—a *farangi*—an infidel."

"Louis, have you not seen the countless tribes amassed in the hills watching this siege? Do you not see that the Druse only wait for the fall of Acre to rise in rebellion? Have not the keys of Damascus already been offered to me? I only stay here until these walls fall, because until then I can derive no advantage from this wretched place.

"If I can do this, I will cut off all interference from the beys, and secure the conquest of Egypt. But, if I do not succeed in this last assault... "

"Then what?" Bourrienne asked.

Bonaparte paused, picked up another stone, threw it, and said, "Then the cost of the cloth will have been too high."

* * * * *

At the same moment, Sidney Smith was aboard the *Tigre* finishing a long letter to Admiral Nelson. It ended as follows:

> Bonaparte will, no doubt, renew the attack, the breach being, as above described, perfectly practicable for fifty men abreast. Indeed the town is not, nor ever has been defensible, according to the rules of art; but according to every other rule, it must and shall be defended. I am not saying that it is in itself worth de-

fending, but we feel that it is by this breach that Bonaparte means to march to further conquests.

It is on the issue of this conflict that depends the opinion of the multitude of spectators on the surrounding hills, who wait only to see how it ends, to join the victors. With such a reinforcement for the execution of his known projects, Constantinople, and even Vienna, must feel the shock.

Be assured, my lord, the magnitude of our obligations does but increase the energy of our efforts in the attempt to discharge our duty. Though we may, and probably shall be overpowered, I can venture to say that the French army will be so much further weakened before it prevails, as to be little able to profit by its dear-bought victory.

I have the honour to be, &c.

W. SIDNEY SMITH

* * * * *

That same night Lucas Walker was making his rounds at the hospital he had set up in the Burj el Hanza. As he walked, the only light came from a few quivering candles in sconces in the walls, and in holders next to a few beds. The only sounds were those made by his shoes on the marble floor, and the occasional groan of a patient dealing with the painful reality of a missing leg, or shattered arm.

He arrived at the end of the long central corridor, opened a creaky wooden door, and slipped into a small private room. It contained Susan Whitney, or what remained of her. She was the only person who had such seclusion, but Walker didn't care. She was special to the people around her; and, above all, she was special to him.

The previous office furniture had been removed and a bed had been brought in, along with a simple chest of drawers and a chair. Walker's every movement was recorded in bizarre shadows cast by a short thick candle on the chest.

Susan was on the bed, completely unconscious. The wet compress that had been on her forehead had slid off to the side, and the blanket was in disarray from her earlier thrashings. Walker automatically felt her forehead, hoping with all his heart that he would detect a change in her temperature. He didn't. The fever had not abated in the least. He tenderly replaced the damp cloth, and placed his fingers on her wrist. Her pulse was highly abnormal. It consisted of alternating strong and weak beats—almost as if the first beat had an echo. His textbooks called it *pulsus alternans,* and said it was a sign of left ventricular impairment. For Walker, it meant that the bubonic infection had reached her heart, and for all practical purposes, she was dead.

There was nothing more he could do.

He replaced the disheveled blanket, quietly sat down next to her, and after a moment gently took her hand.

"Susan, I know you can't hear me, but..." There was a long pause, then he started again.

"We had such times together, didn't we? Do you remember the time..." He grew quiet again, lost in memories.

"But, you know what I remember the best? It was that time you dragged me up to the top of the Rock of Gibraltar." A weak smile crossed Walker's face. "I can still picture you being lead up that winding trail, riding a donkey like you were a queen, and me dragging along behind, complaining with every step. And I remember the smile you had when we got to the top... I've always loved your smile, you know. There's something about it that just..." He stopped again.

"But, you were right. The walk was worth it. To stand on top of Gibraltar and see two continents in front of me, and the ocean, and..." Another, even longer, pause.

"I think that was when I knew for sure that I loved you, girl. It was when I knew that I would always love you. You complete me, Susan. You make me whole."

Walker drew her hand up to his lips and kissed it. Then he did two things he hadn't done since he was a child. He cried, and he prayed.

He sat like that for some minutes, when the quiet of the night was shattered by drum rolls and bugle calls. Yet, another attack was beginning.

Walker glanced over at the open window, and tenderly placed her hand back on the bed.

"They're starting again," he said. "I have to go, Susan—the casualties will start coming soon, and I have to...

"I am sorry. I guess I am not very good at talking to an unconscious person... No. That's not it. I am ashamed that I didn't tell you all this sooner when... when you could have heard me."

Walker choked back a sob and ran out of the room.

On the bed, Susan's eyelids briefly fluttered.

Chapter Seven

Technically, the final assault began about 3:00 AM. It was necessary to start that early because it took so long to get the full army organized and moving. Timing was everything and they wanted to be attacking the wall at sunrise.

In the lead was General Kléber's division. Since their rescue at Mount Tabor, his men had seen only sporadic fighting, and Bonaparte wanted to begin his assault with fresh troops. General Bon's division was next in line, followed by General Fouler, and so on down the French order of battle. There was nothing subtle about the attack. The French Army was drawn up in a single column, 30 men wide—a battering ram of human flesh and bones—that was hurtling itself toward the breach in the wall of Acre.

Between the massed attacks of the French, and the disruptive sorties of the defenders, the Battle of Acre had been raging for fifty-one days, interrupted only when massive fatigue forced the two sides to stand down. In effect, it was a race. Could Bonaparte capture the town before Turkish reinforcements arrived, or would the defenders hold on?

The previous night, French engineers built a traverse, a land bridge that would allow their forces to get across the moat to the breach in the wall. They didn't have enough sandbags for the task so they had to build-in the bodies of their dead, their bayonets and equipment sticking up at odd intervals to mark their dreadful presence.

On the walls, Sidney Smith was directing the placement of the guns. He knew from the ten previous assaults that the most effective weapons were the eighteen- and the twenty-four pounders, loaded initially with ball and later with grape-shot as the attackers drew closer. To this he added two sixty-eight pound carronades from the *Tigre*, and mounted them so they could be brought to bear directly on the head of the French column.

Slowly, almost with regret, the sun rose.

The Frenchmen gathered themselves for the attack then, with the increasing availability of sunlight, abruptly stopped their preparations. All eyes were turned seaward, as in the bay the corvettes and transports of Hassan Bey's Turkish fleet were arriving.

Kléber's grenadiers, primed with equal parts confidence and brandy, raised a shout, demanding the assault begin before the Turkish forces could be brought ashore. Bonaparte hesitated, but finally gave the signal.

It was a magnificent sight. The grenadiers rushed forward. Cannon fire and musket balls rained down on them from the walls. Kléber stood atop a pile of rubble, his unmanageable curly gray hair streaming in the morning breeze, bellowing commands, and banging his sword against his thigh with impatience. Without difficulty, his thunderous voice somehow overcame the pounding and popping of the gunfire, the enthusiastic shouts of the French and the screams of the Turks.

Bonaparte had moved forward to get a better view of the action, and drew the attention of both Turkish and British sharpshooters. A ball passed by just above his head. He brought down his telescope for a moment as if looking for a bee to swat, and then raised the glass again. General Berthier tried to get him to move back, but he ignored him. At the same moment, a sharpshooter's rifle ball struck an aide who was standing next to him. He ignored that also.

Smith took his place on the wall, hatless as usual. "There are a hundred and fifty French marksmen," he once remarked "who are looking for that hat, and hats are too expensive to have holes drilled in them." He cut an inspirational figure, rushing from point to point, his brown hair a wild tangle, his eyes almost blinded by the gun smoke and the hot sun.

Kléber dispatched a group to attack the Commander's Tower, which was right next to the breach. After a brief resistance, they forced their way to the top and broke out a French flag. The sight of that flag fluttering over the tower gave the French soldiers renewed confidence, and they redoubled their efforts.

Smith countered by dispatching British reinforcements to the breach where they found a few brave Turks holding out. They had run out of ball and powder, so they were reduced to throwing rocks at the enemy, which proved to be surprisingly effective. At that close range, the rocks would hit the assailants in the head, knocking them down the slope, and impeded the progress of the rest.

Soon, however, the French troops got to the lip of the pile of rubble that was their last remaining hurdle before entering the town. On the other side of the peak were the newly arrived British and Turks. The muzzles of British muskets were literally touching French bayonets as men from each side stood up to shoot the other at point-blank range. The spearhead of a French flag became entangled with a set of Turkish colors. They were simply that close.

Smith saw the last-ditch defense that was being made at the breach; and, along with his runner Midshipman Janverin, rushed down the stairs to assist. As he was about to round the corner to where the fighting was, he felt a hand grab his arm and swing him around.

"What the devil are you doing?" he cursed as he turned

and recognized the hand as belonging to one of Jezzar Pasha's chief lieutenants. Behind him stood Jezzar, resplendent in his finest silks, with a gold scimitar hanging from a blood-red sash.

"You're not going out there." Jezzar said.

Smith was momentarily speechless. "What do you mean, I am not going out there? My men are there. The fight is there. Of course I am."

"No, you're not, my friend. If you are lost, then all is lost. I will not—I cannot—permit that to happen."

"I don't give a damn what you say. I am..."

Jezzar Pasha made a slight movement of his hand and several of his personal guards surrounded Smith. These were men who had no idea what Smith was saying and, even if they had, wouldn't have cared. The Jezzar had told them to keep Smith from direct participation in the fight, and that is precisely what they would do.

"You are not," Jezzar said quietly. He then signaled again and ten of his personal guards rushed to the breach.

Janverin looked at Smith as if to say: What should I do? Smith nodded at him to continue. The moment he rounded the corner, however, he was hit by a musket ball. It was only a flesh wound to the muscle under his right arm, but it spun him around and dropped him to his knees near Sir Sidney and the Pasha.

Jezzar Pasha glanced down at the wounded midshipman and said, "Now that we've settled that question, what are we to do next?"

Smith stared at Janverin for a long moment.

"Commodore?"

Smith snapped back to the matters at hand.

"We're bringing solders from the ships as quickly as we can, but I don't know if we can get them on shore in time to make a difference. What we need is something to distract the French. Something to slow them down."

"What do you propose?"

"I noticed that one of the first groups off was the Chifflick Regiment."

"Chifflick Regiment? I've never heard of them."

"They're a new unit. They've been trained in western warfare in Constantinople by British officers that I brought with me when I first came out. I want them to sortie through the main gate and take the French column in the flank. Bonaparte will have to divert some of his forces to deal with them."

"But," Jezzar objected. "they're completely untried. You say they're trained in western warfare. That means they'll be fighting in an unaccustomed way, in a way that's not natural to them. How do you know they'll hold together?"

"I don't, but I also don't have time to season them."

Then Smith had an inspiration. "Jezzar, this will only work if you lead them!

"Me? But I... That is..."

"I don't mean lead them into the battle itself. I need you to give them their orders. Form them up. Tell them what to do. Inspire them with your presence and your force of will. Just think what future generations will say about you, and how you defeated the great Bonaparte at the walls of Acre."

This was something Jezzar Pasha could understand. He was no general—deep down he knew that, even if no one would dare to say it in his presence. But he understood giving orders, and if he could safely do that on *this* side of the wall, so much the better.

"It is a brilliant plan, Commodore! I shall make it so. The French will feel the mighty wrath of Jezzar Pasha this day, I promise you that!"

He turned to rush off to the square in front of the main gate, when Smith stopped him. "Wait. If you're going to truly inspire them, you'll need to bring with you the fearsome warriors of your personal guard." Smith gestured at the men standing around him. "Some of the Chifflicks might not know of your formidable reputation, and having them standing with you will increase your credibility."

"Yes. Yes, quite right."

Jezzar Pasha made a gesture, the guards left to follow him, and Smith was once again free to move about as he wished.

Somehow, Jezzar managed to sortie the Chifflicks out the main gate and attack the French from an unexpected direction. This split Bonaparte's forces just as Smith predicted. The column under General Bon was diverted to attack the Chifflicks, while General Fouler's column had to be moved up to attack the breech. All that took time, and time was the thing that Smith needed the most.

* * * * *

Time was also the thing that Maria Corriveau needed the most.

Strange as it might sound, the least busy moments for a military hospital are when a battle is going on. People are wounded in all sorts of ways, but no one has the time to haul them away while the fight is in progress. It's only after the battle that the aid stations and operating rooms are overwhelmed. This pause allowed Maria the opportunity to go out and see how bad things were, which would tell her how bad things were likely to be in the next few hours.

What she learned was not good. There was an air of desperation wherever she went. Men were running to and fro, each on a mission more urgent than the last. She climbed the long stair leading to the top of the wall and quickly looked over the side. It was a terrifying scene. Bonaparte was pushing what seemed like an endless column of men at the breach in the wall; and the fighting had an intensity to it that she had not previously seen. Both sides knew that this was the final act, but no one knew how the play would turn out.

She overheard two men saying that their only hope was to somehow destroy the traverse leading to the breech. If they couldn't do that, or find some way to keep the French off it, all would be lost.

Maria thought about that for a moment, then her eyes widened as she remembered meeting Picard Phélippeaux in the old crusader ruin. There *was* a way to destroy the traverse; there was a room underneath it that could be packed with explosives.

She tried to tell the men on the wall about it but no one would listen—at least not to a woman. Running down the stairs, she started rushing back to the hospital at least to tell Dr. Walker what she knew, when she almost collided with Cecil Durbin and Isaac Pulley.

"Cecil! Isaac! Stop!"

"Maria," Durbin began, "we're in a bit of a hurry. What is it?"

"I know how to win this battle."

"Yes, so does Napoleon—that's why we're hurrying."

"No, I am serious. I know how to destroy that traverse the French are using."

Durbin looked at her with his head cocked, as if to say, "Go on."

She told them about the chance meeting she and Susan had with Phélippeaux, and about the old arms cache room that was underneath the breach.

"So, if we can fill it with gunpowder and set it off, the French would have no way of reaching the wall. They'd have to start their siege all over."

The two men looked at each other.

"Did you actually see this room?" Pulley asked.

"Well, no, not really; but Picard was very clear that it exists, and even mentioned how to find it."

"We could get some casks of powder easy enough," Durbin mused. "Where is the entrance to this place?"

Twenty minutes later, the three had rendezvoused near the Jezzar Pasha Mosque where the crusader staircase was located. Maria led the way with a lantern, followed by Durbin and Pulley who were each struggling with two 35-pound casks of gunpowder, one under each arm, that they had lifted off a wagon.

Their disappearance down the stairwell, however, did not go unnoticed. Across the plaza was a shopkeeper who was zealously guarding his store from any looters who might want to take advantage of the fighting. He was also one of a large number of spies and informers that Bonaparte had inside the city.

Now why would those people be carrying gunpowder into the crusader castle? He thought.

They got to the great hall, went down into the dungeon, and, after a bit of searching, found the tunnel Phélippeaux had mentioned. It was much smaller than Maria had envisioned. Made of rough cut stone, it was about six feet high, but only three feet wide. They would have to go one at a time, with the men shuffling sideways with their loads.

"Why can't you keep up?" Durbin hissed at Pulley as they both sidestepped along the passageway.

"If you haven't noticed, Cecil, I am carrying 70 pounds of explosives, and the lady in front of you is carrying an open flame. You will have to pardon me if I have this strange need to keep as far away from her as I can."

They found the room. It was small, about 10 feet square, but it was there. Putting down their loads, they returned to the wagon for more.

Seeing them offload the last of the powder casks, the shopkeeper came to a decision. Within moments, he had shuttered and locked his store, slid two pistols inside his sash, and followed them.

With a grunt, Pulley dropped the last cask into place. Durbin was feeding a generous amount of fuse into one of the powder charges, while Maria held the spool. When all was ready, the three of them backed out of the tunnel trailing the line.

They arrived back in the dungeon/burial chamber, and cut the fuse from the spool. Durbin held it up as Pulley moved the lantern closer to light it.

"Now, when this thing gets fair alight," Durbin said, "we all run outta here like the devil himself was chasin' us. Understand?"

"Except I wouldn't light it if I were you."

Their heads snapped around to see the shopkeeper standing by the stairway, pointing two pistols at them.

"That could be very bad for your well being."

The three were in shock, but Pulley was the first to recover. He held the lantern up as if to see the intruder better and asked, "And who might you be?"

Before the man could answer, he blew out the lantern, pitching the room into absolute darkness. Durbin drew his sword; Pulley drew his pistol, and both instantly moved to new positions.

After a few moments, Pulley tried to cock his pistol as quietly as he could, but to no avail. The inevitable "click" occurred, causing the intruder to fire one of his weapons just as Pulley moved to his left. He both heard and felt the ball go past his head.

Now, a deadly standoff occurred. There was no light whatsoever, only blackness and complete silence. All three men were slowly and silently maneuvering trying to determine the location of their enemy.

Pulley continued to his left, hoping to reach the wall; that way he would know where he was in the room and would eliminate one possible attack direction. It was a painstaking process. He would move one foot, gently set it down, test his weight on it to make sure no sound would be made, then move the other. Slowly, soundlessly, he was moving; but, then again, so was everyone else.

This process continued for about ten minutes, but it seemed like an eternity to the participants. Finally, Pulley heard something. It was the sound of a foot dragging across sand-covered stone. It was in front of him, slightly to his right; and it only lasted for an instant.

He slowly raised his pistol, but had no idea what to do. Yes, he heard a sound, but who made it? Was it the intruder? Cecil? Maria? If he were to shoot, he only had a one in three chance of hitting the right person.

A lifetime of cautious living now weighed down on him like a rock. This wasn't the way it was supposed to be. Durbin was the decisive one, not him. He wanted to call out, "Cecil, what should I do?" but that would mean his instant death. On the other hand, if he pulled the trigger it could mean the instant death of an innocent woman, or a man he loved like a brother.

There was a very long moment of complete silence, which was shattered by the sound of a pistol going off. The muzzle flash revealed a look of astonishment on the face of the intruder as a ball entered his chest just to the left of his sternum, producing a shockwave behind it that tore out the right side of his heart.

With a hand that was trembling like a leaf, Isaac Pulley lowered the still smoking gun.

* * * * *

All morning the battle continued, with the French gaining purchase inside the town, only to be pushed back, then to regroup, renew their attack, gain a foothold, and again be pushed back.

At about 2:00 in the afternoon, the battle suddenly stopped. It was not planned that way; it happened when both sides felt a tremor in the earth unlike anything they had previously experienced. Smith grabbed on to a piece of the wall. Bonaparte steadied himself and moved even closer to the battle to try and see what was going on. The tremor grew in intensity, and a deep groan welled up from the ground, as if the earth itself was in pain.

Suddenly, in front of the wall where the soldiers were stopped, the ground erupted in a huge explosion, and the ditch started vomiting flame. Sand and body parts from both the living and the dead flew high into the sky and showered down on both attackers and defenders.

Bonaparte looked on in stunned disbelief. His traverse, his bridge into the city, was gone. In it's place was a hole that was belching flame and smoke. It could have been the entranceway to hell. He stared for a moment at the inferno, and then looked out to sea where 20,000 Turkish troops were being disembarked, and he knew the battle for Acre was over.

* * * * *

The sounds of the battle were penetrating Susan Whitney's hospital room, but she couldn't hear them. It wasn't that she was unconscious; quite the contrary. Her mind was locked in a very active war of its own. The Army of Pain was battling the Militia of Laudanum for control over her consciousness. In a strange way, pain was losing; not because the laudanum was so effective, but because the pain had become a routine way of life. It had become a given in the same way she had previously accepted the presence of air. It was no longer a thing to be examined.

Occasionally, however, there were a few golden moments when the fog of laudanum exactly canceled out the pain. These were precious to her. She clung to them like a drowning man clings to a log, only to eventually, inevitably, have them cruelly snatched away.

She was experiencing one of those moments now, but somehow it seemed different. It wasn't just the fog being equally matched with agony. There was a clarity to things that she hadn't experienced before. She looked down at the foot of her bed and could see the candle flickering on the chest of drawers across the room. She marveled for a moment at the shadows it was casting on the wall behind it, and wondered why she hadn't paid more attention to that marvelous phenomenon in the past.

There was a loud explosion followed by screams somewhere in the distance outside her window, and her head automatically turned to track the sound. It was then that she saw a man sitting in a chair next to her bed. He was a very old man, in a monk's hooded robe, and had a bright red birthmark on the left side of his face and neck.

"Father John, you startled me. I had no idea you were here."

"I know." And he said nothing more.

There was something about him that Susan found unbelievably comforting. It had been that way since she and Lucas first met him years ago when they were on a brief vacation, visiting Ephesus in Turkey. [1] He was John; she firmly believed that. Not any John, but *the* John—as in John 21:21

21 When Peter saw him, he said to Jesus, "Lord, what about him [the disciple John]?"

22 Jesus said to him, "What if I want him to remain until I come? What concern is it of yours? You follow me."

23 So the word spread among the brothers that that disciple would not die.

Lucas mocked her for it, but she believed he was the same John that had once walked with Jesus.

"I am sick, father. I know I am not of your faith, but... would you pray for me?"

"And of what faith do you think I am?"

"I... Well, given your robe I assumed..."

---

[1] See *HMS Diamond* - Chapter Three

"Are you a Christian, my child? Are you a follower of Christ?"

"Yes, certainly I am... or, well, I try to be. But there are sometimes when I..."

"Then you are of my faith; and I *have* been praying for you."

There was a long period of silence. Finally, Susan broke it.

"Father... Am I going to die?"

He looked up. There was a gentleness in his eyes that riveted Susan. She had never seen anything like it.

"No, my child, you are not—at least not in the immediate future."

"But Lucas thinks so... everyone thinks so."

"They're wrong." He said simply.

"I want to believe you, father. I really do. I can't tell you how much I want to live. I want to breathe fresh air again, and see the ocean, and feel the sun on my skin. I want to... well, maybe someday have a..." She broke off for a moment, and then continued, "And I want to be with my friends, with Sidney, and with..."

"...and with Lucas."

"She looked away and quietly said, "Yes."

"You shall do all of those things and more, my dear, for your work is not yet done. None of you has finished your work."

"Father, you said that before. When we were in Ephesus, you said, 'God's hand is on you, my child, and on your friend, and your captain.' And you told us that story about those children who were asleep in a cave somewhere. You said, 'God protected them because he had other work for them to do. It was their fate to live on.' [1] Is that what you're saying to me now? That God has... I don't know what to call it... a mis-

---

[1] See *HMS Diamond* - Chapter Three

sion for me or something? A mission for all of us?"

John sighed deeply and replied, "Susan, look at the way your life has become intertwined with Sidney and Lucas. Look at the way you three met. [1] Sidney Smith is assigned to HMS *Richmond* seemingly at random. You follow your gunner's mate husband to sea; he's assigned to the *Richmond*, and dies in battle. Lucas Walker's ship sinks in a storm; and he, the only survivor, is picked up by the *Richmond*. Together you three save Prince William from certain capture via a series of amazing exploits. For this, you, a girl raised on the streets of Portsmouth, become Lady Whitney, a wealthy woman with a very nice estate. And this doesn't even get into your escape from Toulon, [2] or Sidney's escape from the Temple, [3] or a dozen other adventures.

"Don't you see, Susan? Your whole situation is preposterous! It's absurd—but that is exactly the point. It... is... absurd... and in that very absurdity can you not see the hand of God at work?"

Susan did not speak. She could not. She had no words to accompany the enormity of what John had just said to her. She had indeed started out life as a street urchin in Portsmouth. Yes, she had been lucky—very lucky in many ways—but...

"Father, are you saying... are you saying God even knows I exist? That he has some plan for me? For all of us? Some purpose?"

The old monk could not suppress a smile. "I can assure you, Susan... God indeed knows you exist, as well as Sidney, and Lucas. He knows everything there is to know about all three of you, and what will happen in your futures." Then he paused, looked off into the distance, and quietly murmured, "As do I."

------

[1] See *Midshipman Prince* - Chapter One
[2] See *HMS Diamond* - Chapter Five
[3] See *The Temple* - Chapter Two

He slowly stood up, as if to leave.

"Wait, don't go. Please, you must tell me our mission. What purpose does God have for us? What do we need to do to..."

The old man continued to shuffle out of the room.

Susan now had a touch of desperation in her voice, "Father, before you go, would you bless me?"

That was one appeal he could not ignore. The old monk smiled, shuffled back to Susan's bedside, sat down, made the sign of the cross, and prayed for a moment. Then he gently placed his hand on her head.

"May the Lord bless you and keep you, Susan. May He make his face to shine upon you, and be gracious unto you. May He lift up His countenance upon you, and above all, give you... peace."

He started out of the room again when Susan asked, "Do you think he heard you, father? The Lord, I mean?"

"Whatever you bind on earth will be bound in heaven, and whatever you loose on earth will be loosed in heaven."

"But that was Jesus speaking to Peter."

The old man chuckled. "Well, that's what *Peter* says anyway," and he walked out of the room.

* * * * *

King Ferdinand's palace in Caserta, 20 miles north of Naples, was his favorite place. It was his favorite not because of its considerable beauty, but because it was begun by his father and carried to completion specifically for him.

The model for the palace was Versailles in that it was to be the administrative headquarters for his kingdom as well as the home of his court. It consisted of 1200 rooms, including dozens of apartments for visiting dignitaries, a huge library, and a theater modeled after the Teatro di San Carlo in Naples. Like Versailles, it had an unbroken balustrade running along the top of the building, with pavilions breaking up the long facade. The rooms were opulently decorated with the finest fabrics, furniture, and artwork that his taxation could provide. Gold and silver inlay could be seen everywhere. In short, like Versailles, it was designed to inspire awe by displaying the utter power and grandeur of a Bourbon monarchy.

However, Ferdinand's main source of pride was not the palace per se, which was viewed as nearly the equal of its French counterpart. It was the garden, almost 2 miles long, which was considered its superior.

Immediately behind the palace was a large park, crisscrossed by avenues, and containing a flower garden displaying what seemed like every color and hue that nature had to offer. On the left was the "old woods," so-called because they predated the construction of the palace. On the right was a meadow, framed by stands of trees. Beyond this initial park was a long stepped canal with wide walkways on either side. Spotted at various intervals were fountains and artificial cascades, providing an unending display of water patterns to delight the eye.

At the end of this alley was the Grand Cascata waterfall, called the Fountain of Diana and Actaeon, almost 260 ft. high. Next to it, however, was the highlight of it all—the English Garden.

This latter feature was not included in the original palace design, but was added by Ferdinand himself in the 1780s. It was designed by Carlo Vanvitelli, assisted by the London-trained garden designer John Graefer, who had been recommended to Ferdinand by Sir William Hamilton. In contrast to the very formal European style, the English approach was considered much less ordered—but much more romantic.

It was here that the cream of the Neapolitan aristocracy was congregating.

At precisely noon, King Ferdinand and Queen Maria

Carolina arrived in a gilded carriage, drawn by four magnificent white horses. In a second carriage was Admiral Nelson, plus Sir William Hamilton and Lady Emma.

The carriages stopped at an open pavilion called the Temple of Fame, which was surrounded by the hundreds of glittering guests. Inside the pavilion were three life-size wax figures of Nelson, Sir William, and Emma. Sir William's figure was leading Nelson to Emma, who was holding up a wax Wreath of Victory.

The King sat down on a small throne situated on a dais before the wax figures. The Queen sat next to him, and was beaming with pleasure.

Emma, the real version, was resplendent in a flowing silk gown that was being insistently tugged by the gentle garden breeze. It was part of two coach loads of magnificent dresses that had been given to her by the Queen, along with a richly jeweled picture of the King valued at more than £1000. However, the thing that drew everyone's attention was another gift from the Queen that Emma wore around her neck. It was an impressive gold chain, with a miniature picture of herself set in diamonds, with the motto *Eterna Gratitudine* inlayed around the frame.

On the other side of Nelson was Sir William in formal dress. Around his waist was a thick red sash, and over it a gold and diamond encrusted sword was buckled, fully the equivalent in value of Emma's bejeweled portrait and pendent.

Between them stood Nelson, in full uniform and covered with his various orders and honors.

The King stood, dramatically looked around for a moment, focused on Nelson, and began, "My dear Admiral, the expressions that are generally used to express gratitude are completely inadequate to describe how I feel. The service, which you have rendered the Two Sicilies and me, can simply never be equaled. With an active and imposing force, you organized a most judicious defense of my kingdom, preserving it for my family and me. Your powerful cooperation made the force of my faithful soldiers effective, along with that of my allies who united with them. In recounting these services, I hope you will permit that some lasting marks of my gratitude may be presented to your Lordship in my name, which I hope will not hurt your elevated and just delicacy.

"When my august father took leave of me, he gave me, along with these Kingdoms, a sword as a symbol to preserve what he had entrusted to me. To you, my Lord, I now give that sword as a memory of the obligation I then contracted, and which you have given me the opportunity of fulfilling. It was you, sir, and your brave followers, who liberated Naples and it's coasts from the enemy. It was you who have supported my efforts to re-establish quiet and order."

With this, a page stepped forward bearing a pillow with a sword laid across it. It was even more magnificent than the one that had been given to Sir William. The King handed it to Nelson, who received it with a respectful bow.

The King continued, "To your magnanimous Britannic sovereign, my best ally, and to your generous nation, I owe an avowal of immense gratitude. Rest assured, my Lord, that this gratitude will never cease.

"But there is one more step I must take. I have a document that I would like Prince di Luzzi to read." With that, the King returned to his throne and sat down. From the crowd of courtiers stepped a thin, elegant old man, who opened up a document and started reading in a surprisingly strong voice.

"Whereas, the glorious enterprises of your Excellency, which gained the admiration and applause of the greatest and wisest part of Europe, has excited in His Majesty the most lively sentiments of approbation, gratitude, and esteem toward your illustrious person.

"Whereas, His Majesty is desirous of giving your Excellency a public and lasting proof of these sentiments—one that will transmit to future generations a remembrance of your merits and your glory.

"Therefore, be it resolved and ordained, that the ancient and famous Town of Brontë, on the skirts of Mount Etna, with its territory and dependencies, shall be constituted a feudal tenure, and shall be raised to the dignity and title of Duchy. The right of absolute jurisdiction, both civil and criminal, and the Duchy and Title, with its revenues and jurisdiction, shall be conferred on your Excellency, and on the heirs of your body, in a right line, according to the laws of this Kingdom.

"It is hoped Your Excellency will accept this Royal Patent, and the actual concession of the before-mentioned Duchy."

Nelson was in rapture, even though he knew this was coming. Two days after the King's return to Palermo, Nelson was informed by Lady Hamilton that His Majesty intended to make him the Duke of Brontë; but now it had actually happened. He had only to accept it.

"Your Majesty, I am humbled by your most gracious ap-probation of my conduct, and also that Your Majesty has been pleased to confer upon me the title of Duke of Brontë together with the estate attached to it.

"My only request is that your Excellency will lay me, with deep humility and full of gratitude, at your feet; and under-stand my attachment to your sacred person, the Queen, and the Royal Family. It shall be my life's work to continue the conduct which has gained me your royal favor, and to merit the continuance of it."

And it was done.

The man who cruelly mocked Sir Sidney Smith for being a "Swedish knight" was now—proudly— a "Sicilian Duke," with an expected income of over £3,000 a year from his es-tate.

Several days later, he wrote a letter to Alexander Davison, an old friend and his prize agent after the battle of the Nile.

After describing the ceremony in which he received his Dukedom, he wrote:

> You will observe in a part of the King's speech, an observation is made, that he hoped this present would not hurt my delicate feelings. That is, I might have previously received money and jewels, but I rejected them, and never received even one farthing for all the expenses of the Royal Family on board the *Vanguard* and *Foudroyant*. This I expect to be paid from the Board of Admiralty, and that they will order me a suitable sum.
>
> It has been honor, and not money, which I have sought; nor, it seems, have I sought it in vain.
>
> Brontë Nelson

He folded the letter, sealed it, and placed it in the mail sack. It was time to get ready to go into Naples where Sir William was holding a party in his honor, and where the executions were finally wrapping up.

* * * * *

At the far end of the Mediterranean, Sir Sidney had written a letter of his own—only this one was to Bonaparte.

> General,
>
> I am acquainted with the dispositions that for some days past you have been making to raise the siege. The preparations in hand to carry off your wounded, and to leave none behind, do you great credit.
>
> This last word ought not to escape my mouth, but circumstances remind me to wish that you would reflect on the instability of human affairs.
>
> Could you have thought that a poor prisoner in a cell of the Temple prison—an unfortunate for whom you refused, for a single moment, to give yourself any

concern—could you have thought that this same man would someday become your antagonist, and compel you, in the midst of the sands of Syria, to raise the siege of a miserable, almost defenseless town? Such events, you must admit, exceed all human calculations.

Believe me, general, adopt sentiments more moderate; and that man who now tells you that Asia is not a theater made for your glory, will not be your enemy.

This letter is a little revenge that I give myself.

Bonaparte stood before the fireplace reading the letter. His face was haggard and drawn, his uniform was rumpled, and he seemed strangely spiritless—almost like a man awaiting a death sentence and resigned to his fate. For the past several days he had been organizing his army to retire in defeat. It was something he never seriously thought would happen; yet it had, and he was not good at it. In his own mind, and in the minds of others, he was all-powerful and predestined for greatness—and now this.

Suddenly he crumpled the letter, and threw it on the floor in disgust. "That bastard," he spat under his breath.

Across the room, his secretary, Bourrienne, was finishing the final draft of some correspondence, and General Kléber had just walked in to make a report to Bonaparte. The two looked at each other in surprise.

"General?" Bourrienne asked with concern in his voice.

"That letter is from Smith. He is such a... such an insufferable..." his words trailed off.

"Did he challenge you to a duel again?" Kléber finally asked, trying to lighten the mood. Bonaparte did not see the humor, and only glowered in reply.

"What is it Kléber? I assume you have some business here, or did you just stop by to display your skills as a comedian?"

Kléber immediately sobered up. "Yes, sir. I have the list of sick and wounded you wanted."

"How bad is it?"

"There are about 2000 wounded, but they can be evacuated. The thing that worries me is that we have over two hundred cases in the plague hospital on Mount Carmel. I am not sure what to do with them."

"What are your plans for the wounded?"

"Our scouts report that there is a small squadron of our frigates laying just south of Carmel. The British have held off chasing them away, assuming they will serve as the customary evacuation cartel ships."

Bonaparte turned to the unlit fireplace and thought for a minute.

"No," he finally replied.

"No?" Kléber asked. "No to what?"

"No to the evacuation of the wounded by ship. Those that can walk, will walk. Those that cannot will have to be transported in carts."

Kléber was surprised and confused. "But sir, hundreds will die if we do that."

"I know, general, but it can't be helped. We have two problems. First, when we get back to Egypt we must find a way to portray this debacle as a victory. We can't do that if we have a seemingly endless line of ships pulling into Alexandria before we get there, filled with wounded."

"And second?"

"Second, to use our ships for evacuation purposes we will have to ask permission of the British. I won't do that. I won't ask that beef-eating bastard Smith for a damn thing."

Kléber was taken aback not only by the words, but also by the vehemence with which the last sentence was spoken. After a long pause, he ventured another question.

"And the plague cases? What about them?"

Bonaparte gave a deep sigh. "They must be left behind."

Kléber and Bourrienne looked at each other in genuine

alarm. "Left behind? Sir, do you realize what these barbarians will do to them once we leave?"

"I am aware of that Kléber, but we can't take them with us and risk having them infect the whole army."

"So we leave them to be massacred, if not tortured to death?"

"No, we will kill them ourselves."

Kléber was now wide-eyed with horror. "Sir, I would never be able to muster the troops to shoot our own men—men whose only fault is that they have the plague." He then drew himself up to his full six foot three inch height and said, "Indeed, I am not sure I would even give the order."

"We will not shoot them. I will order Desgenettes to give them all a fatal dose of opium before we leave."

Kléber stood there, mute, all remaining respect for Bonaparte draining from his eyes.

After Kléber had gone, Bonaparte put on his hat, called for his horse, and rode out of camp. He proceeded toward the city and stopped at one of the batteries that was close to the city.

Dismounting before the amazed gun crew, he ordered, "Sergeant, I want you to load this gun with round shot."

The crew quickly complied, but before the ball could be run down the barrel, Bonaparte stopped them. He took the ball, wrapped his hat around it, and gave it back to the gun captain. "Now, complete your loading, and fire that ball inside Acre."

The men stepped back and a loud crash was heard as the gun fired. Bonaparte, who was standing away from the smoke, followed the flight of the ball. When it had landed over the wall, he turned and shook his fist at the *Tigre*, knowing that Smith was aboard.

"Try stopping that, you bastard! I said I would enter Acre, and a part of me just has!"

* * * * *

Smith had the gallery windows wide open in his cabin aboard the *Tigre*. He loved it whenever he could do that. He loved the breeze that was coming through, and the smell of the ocean. He even loved the sounds of the gulls that were squabbling over some nameless scrap floating on the water.

He adjusted a window sash and walked back to his desk, where piles of papers were spread over every square inch of surface. This was the other side of warfare, the paperwork. There were reports to file, and logs to sign, and stores to account for, and... out of nowhere, another paper was dropped in front of him.

Smith looked up and saw Lucas Walker turning to go over to the water pitcher on the other side of the room. He poured himself a glass then took out a small lime from his pocket, cut it in half, and squeezed each half into the water.

Returning to Sidney's desk, he flopped down onto the overstuffed chair in front of it.

Sidney picked up the newly deposited paper. "And this would be?"

"It's a report on our dead and wounded—at least as of this morning. What it might be tonight, or tomorrow, or next week, I have no idea."

"How bad?"

"From the *Tigre*, the *Theseus*, and the *Alliance* combined... 53 killed in action, 13 drowned, 113 wounded, and 82 taken prisoner. We're working out the prisoner exchange details now."

"That's not as bad as I had feared."

"It's *not* bad—unless you're one of those 261 people."

"And what about..."

"Susan? Sidney, it's the damnedest thing. That headstrong, willful, thoroughly impossible woman actually beat the plague. I think the disease just couldn't take her any more and decided to leave. She's going to be brought aboard this afternoon."

"Beating the plague is not impossible, is it?"

"No. I've heard of it. I've never seen it; but I've heard of it."

Smith studied Walker for a long moment. "You're delighted, aren't you."

Walker looked a bit embarrassed. "Yes, more than I can tell you," he sheepishly admitted; then quickly added, "But if you ever tell her that... well, don't come to me if you get a musket ball in the gut."

Smith just grinned.

"So, what are you doing?" Walker asked, while surveying the piles of paper. "You've decided to resign your commission and become a clerk; or perhaps a scrivener for some wealthy lawyer?"

"No, I am just savoring the joys of being a commander in the Royal Navy. For example..." Smith rummaged around in a stack. "Here is a letter from Lord Spencer demanding that I explain my insubordination to Lord St. Vincent."

"What insubordination?"

"I have no idea.

"Then there is this reprimand from Lord St. Vincent himself. It says that I gave orders to ships not put under my command by Nelson."

"What ships were those?"

"I have no idea.

"But the prize goes to this stack. They are copies of correspondence from General Koehler in Constantinople to anyone who will listen—from parliament on down—expressing his outrage that I, a naval officer, should be fighting a land battle with Bonaparte. That, it seems, should be his province. Never mind that in two months he has not seen fit to travel the couple of days needed to get here."

"Do they know that you've won?"

"No, that's this stack," Smith said, grinning with satisfaction.

* * * * *

If there is one thing that is ubiquitous among armies, it is the presence of rumor. It was true in the time of Julius Caesar. It was true in the time of William the Conqueror; and it was no less true of Bonaparte's army.

For several days the army had been abuzz with the rumor that the siege was finally over, and they would be heading back to Egypt. It dominated the conversations when they were working, when they were eating, and around the campfires at night. Still, nothing official had been announced, so there was plenty of room for the inherently pessimistic to claim that their bones would soon be mingling with the Syrian sands, no matter what the rumor said.

It was therefore with some anticipation that they heard "assembly" being played by regimental buglers throughout the camps. Each man was to put down whatever he was doing, and immediately go to his unit's area and form up in ranks.

At approximately the same moment, dozens of officers along a half-mile stretch of wind-swept ridge began reading the following message from their commander.

Soldiers, you have crossed the desert which separates Africa from Asia with more rapidity than an army of Arabs.

The army which was on the march to invade Egypt is destroyed. You have taken its generals, its campaign outfits, its water-bags, its camels. You have seized on all the strong places which defend the wells of the desert. You have dispersed on the field of Mount Tabor that cloud of men which had come from every part of Asia in the hope of pillaging Egypt. The thirty vessels you saw arrive before Acre twelve days ago carried the army which was to besiege Alexandria; but, obliged to hurry to Acre, it has finished its destiny. A part of its flags will decorate your entry into Egypt.

After having with a handful of men nourished war for three months in the heart of Syria, taken forty pieces of cannon, five flags, six thousand prisoners, having razed the fortifications of Gaza, Jaffa, Haifa, Acre, we are about to return to Egypt. The season of year calls me there.

Cheers erupted from units all up a down the line when this last paragraph was read. After a moment, the various commanders continued:

A few days more and you had the hope of taking the Pasha himself in the middle of his palace, but at this season the capture of the castle of Acre is not worth the loss of a few days. The brave men who would have been lost are, moreover, necessary today for more essential operations.

Soldiers, we have a career of toil and danger to run. Having put the Orient out of condition to essay aught against us this campaign, we may have to repel the efforts of part of the Occident. You will there find a new occasion of glory, and if, in the midst of many combats, each day is marked by the death of a brave man, new brave men must gather and take rank in their turn among the small number who give *elan* in danger and bring victory.

Bonaparte

Bonaparte had simply declared victory and announced they were leaving. The men didn't believe the victory part for a minute, but leaving the accursed walls of Acre had their full support. However, before they could leave, there was work to be done.

To the puzzlement of the men, Bonaparte ordered that the trenches be repaired, not destroyed. He wanted to give the impression that he was staying, and preparing for another attack. While these repair efforts were underway, however, the rest of the army was discretely gathering their equipment for departure. Unfortunately, there was more ammunition than they could reasonably carry, including 1000 mortar rounds that had just arrived. Bonaparte's solution was to fire everything they had—not at the walls of Acre, but over the walls into the town. For four straight days, the cries of the *muezzins* to prayer, were punctuated with bursting shells.

Finally, on the night of 20 May, the retreat began along the road to Haifa. Junot covered the left flank, the ocean protected their right, and Kléber along with Murat's cavalry guarded the rear. It was a well-organized withdrawal, except for the assumption that the ocean was their friend.

The following morning Smith and his flotilla got underway to follow the French army down the coast. He sent the *Theseus* to chase away the French ships that they originally thought would serve as cartel ships for the wounded. Bonaparte rejected that option; and it was the wounded who were now causing Bonaparte his greatest problem.

The first town they came to was Haifa, which was at the opposite end of the long, sweeping, Bay of Acre. They couldn't see much, because it was still the dead of night; but they could hear just fine. That was the problem.

As they approached the town's central square, there were about 100 sick and wounded men who were considered non-ambulatory and too ill to move. They were told they would be left behind. As the army passed by, they were assailed by their screams and curses. Some of the wounded men tore off their bandages and rolled in the dirt like madmen. The sight terrified each soldier that walked by.

Things did not improve the following day.

As the sun rose, they could see the new threat they were facing. Smith had moved his gunboats in close to shore and started peppering the advance columns with grapeshot. This made the column move inland along a much more difficult road.

The worst part for Captain Joseph Moiret was the sun that was pounding down on him with an invisible fist. There was no escaping it. Combine that fact with the inadequacy of water and the sand that was burning his feet through his broken-down leather shoes, and he was in misery—as was everyone around him.

His once bright red coat was stained and torn. Sweat had turned his sky-blue collar into a pasty blue and white smudge. His body ached for relief, yet he had no choice but to keep going. He had to continue to place one foot in front of the other, for if he faltered, absolutely no one would care. He would simply be left on the side of the road.

He kept his eyes looking forward as he walked. He had seen officers, with their limbs amputated, thrown off of litters by bearers who had grown tired of their load. He saw people with amputated limbs, bullet wounds, those infected with plague, or those who were only suspected of the plague, deserted in the dust and left to fend for themselves.

As they marched past, he had learned to ignore the cries of these men; but suddenly he heard a voice that made him look up.

"Someone please help me. I am not infected—I am only wounded. Look for yourself. Please help me!" The man's dry throat could barely get out the words.

No one attended to him. No one even looked over at him. If anyone said anything it was only a mumbled "It's all up with him. Leave him be."

However, Moiret did look over, and couldn't believe his eyes. He saw a man who was little more than a pile of rags. His coat was in tatters, and his pant leg was slit up the side revealing a deep gash on his lower leg. The man had ripped off his bandage so the passers-by could see his wound, which was now starting to bleed profusely. Next to him was the litter from which he had been dumped.

"I swear to God, I don't have the plague! Help me please. I can't walk."

Moiret glanced at the man's collar, and saw the flash of an engineer in the 75th Demi-Brigade. Suddenly, the pieces fell into place.

"Horace? Is that you?"

"Joseph, thank God... Oh, thank God. You'll help me? Please, Joseph. You'll help me, won't you?"

Moiret didn't reply. He knelt down and gave his friend a sip from his dwindling supply of water.

"What happened?" Moiret asked. "I didn't know you had been wounded."

"It happened after our last attack. I was moving back from the wall when a Turk—one of those bastards who took us in the flank—reached out and got me with a pike. My litter bearers abandoned me over an hour ago."

Moiret smiled, "Hmm, I seem to recall telling you about a date I have with a case of wine, a wheel of cheese, a maiden, and a cold mountain stream. I'd like you to be there with me, Horace; so let's get you moving."

Moiret looked up and spotted one of his men. "Poupard, get over here. I need you to take the other end of this litter."

The private gave his captain a look that was verging on outright mutiny. Moiret walked over and quietly said,

"You listen, Poupard. If it wasn't for me, your head would be lying somewhere in that miserable city right now. I led you to that mosque; and I got us out of there, with Commodore Smith's help.

"Now, that man laying over there is Captain Say. He's a friend of mine, and I am not going to leave him to die—just as I didn't leave *you* to die."

The private was not happy about it; but he took one end of the litter, Captain Moiret took the other, and they set off with the thousands of other wretches who were what remained of Bonaparte's *Grande Armée*.

* * * * *

The *Tigre* was about a mile off shore, and that was as close as Smith wanted to get. He had an unknown shore before him, with unknown depth, and he feared that a shift in the wind could pin him against it. However, that didn't stop his shallow drafted vessels from going in and periodically lobbing airbursts at the beach. It would remind Bonaparte that he was still there; and serve as great experience for the midshipmen and master's mates who were commanding those ships.

Susan was on deck sitting in a wood frame canvas chair the men had rigged for her. There was a look of sheer ecstasy on her face as she drank in the sea air and again felt the gentle kiss of the sun. Walker came up the aft ladder, wiping his hands on a blood stained cloth, and joined her.

"Susan, I said you could briefly come up here once or twice a day. I didn't say you could take up residence here."

"I feel fine, Lucas. Really. Give me another day or two and I'll be ready to resume my duties."

"I'll be the judge of that, young lady."

"*Young* lady? Flattery? From Lucas Walker? Acre must have mellowed you when I wasn't looking."

"All right, then I stand corrected. I'll be the judge of that, you old bat."

Susan made a pretense of looking thoughtful for a moment. "Nah, let's go back to the first version."

The two looked out at the ocean sparkling before them, as they had so many times in the past. They didn't say anything to each other for several minutes. They didn't have to. They were quite capable of communicating with each other without ever saying a word. Finally, Lucas broke the silence.

"Susan, what happened to Maria Corriveau? I assume she's on the *Theseus*."

"No, she's back at Acre."

"What?" Walker was genuinely alarmed. "How did she miss the sailing? What happened?"

Susan slowly shook her head. "She didn't want to go.

"She was helping to get me ready for transport out to the ship, and I asked her if she had her things packed. She seemed surprised by the question, so I restated it. 'Are you ready to go?' I asked her. She said, 'Go where?' She explained that there was nothing for her in France, and she'd never adjust to England 'Too cold,' she said. She pointed out that her life was here now."

"But what's going to happen to her?" Walker asked. "Weren't you the one who said Jezzar Pasha viewed his women as 'contaminated' because they've had contact with the world outside the harem?"

"Yes, I asked her about that too. She said it was true that she could no longer be owned by Jezzar Pasha, but that she was a western woman and still had at least some of her looks. Jezzar would probably give her away to some other Pasha, or to a particularly gifted tax collector. She would again be a prized possession, and her life would be far better than it could ever be in France."

Walker just shook his head, and silence descended again. After a few minutes, Susan broke it.

"I saw John again."

"John who?"

"John! You know, the monk from Ephesus."

"Oh yes, the one-man tourist trap."

"Lucas, I am serious!"

"So, you saw Father John... in Acre?"

"Yes, he visited me in my room. He told me that I wasn't going to die, and he blessed me, and right after that I started feeling better! He's amazing, Lucas. Truly amazing."

"Yes, my dear." Walker tried to keep the patronizing tone out of his voice, but failed miserably.

"That's not all he said. He said that God had a mission for

us—for all three of us, you, me, and Sidney—and our work isn't done. That's why I wasn't going to die."

Walker turned. "Susan, I had you on very large doses of laudanum—so large that I was worried I was going to kill you with them. Now, you know as well as I that laudanum is a funny drug. It can easily cause people to see and hear things that aren't there."

"It was not a dream, Lucas. I am telling you, he was there!"

"All right, fine. He was there. I believe you."

Susan was not happy with that answer.

"I had another dream; this time not involving John."

"Really? What was that?" Walker asked as he idly looked out to sea.

"I dreamed you had visited my room."

Walker's head quickly turned around. "I was in your room lots of times," he said cautiously.

"I know, but this was just before the last attack. It was just you."

"Really?" Walkers face was coloring.

"Yes, and you had lots of... well... lots of really sweet things to say."

Walker turned to look out over the ship's side again. "Yes, as I said, laudanum is a funny drug. It can cause all sorts of strange dreams. I am sure that's what you were experiencing."

Walker was a terrible liar. Susan had learned years ago to know when he was telling a fib, and Walker knew it.

She smiled contentedly and looked at some gulls that were lazily soaring overhead.

After a moment, Lucas too smiled, and gently put his hand on her shoulder.

* * * * *

Each day was much the same as the previous one. Smith's gunboats would harass any French troops that attempted to use the coast. When they moved inland, they were harassed by Nablousians—fierce tribesmen from the City of Nablus who ironically, according to legend, were descended from the Good Samaritan. In reply, Murat's cavalry would raid the local villages, killing the inhabitants and setting fire to crops and buildings.

A few days later the French column reached the conical hill upon which sat the city of Jaffa. It's white walls were surrounded by gardens and orchards; it had food in abundance; and, above all, it had an ample supply of water. The men were allowed to rest there for four days, but their break was something less than idyllic. On their way to Acre, they had slaughtered thousands of prisoners at Jaffa, and those bodies still lay on the beach unburied. Each night, as the wind came in off the ocean, the odor of putrefying bodies wafted over their campsite, reminding them of what they had done and providing the massacred prisoner's a kind of revenge.

The port was also littered with additional French sick and wounded who would plead with anyone who would listen, begging them not to leave them behind. Eventually, it reached the breaking point and a delegation was sent to Bonaparte led by Jean-Paul Daure, his transport officer and formerly the director of the hospital at Jaffa.

"Mon Général! Sir, may I have a moment with you please." Colonel Daure nearly tripped over a water bucket as he rounded the well where Bonaparte had paused to get a drink. Trailing behind him was Réne Desgenettes, the physician-in-chief of the army, and two younger officers Bonaparte had seen before but did not know.

"Sir, I need to talk to you about our wounded and our men who have the... ah... who are sick."

"What about them, Daure?"

"They need to be evacuated, Général. There is no way they will survive the rest of this trip."

"And how do you propose to evacuate them?" Bonaparte's arm swept out toward the ocean. "Do you see any of our ships out there?"

"No sir, but there are ships here in Jaffa, smaller ones—fishing boats and the like—but they're seaworthy."

"Seaworthy enough to get to Alexandria, especially while loaded to the gunnels with wounded? I hardly think that's the case."

"They don't have to make it to Alexandria, sir. All they have to do is find Sir Sidney Smith's ships, and put the sick and wounded under his protection."

Bonaparte turned to Daure and spoke very softly, "You want me to communicate with Smith—to open negotiations, to beg him to take our wounded? Is that what you want?"

Daure knew he had to be careful. He didn't overly fear Bonaparte when he was screaming and yelling; he feared him the most when he was speaking softly. *That* was when he was the most dangerous.

Without waiting for an answer, Bonaparte snapped, "No! Never! I will never treat with that dog. Besides, your plan will not work. How would you even find Smith? We haven't seen a British ship in several days. We have no idea where he's gone, and our wounded would be dead before you could locate him."

"But, sir..." Before Daure could complete his statement, one of the young junior officers pushed to the front.

"*Bâtard!* [Bastard!] And why didn't you think of that when we were still at Acre, Général. Was your pride so great that you couldn't bring yourself to even send a message to Smith?

"He was prepared to let our cartel ships in so our wounded could be taken to Alexandria. He even offered to transport them in English ships, to keep the Turks from interfering. He was prepared to collect our plague victims as well as our wounded.

"But no, you wouldn't even negotiate with him on the

subject. You rejected his offers, then forbade us, on pain of death, to even communicate with the British.

"I have wounded friends here, Général—some of whom I've known most of my life. I have men who served under me—who received their wounds in your service—and you just abandon them. You abandoned them at Acre; and you are abandoning them again now."

Bonaparte stared at the officer for a long time; but the young man did not flinch under his gaze. Finally, he said, "All right, Daure; you can have your ships; but you can only have six vessels. Six! Do you understand me?"

"Yes, sir," Daure said through his smile.

"And," Bonaparte continued, "they are *not* to seek out the British. They will proceed immediately to Egypt, then return to me. If this works out, I *might* send some more. But no British—no Smith—is that clear?"

The following day six small ships left Jaffa harbor, made straight for Sir Sidney Smith's flotilla, asked for asylum, and it was granted.

* * * * *

Standing on the quarterdeck of the large polacre-xebec was one of the proudest officers in the Royal Navy. Richard Janverin was only a midshipman by rank, but on this day, he was the captain of his own ship. *No, more than that,* he thought. *If I am also responsible for the other five ships in this group, does that not make me a commodore?*

It was the kind of intoxicating thought that would find a welcome home in any midshipman's mind; but further savory consideration was quickly banished by the dark clouds that were forming on the horizon.

He walked over to the weather side of the deck, patting for the hundredth time the letter in his coat pocket. It was from Sir Sidney to the Commandant of the Port of Damietta. It stated that the wounded being carried by Janverin's ships were French soldiers, but were not to be considered as prisoners. They were to be treated well, and given back to the French forces at the earliest opportunity.

He glanced upward at his sails, then to the horizon, then to the sails again. His ship was unlike anything he had ever sailed. It carried square sails on the foremast, and lateen sails on the main and mizzenmasts. Add to that a bowsprit with two headsails, and his ship's suit was complete.

He knew perfectly well how to handle the square and the headsails, but the lateens were something else entirely. These were large triangular sails, hanging from a single long yardarm, fastened at an angle from the mast, and running in a fore-and-aft direction. They had been used in the eastern Mediterranean since the second century; but, to put it mildly, they were something less than standard equipment in the Royal Navy. That made him nervous, along with the approaching storm.

"Davis," he said to the helmsman, "come two points to larboard, and keep her about a half-mile from the shoreline."

"Mr. Milliston," he said to the very junior master's mate, who was now his first lieutenant, "send a message to the other ships to follow in line behind us. I don't like the looks of those clouds, and I want to get us closer to shore in case we have to duck in somewhere."

Milliston had barely run up his signal flags when a call came from the foremast lookout.

"On deck thar!"

"Deck, aye," Janverin replied.

"Capin', there is some men on the beach ahead tryin' to signal us; and I see smoke risin' somewhere back off behind'em."

"Where away?"

"About three point to larboard, sir."

Janverin snapped a telescope to his eye, and immediately winced with pain. The flesh wound to his arm was still very raw and tender. Sure enough, there were at least three men on the beach, and it looked like they were waving their shirts at them. It was hard to tell at that distance.

"Davis, take us as close as you can get to the shore. Mr. Milliston I'll have a man in the chains swinging a lead. I want continuous depth measurements."

As Janverin's small ship's boat reached shore, he was sure of only three things. First, the men were French; second, they were extraordinarily glad to see him; and third, they had all been wounded.

Their initial contact consisting of the refugees babbling expressions of gratitude, mixed with foul oaths directed at their officers. After he got them calmed down, he was able to use his limited French skills get a coherent story out of them.

"We were part of the column retreating from Acre, monsieur," said the spokesman, a young sergeant. "We got to the outskirts of Caesarea, and camped for the night. But the following day the order was given to leave the worst of the wounded in a nearby abandoned village, while the rest of the army went on."

"What do you mean by 'leave you'?" Janverin asked. Do you mean abandon you? Did they not leave troops to protect you until you could be picked up?"

"No, sir. Nothing. They just left us. No weapons. Nothing."

"Well, they did leave us with something," a second man chimed in. "They issued all of us small bottles of what they said was laudanum for the pain, but I think it was poison."

Janverin stared opened-mouthed from one man to the other. Finally, he was able to say. "But... but what about the tribesmen? They left you with no weapons, no protection? There are..."

"Yes, sir. It took them about six hours to find us."

"Then what happened?"

Neither man would speak. They just looked downward

and Janverin could almost see the scenes of horror that were flooding back into their minds.

After a long moment, Janverin said, "All right, you two men get into the boat. You..." he said pointing to the sergeant, "I want you to take us to your campsite. I have to see if any others survived."

The man looked more than a little afraid.

"Don't worry," Janverin assured him, "the tribes would never attack a British uniform." Although in his mind he secretly added the words, *I hope.*

The party set off and, after stumbling over a half-mile of sand dunes and barren, rocky ground they came to a village that had obviously been taken over by the French as a makeshift final hospital for their wounded. What they saw stunned them.

Most of the huts were at least half burned. Corpses lay throughout the compound, some inside the sill smoldering huts, and some outside. In one area, about six yards square, were the mutilated bodies of thirty-two soldiers; some had evidently received amputation at the hands of French surgeons—others, less gently, at the hands of the Turks. Almost every body they saw showed evidence of poisoning and was swelled from the heat. All together, Janverin estimated there were about 300 dead; and the British sailors had to tie bandanas over their noses and mouths to try to keep the stench at bay.

From behind one building, however, came the sound of shouted orders being given in Arabic. Janverin rounded the corner to find several Nablousians with muskets leading away a group of wounded French soldiers. Janverin know what would happen to them whenever they got to wherever they were going.

"Halt!" Janverin snapped in as authoritative a tone as his 22-year old voice could muster. "Those men are our prisoners."

The Turks turned and were obviously surprised to see a

British officer and four armed sailors pointing weapons at them. Finally, one man emerged from the group and asked in broken English.

"Who are you, and what are you doing here?"

"I am Cap..." and he checked himself. If the man spoke English, he could probably tell the difference between a captain and a midshipman's uniform. "I am Midshipman Richard Janverin. I command the *Negresse*, one of the ships you will find anchored off-shore." Actually, the ship he was in charge of didn't have a name, so he decided to use that of the gunboat he had formerly commanded.

"You didn't answer me. Why are you here?"

Janverin had to think fast. "I am here at the orders of Commodore Sir Sidney Smith to pick up some prisoners. We want to... ah... interrogate them to see what Bonaparte's plans are."

This caused some debate among the tribal warriors. Interrogating prisoners as to Bonaparte's plans was patently ridiculous. It was perfectly obvious what his plans were. On the other hand, he *was* a British naval officer, he *could* have been sent by Smith, and who knew what connections Smith still had with the Pasha.

"No, you will not have these pigs. They will receive the justice of Allah, as we have sworn, and as they deserve."

Janverin now had a decision to make. Were these men bluffing, or would they really open fire to preserve the sanctity of "Allah's justice." He glanced over at the French prisoners. All were wounded, all were bleeding, several were crying, and even more were praying. He knew he had to go all in.

"You will NOT," he barked, his voice crackling with nervous emotion. The sailor's behind him tightened their grips on their muskets.

The English-speaking tribesman stared hard at Janverin for a long moment, then broke his gaze, and looked over at the man who was obviously their leader. He received a subtle nod.

"If you have been sent by Commodore Sir Sidney, peace be upon him, we will allow it. But only if you promise that when you are finished you will cast these animals into the sea."

Janverin could now finally exhale. "I give you my word of honor that justice will be done."

* * * * *

The return of Bonaparte to Cairo was a sight unlike any that had been seen before. Every musician in the city had been summoned to participate in the massive parade. Every person of consequence in the city, or anywhere nearby, had been ordered to be present with gifts and congratulations. Failure to attend meant imprisonment.

With drums beating and flags flying, Bonaparte, riding a magnificent white stallion, was the first to appear through the Bab el-Nasr gate—the Gate of Victory. Behind him were his troops, each wearing a palm frond in their cap. The street in front of them was strewn with palm leaves that had been laid down earlier by a small army of women.

The procession advanced through the streets to the Esbekiya Square, where the French garrison, the local militia, the members of the *Dewan,* and other officials were drawn up. Bonaparte did a quick inspection of the local troops, and took a seat with the major officials on a dais that was covered by a spectacular white and gold canopy.

Captured Turkish flags were paraded, along with military bands, drummers, buglers, and of course the troops—starting with the demi-brigades and ending with Murat's superb cavalry. In the square, solemn Muslim prayers of thanks were offered by black robed mullahs, while trained monkeys and dancing bears were exercised on the streets leading up to the square. The celebrations and feasting lasted for the next three nights; and concluded with a fireworks display that for the most part fizzled because of the poor quality of the powder with which the engineers had to work.

The only uncomfortable moment for Bonaparte came when a local pasha asked him why the number of soldiers in the parade was so small. He covered it well by saying that he only brought a small number of men with him; and that most of the units had been left in Alexandria and in the delta to guard against a possible Turkish invasion.

It was true that a large part of his force had been left behind. At Acre, they were still sending out burial parties.

* * * * *

Sir Sidney had assigned the *Theseus*, under Lieutenant Canes, to continue harassment of Bonaparte's troops as they made their way back to Egypt. He had received word that there had been an insurrection of janissaries, mostly Arnauts and Albanians, on the island of Cyprus. Because the Sultan had made him the commander of his land and sea forces on the coast of Syria and Egypt, he was responsible for representing the authority of the Sultan in that region and maintaining order. Thus, he had to leave station to take care of the insurrection.

On Cyprus, some insurgents had murdered their local chief on the island, and the Greek population was at their mercy. Small towns and villages were being plundered, and Christian Greeks were being massacred. Sir Sidney landed and, wearing the imperial aigrette of the Sultan, quickly restored order. He took with him the complete marine complement of the *Tigre*, rounded-up the outlaws, led them down to the beach, and sent them into exile aboard several somewhat leaky ships.

He expected some measure of gratitude from the local population, but was completely unprepared for what he received.

Prior to his arrival, he was already the "Hero of Acre," the man who defeated Bonaparte and almost certainly kept Cyprus from eventually becoming a French vassal state. Now, he had come directly to their island to save them from their own homegrown brand of terror. To them he was more than a hero—he was a saint.

He had received word that the Archbishop of Cyprus wanted to travel from Nicosia to Larnaca, where Smith's ship was anchored, to honor him. Smith thought that the Archbishop would be disgracing himself by coming to him, so Sidney gathered Lucas Walker and Susan Whitney, who insisted on coming along, and rode to Nicosia to see the Archbishop.

He was met at the gates of the city by a group of some thirty priests, monks and prelates. As the three dismounted and approached the group, a young monk disengaged and introduced himself.

"Top of the mornin' to you, Commodore. I am Father Bartholomew and I'll be your interpreter."

Smith could not have been more surprised if the priest had hit him over the head with a board.

"You're... Irish?" Smith asked in disbelief.

"I am that," he said, then added as an aside, "Trust me, it's a long story," and continued, "Let me introduce you to the Holy Father."

The three were led to an elderly man with the gentlest blue-gray eyes Smith had ever seen. He wore the same simple robe as the others, except for an impressive cross that hung from a gold chain around his neck and a silver tipped cane that he carried.

"This is Father Chrysanthos," Father Bartholomew began "who is the Archbishop of the Greek Cypriot Orthodox Church."

The three bowed as they stood before him and Bartholomew continued.

"Our church is an autocephalous one within the communion of Orthodox Christianity. In other words, Archbishop Chrysanthos does not report to any higher-ranking authority. Although the analogy is not a perfect one, within the Cypriot Orthodox Church he is essentially the equivalent of the Pope in Catholicism."

After the introduction, the Archbishop began to deliver a surprisingly animated speech, with Father Bartholomew standing off to the side and translating. It contained all manner of gratitude for saving the lives of the clergy, laymen, citizens, peasantry, and everyone else on the island.

At the end of the address, he stepped forward, embraced Smith paternally, and, at the same moment, adroitly placed around Smith's neck the cross that he had been wearing.

"Commodore, this cross once belonged to an Englishman, and I now restore it to an Englishman. It belonged to the man you call Richard I, and we call *Agio Ricardo*, Saint Richard, surnamed Coeur de Lion. He left it in this church when he departed in 1191 for Acre, and it has been preserved in our treasury ever since. Eighteen archbishops in succession have signed for the receipt of this cross. I now give it over to you, in token of our gratitude."

The Archbishop continued to talk but Smith was not really listening to him, or to the translation of Father Bartholomew, any more. He caught the word "Templar" being used several times, but it didn't really register. His attention was fixed on the cross he held in his hand. It was not just any cross. This one had once been owned by Richard the Lionhearted... held by him... perhaps even treasured by him. He left it on his way to take Acre from Saladin; and Smith was receiving it on his way back from defending Acre from Bonaparte. The cross had come full circle.

After the ceremony, Father Bartholomew walked the three back to their horses, where Smith asked him, "Father, at one point the Archbishop was saying something about the Templars. I am sorry, but I didn't quite catch what that was about."

"Commodore, you are now a Knight Templar."

Smith stopped and turned to the priest. "What? What did you say?"

"Yes, you are now a member of the Knights Templar. You see, at one time the Templars owned this island. It was conquered in 1192 by Richard I, and later he sold it to the Templar order. In fact, they had their headquarters here because Cyprus was so important to protecting the sea-lanes to the Holy Land. Anyway, it was in Christian hands until 1570 when the Ottomans invaded."

"That's fine, but how could the Archbishop make me a Templar Knight?"

"He can do it because he is, in effect, the ruler of this island, and this island has never been stricken from the books as a Templar holding."

"What Templar holdings? The Templars don't exist any more."

"Oh yes they do, Sir Sidney. They most certainly do.

"The Grand Master of the Templars, Jacques de Molay, was a resident here until he was called back to France in 1305. There he, and almost every other Templar in France, was arrested on trumped-up charges of heresy, tortured into making false confessions and, in de Molay's case, burned at the stake. Basically, the King of France wanted to be free of the debts he owed the Templars, and the Pope wanted the Templar land holdings; so Pope Clement V dissolved and outlawed the order, and King Phillip IV had them killed.

"What you might not know is that Phillip didn't get them all. The surviving knights realized that the Pope had no authority to dissolve their order. They were not created by the church—they were essentially a private organization—and were therefore totally independent of papal authority. The Pope's *Suspendo In Perpetuo* was meaningless.

"So, they quietly elected another Grand Master to replace de Molay—Jean-Marc Larmenius, I believe was his name—

and the order continues to this day.

"You, sir, are indeed a Knight of the Poor Fellow-Soldiers of Christ and of the Temple of Solomon. You are now a Templar."

* * * *

Later that night the three were back aboard the *Tigre*. Susan really had exerted herself too much that day and had retired. Sir Sidney and Lucas Walker were in Sidney's cabin relaxing.

"Well, Sidney, I rather suspect you've done it all now," Walker began. "You won the war with Bonaparte in the East, rescued an entire island, received Richard I's cross, and somehow became a Templar in the bargain. What do you plan to do for an encore?"

Smith smiled, took another sip of his sherry and a long puff on his cigar, a newly acquired habit, and replied: "My friend... I will treasure that cross always; I am still somewhat dubious that I am really a Templar; and yes, we've won the war, but that was the easy part. The real question is, can we win the peace?"

Within a year, Sir Sidney Smith's efforts to do just that would see the hero of Acre's name vilified from the eastern Mediterranean to the halls of Parliament.

ɧistorical Postscript

As with all of my other Sir Sidney Smith novels, I am including a historical postscript. Intellectual honesty requires it.

You see, the actual events that occurred in Sir Sidney's life outstrip anything I could possibly imagine; therefore, in each book, I feel compelled to fess-up. My plots are mostly driven by actual events, not by my creativity. My characters literally tell me what they are going to do and say. I know that sounds strange; but I swear it's true. All I do is take dictation, and cash the royalty checks. (Who knew there was a racket like this out there?!)

In general, the first thing I should admit is that I shifted some dates a bit. The Siege of Acre and Nelson's machinations in Naples all took place over a seven-month period, but not at the same time. The Siege of Acre ran for two months, from 20 March to 21 May 1799. Nelson's evacuation of the royal family out of Naples took place at the very end of 1798 (December 23rd to be exact), a few months before Acre. Ruffo's recapture of Naples, the ensuing bloodbath, the hanging of Caracciolo, Nelson's annulment of the surrender, and the bloodbath following that, all took place in late June and early July, a month *after* the Siege of Acre. I placed everything on top of everything else because... well... it's more dramatic that way. Call it poetic license, or prosaic license, or whatever.

In any event, here is what actually happened—and what I made up—in *Acre*.

Chapter One

Captain Joseph Moiret and Captain Horace Say were actual officers in Bonaparte's army who were at the events I describe. I know because, blessedly, they left memoirs.

El-Arish and Jaffa fell as described. The slaughter, rape, and pillage of Jaffa actually happened. It was designed to send a message to any future city that, should they resist, this could happen to them as well.

The holdouts were in fact talked into surrendering by Bonaparte's stepson, Eugene de Beauharnais, and his friend, Jean-Louis Croisier. Bonaparte was furious, because it left him with the problem of what to do with the prisoners. The meeting with his staff occurred, although I have no idea exactly who was there. The people I placed in the room are all likely candidates, and the dialogue is probable.

Even though they had laid down their arms in response to Beauharnais' offer, the prisoners were nevertheless slaughtered on the beach as described. The only departure from actual events is that I had the executions occurring in one day. It actually took two. Later Captain Croisier did everything he could to get himself killed at Acre (and eventually succeeded) to assuage the blot upon his honor.

The letter from Lady Emma Hamilton to Admiral Nelson is not made-up. It is word-for-word what she wrote to him, complete with the actual misspellings and faulty grammar. The letter from his wife, Fanny, is also accurate. It doesn't take a rocket scientist to figure out which letter would have interested him more.

Topkapi Palace in Constantinople is laid out as described, as is the Hagia Irene. Both can be seen today, and are major tourist attractions. The description of the Sultan's procession is quite authentic and taken from an eyewitness account.

The game of jereed was played exactly as described; and yes, Sultan Selim III was in fact a big fan of the Cabbagemen. Go Green!!

Chapter Two

The provisioning of the *Tigre* is based on actual records for the supplying of a similar sized warship, the 80-gun *Foudroyant*. The balancing act represented by its stowage was a serious and ongoing concern.

As you probably know from previous books, (you *have* been reading the other books in this series, haven't you?) John Wesley Wright, Picard Phélippeaux, and Sir Sidney's brother, Spencer Smith, are real people and played significant roles in his life. The meeting on board the *Tigre* did not take place, but Spencer Smith's assessment of the situation is accurate. Here I must also give credit to a wonderful historian (and even better writer), Tom Pocock, for the whale and elephant analogy. Bonaparte was far from defeated by Nelson's victory at the Nile. Rather, he believed he was in a position to carve out conquests on land that would have put Alexander the Great to shame.

But the really important element of that scene is Sir Sidney's description of his chaotic, multilevel chain of command. No one really knew exactly what Smith's authority and responsibilities were, including I suspect Sir Sidney himself. On one hand, this was good, as it allowed Sir Sidney to adopt whatever role he needed, when he needed it. On the other hand, it gave his enemies plenty of ammunition with which to criticize him, by contending his proper role was something other than whatever Smith chose.

The account of the rat dying of the plague is, of course, fictional; but I am pretty proud of it. I mean, how many people can make the death of a rat sound even mildly interesting? Okay... Okay... moving right along.

The change of command between Smith and Troubridge actually occurred. While my details are fictional, the ships Smith was given to blockade Alexandria are not. As I have him saying in the novel, he had, "... two third-rates, a store-ship, a captured sloop, and an attack canoe..." to work with. That's it.

Nelson's rescue of the Neapolitan Royal Family is accurate, and raised my generally negative opinion of him somewhat. It was a reasonably heroic act; although later events justifiably lowered my opinion again.

Wright's intelligence excursion into Alexandria happened; but I have no knowledge whether this was how Sir Sidney learned of Bonaparte's departure from Jaffa. What is known is that Smith learned of it the day after he relieved Troubridge, and sent the ships and personnel off as described.

There is one part of the storyline that you might have missed because it was so brief. It was when Susan tried to find out whether Sir Sidney was on a spying mission the night he was captured at Le Havre. He successfully evaded the question, and that is important because it relates to one of the great unknowns about Sir Sidney.

We know he was heavily involved in espionage work throughout his entire career, and we know much of it was done in conjunction with John Wesley Wright. However, we have almost no clue as to what, where, how, or why he was doing it. Unfortunately, it's in the nature of intelligence work that people *not* know what's going on—not when you're doing it—not ever. That's a shame, because I suspect it might shed a whole lot of light on why Sir Sidney did many things he did.

You might remember Dr. Dominique-Jean Larrey, from my previous book, *The Temple*. Larrey was in fact Bonaparte's chief surgeon, and was continually at odds with his boss, Réne Desgenettes. He was also a brilliant pioneer in the field of military medicine, and many of his innovations are still used to this day.

Bonaparte's visit to the plague victims actually occurred, and occurred for the reasons given. That being said, it should be pointed out that Bonaparte very rarely visited his sick and wounded men. He claimed that he had a very sensitive nose, and the odors of the hospital made him ill.

General Grézieux, the man who, in the story, was so afraid of shaking hands with Larrey and to whom Bonaparte said: "Grézieux, if you're that worried about the plague, you will surely die from it" eventually did die, at Acre, of the plague.

Chapter Three

Ahmed al-Jezzar (The Butcher) was a real person and acquired his nickname as described. In addition to the fun sport of lopping off body parts from assorted victims, he reportedly walked around with a mobile gallows following behind him. That was so that, if anyone displeased him, justice need not be excessively delayed. Still, he is viewed today as one of the better rulers of Acre, primarily because of his building campaigns. His major accomplishment was the building of the al-Jezzar Mosque, a magnificent structure which is today another significant tourist attraction in modern Acre. To my astonishment, he is also credited by many modern sources as the person who stopped Bonaparte at Acre (you've *got* to be kidding!), with Sir Sidney given scant, if any, mention.

Haim Farhi was Jezzar's chief financial advisor and, because of the Pasha's many other interests, was the de facto ruler of Acre. From this position, he was able to provide taxation relief to the Jewish population, and is today regarded by them as a hero. His utility did not make him immune from the Pasha's whims, however, and he was disfigured by Jezzar as described.

The meeting between John Wesley Wright and Jezzar Pasha happened. Although I don't know exactly what transpired, I do know that Wright secured Jezzar's permission for Sir Sidney in effect to take over the defense of the city.

Bonaparte had to have been stunned to find Smith's ships in the Bay of Acre when he got there. He desperately tried to head off the ships that were transporting his siege equipment, but failed to do so. As a result, Smith captured them as described. The guns, shot and powder he found on those ships were immediately transported to the walls of Acre, to be used against Bonaparte.

Emma Hamilton was truly one of the most beautiful, and most amazing, women of her day. [1] She was especially known for her singing voice and for her dramatic posed "attitudes," which I described here. I don't know if she ever sang, "See the Conquering Hero Comes" to Nelson, but I'd be surprised if she didn't.

Cardinal Ruffo was a real person, and was assigned the task of forming the *Armate della Santa Fede* to kick the French out of Italy. I doubt that anyone seriously thought he could do it, so it must have come as quite a surprise when he did.

The description of Acre, it's fortifications, and the make-up of Jezzar's harem, are all accurate. It seems the Pasha really did have a weakness for light-skinned women, which might not be surprising as he was originally from Bosnia himself.

The first attack on the wall happened exactly as described, and Jezzar Pasha's primary role in the defense of the city seems to have been paying people for cut off heads.

Cecil Durbin is a fictional person, but the incident of burying the headless French general was not. The actual person who did it was one Daniel Bryan, the captain of the foretop on the *Tigre*. From "Mounseers, a-hoy!" to "Here you lie,

---

[1] For a fascinating fictional account of Emma Hamilton, you might want to check out *Bride of Glory: The Emma Hamilton Trilogy* by Bradda Field and published by Fireship Press.

old Crop." to the promise: "I'll take it this time, sir. But I pledge to you that if we're ever on a battlefield, and I spot ya dead, I'll bury ya—for nothin'." — it all happened as described. As a result of his actions, Bryan became something of a celebrity when they got back to England. When his sailing days were over, he retired to the Royal Hospital Haslar near Portsmouth on a very nice pension.

Chapter Four

The account of the rape and pillage of Naples by Cardinal Ruffo's royalist forces is, I believe, accurate. It was taken from a secondary source, which I try not to do, but that work was based on some reliable primary sources—letters, diaries, etc. of eyewitnesses.

In any event, the whole thing was bizarre. It was as if Naples was wearing a target on its back. First, they were looted and despoiled by the French and Jacobin sympathizers, and then they were ravaged by the royalist army and their supporters. Then a settlement is reached and everyone feels safe, when Nelson cancels the surrender and the killing starts again. I mean, good grief.

Next up is a series of interludes, just to vary the rhythm of the plot a bit. (Did you know that plot lines had rhythms? Yup, they do, just like poetry; but you're not supposed to see them—just feel them. It's a long story.)

Bonaparte paying his men to gather cannon balls—happened, right down to the amounts they were paid.

Sir Sidney reprinting and switching Bonaparte's proclamations happened, and I laughed my tail off when I first read about it. I could not locate the exact wording of those documents, however; although what I quote here is based on a proclamation Bonaparte made the previous year in Egypt.

At one point, Sir Sidney really did challenge Bonaparte to a duel, and the wording of his insulting reply is accurate.

The last interlude might well be the answer to a trivia question. Who was the first major figure to offer the Jews a homeland after the Diaspora? Answer: Bonaparte. The exact wording of his letter has only recently surfaced, and is included here. It's somewhat ironic that, although Bonaparte wrote the letter, it was the British who, in 1947, were instrumental in making it happen.

The French did indeed try to undermine the walls, and they were stopped by a daring raid conducted by John Wesley Wright, and Major Oldfield. Oldfield was killed and Wright wounded in the action.

Once again, that intrepid old tar Cecil Durbin does something crazy, like go out and fetch the wounded John Wesley Wright, and the body of Major Oldfield, from the moat in front of the whole French army. The thing is, it actually happened. The British sailors wrangled with the French over Oldfield's body as described, and the situation was resolved only when Oldfield's neckerchief snapped and the French won the tug-of-war.

Nelson, in fact, was suffering major headaches, weakness, and sleeplessness from the head wounds he received at the Battle of the Nile. Indeed, there is a great deal of speculation that those wounds might have caused some brain damage, and were the source of some of his more erratic later behavior.

The quotes from his letters to Emma and to his wife Fanny are accurate.

Cardinal Ruffo had negotiated the armistice with the French and rebel forces as described. The document was signed by him, and Captain Foote, and several Russian and Turkish Admirals. I should point out that the Russian and Turkish Navies played a role in Ruffo's successful campaign. I didn't include them because... well... you just can't include everything, or your novel will turn into yet another dry history book and some fool will make you read it as part of a class.

Nelson and Ruffo met shortly after Nelson arrived at Naples. It is known that Nelson was furious at the Cardinal for negotiating the truce, and Ruffo was furious at Nelson for trying to cancel it. No one knows exactly what they said at that meeting, so... yeah... I made it up. Hey, this is a *novel*, remember?

Lost in all of this is poor Captain Edward Foote. He was the senior British officer on the scene before Nelson's arrival, but had been given no directions other than to keep the Cardinal happy. When Nelson initially annulled the armistice, it was Foote's honor that was being compromised. He never said much about the incident while Nelson was alive; but years later, after Nelson's death, he ripped into him for his disgraceful handling of the Naples affair.

The scene with Maria, Susan, and Colonel Phélippeaux was fictional, but the crusader city underneath Acre is not. Except for the arms cache under the wall, it is as described and can still be seen today.

Chapter Five

Sidney Smith did indeed send messengers to Sultan Selim III begging for reinforcements. As you now know from reading this book, he got them, and just in time.

The letter from Smith to Jervis and Nelson pleading for support was made up; but I have to believe that a message like that was sent. Smith knew that the arrival of Turkish reinforcements was uncertain at best, and their performance once they got on site was unpredictable. His natural instinct would have been to go with British troops, not Turkish. Yet, there is no record of such an appeal being made. As with much of Sir Sidney's life, there are gaps caused by the loss of many of his personal papers in a fire circa 1816. (I know where that fire happened, but I am still trying to find out exactly when.)

However, this much *is* known. First, both Jervis and Nelson knew that Smith was engaging Bonaparte at Acre—Smith sent them frequent reports. Second, they knew that the odds against Smith winning were overwhelming. Bonaparte had never lost a battle against some of the finest armies and generals in Europe. What chance did a naval officer have of beating him? And third, they had the resources to come to his aid; but they didn't.

All three of those points are facts; to which I would add—and this is the part where I get into trouble—I think their failure to reinforce Sir Sidney was intentional. No, I am not saying that Jervis and Nelson set out to overtly kill Smith; but I do believe that—by omission—they hoped it would happen.

Think about the situation for a moment.

Smith had Bonaparte pinned down for two months! It was plenty of time for ships and men to be sent to reinforce Smith, and for an expeditionary force to attack Jaffa. In that only a token French force was maintained there, it would undoubtedly have fallen, leaving Bonaparte utterly trapped. Indeed, two months would have been enough time to send ships and troops from England, let alone Sicily (Nelson) or Gibraltar (Jervis)!

Bonaparte would then have had British troops at Acre, cutting off his advance to the north; and British forces to the south at Jaffa, who would be cutting off his return to Egypt. To the west would be the Mediterranean Sea, which was owned by the Royal Navy; and to his east would be hordes of hostile tribesmen.

What, pray tell, could Jervis and Nelson have been doing with their assets that would have been more important than nailing Bonaparte once and for all?

On the other hand, by doing nothing, they would have Sir Sidney twisting in the wind. The probability was high that Smith would attempt something insane to make up for his lack of resources, and both Jervis and Nelson knew it. Should Sir Sidney meet his maker in the process, it would be a "very regrettable loss"—but I believe not too many genuine tears would have been shed by either man.

Can I prove that it happened that way? No, I can't. Most

of Sir Sidney's important papers were lost in the fire mentioned above and, with them, perhaps the smoking gun. To the contrary, most of Smith's biographers—and even some of Nelson's—suggest that, after the Battle of Acre, he and Nelson reconciled and formed some kind of mutual admiration society. I don't believe it for a minute.

Consider: when Nelson died at Trafalgar, his body was brought back to London where he received a funeral that would normally be reserved for a king. Anyone who was anyone in the Royal Navy attended—except Sir Sidney Smith. He was in London at the time; but he didn't go. He was, alas, "too busy."

The Battle of Mount Tabor took place as described. Kléber, with 2000 French troops, engaged an Arab force variously estimated at 25,000 to 30,000. He was about to be overwhelmed when Bonaparte appeared, seemingly out of nowhere, with 2500 reinforcements and two cannon, which scattered the Arabs. The middle-eastern military forces, from Egypt to Constantinople, simply had no answer to the disciplined, bayonet studded, Western square.

This battle also reinforces yet again the fact that, had Bonaparte not been stopped at Acre, he would have had no trouble making it all the way to Constantinople—and who knows how history would have changed if he had taken it.

Nelson's duplicity regarding the French sympathizers trapped in Naples has been widely documented, although rarely mentioned in modern times. The meeting between Cardinal Ruffo and Captains Ball and Troubridge actually occurred; and all documents presented in this section are quotes from the original documents.

To be fair, Nelson did not lie in those documents. He did not in any way "... oppose the embarkation of the rebels..." He waited for them to lay down their arms, come out from behind their fortifications, board the ships, and *then* made them prisoners. The embarkation was not opposed at all.

Sir Sidney's ships were indeed blown off station by bad

weather, and while he was gone, Jezzar Pasha was in charge. He sawed off the head of the French officer, and threw the other prisoners into the sea, tied up in sacks, as described. The sacks washed ashore for weeks afterward, which did not amuse the French at all.

The trial of Francesco Caracciolo occurred as described. Indeed, all document citations and much of the trial dialogue is taken from an eyewitness account of the court martial, and from public records. On the surface, it might seem that Caracciolo was indeed guilty of being a traitor and deserter. If so then, as Caracciolo points out, the same charges could be laid against the King. When the King fled Naples with the royal treasury in tow, he effectively sealed the fate of both his army and his people. That Caracciolo was not given the time to prepare a defense, that he was not allowed to call witnesses, that there was no appeal, that he was disgracefully hung instead of shot, that he was not given time to prepare for his death, that his body was simply dropped into the sea instead of buried ashore, all happened; and Nelson knew of, and approved it all. The trial of Francesco Caracciolo is another item in Nelson's career that is widely documented, but rarely mentioned these days.

Chapter Six

No one knows for sure what caused the *Theseus* to blow up. It is believed, however, that it was caused by two midshipmen playing with fuses by striking them with a hammer and nail (a common, albeit disapproved, game). Jimmy Webb and James Bigges Forbes were the only two midshipmen I could positively identify as being aboard the *Theseus* at the time, so they get the blame. (My apologies to any collateral descendants if I am wrong.)

However, the explosion did occur, Captain Miller was killed, and the damage to the ship was as described. The damage reports I cite are all from original sources.

Picard Phélippeaux died as described on May 2, 1799 of

overwork, or heat stroke, or the plague (take your pick and there will be an authority who will agree with you) on the 46th day of the siege.

Walker's probing of Smith concerning the reason reinforcements hadn't arrived is discussed in the notes to Chapter Five.

George Parsons and George Antram were both Midshipmen aboard the *Foudroyant* at the time of Nelson's Naples affair. Indeed, it is through writings left by Midshipman Parsons that we are able to know much of what happened on the *Foudroyant* during that period.

The description of the festivities surrounding the first anniversary of Nelson's victory at the Nile are accurate, right down to the Roman galley with the 2000 lights. It was held on August 1, 1799, but I had to time-shift it back a couple of months to bring it into the Acre timeline.

But here's where things *really* get strange.

Do you remember that incident where Caracciolo's body floated back to the *Foudroyant,* and was discovered by the King? I would *love* to say that it was a brilliant plot segment that came out of my fertile imagination, but I can't. It actually happened. Every bit of it. It was recorded in several sources, and George Parsons writes a detailed eyewitness account of it. The only thing I made up was the fog and the King blaming Nelson. Like I keep telling you, I can't make this stuff up. I am not that good.

The incident where Bonaparte was confronted by the soldier over the death of his friend, André Gilles, happened—including Bonaparte's later comment, "If he starts again, have him shot."

The "garden trap," where the French were allowed into the city and then ambushed occurred as described, including the death of General Rambeaud, and the wounding of General Lannes.

Emma Hamilton did indeed hold court to hear pleas for clemency from the Republican prisoners. However, as one observer put it, "I grieve to say that wonderful, talented and graceful beauty, Emma, Lady Hamilton, did not sympathize in the manner expected from her generous and noble nature."

Eleonora Fonseca Pimentel was a real person, and one of the leading literary figures of her day. I don't know if she was ever personally seen by Emma Hamilton, but the reason for her condemnation was as stated. While it was bad enough that she had published a Republican newspaper, it was her pamphlet suggesting that Emma and Queen Maria Carolina were in a lesbian relationship that, most observers believe, pushed her over the edge (or off the ladder, as the case may be). Her manner of death, and the people she died with, is all accurate.

There are times I wish I hadn't started doing these historical postscripts. That way I could take credit for writing a hanging scene, in which a crowd roars it's approval while waiting for a lottery drawing to begin, and a dwarf sits on the shoulders of the condemned as they are swinging from the gibbet. I would be hailed throughout the nautical fiction community as a creative genius. Alas, it happened just as I described it. I didn't make it up at all.

While, as mentioned, Captain Moiret was a real person, he was not a part of the barricade in the mosque. However, the barricade did happen, and the Frenchmen were saved from a truly terrible death by the intervention of Sir Sidney. It was an example of why he was so respected by the French when he went to live in Paris after the war. But, if you think his action here was honorable and noble, wait until you see what he does in the next book, and what happens to him for doing it.

Bourrienne was a real person and his background was as described. Bonaparte's walk on the beach with him prior to the assault actually happened, along with almost all of the dialogue I used. The scene was recorded in Bourrienne's book *Memoirs of Bonaparte*. I only changed a few words of the dialogue to modernize it a bit.

And Susan Whitney's "death scene" was, of course, fictional; but it's my reply to about ten zillion female readers who have written to ask, "So, why doesn't the jerk just tell her that he loves her, and be done with it?" Well, he finally does... sort'a.

Chapter Seven

The final assault on Acre took place more or less as described. I say "more or less" because we again run into the problem of varying accounts of the same event, even when you are dealing with primary sources. In addition, I combined the events of some of the attacks to heighten the drama.

The scene where Jezzar Pasha stops Smith from plunging into the battle was fiction, but Jezzar's concern that Smith might be wounded or killed was very real. He was the key to victory; and several times during the siege Jezzar headed off Smith from executing some of his more foolhardy plans.

The newly arrived Chifflick Regiment was real, and attacked the French flank as described. They were the first Ottoman regiment to be trained in western fighting methods, and did quite well.

Richard Janverin was a real person, a midshipman aboard the *Tigre*. He was with Sir Sidney on the raid outside the walls; he was wounded in the arm; and he pried the wounded Frenchmen from the Nablousian tribesmen in a tense standoff at Caesarea. Because the specific details of each event are not known, I placed them in a fictional context of my own devising. However, I'd like to thank Jan McCombe, the 4X niece of Midshipman (later Post Captain) Janverin for providing some of the key information on him.

The laying of the powder kegs by Durbin, Pulley, and Corriveau was, of course fictional. But I had to arrange an explosion, and people seem to really like the Durbin/Pulley characters. Pulley was the hero of this scene because I couldn't give all the good parts to Durbin. Jack would never forgive me (see the dedication to this book).

In any event, by placing the powder kegs the traverse was blown up. That actually happened... I think. I can only find one account that even mentions it; but that account is a primary one, from an eyewitness—Antoine Lavalette, a key aide-de-camp of Bonaparte. So, I put it in. After all, you can't have too many good explosions in a book like this, right?

Nelson was indeed made the Duke of Brontë by King Ferdinand. The investiture ceremony was made up—as far as I know, there was no ceremony. In fact, it appears it was all handled by letter. On the other hand, the description of the palace grounds at Caserta is accurate, and the speeches made by the King and Prince di Luzzi are based on the wording of actual correspondence exchanged with Nelson.

Nelson's elevation to ducal status had two effects. First, all snide remarks about Sir Sidney being the "Swedish knight" ceased. It would not due for aspersions to be cast on the Swedish knight, by the "Sicilian Duke" and his friends. Second, back in Yorkshire an obscure parson by the name of Patrick Prunty changed his last name in honor of Nelson. He became Patrick Brontë, as did his daughters Anne, Emily, and Charlotte. Yeah, the ones you studied in high school (or at least I did)—*Jane Eyre*, *Wuthering Heights*, and a bunch of poetry I don't remember anymore... those Brontës.

The letter from Sir Sidney to Bonaparte to give himself "a little revenge" was actually written. I edited it somewhat to make it more readable to the modern eye, but that's about it.

Bonaparte indeed declined to have his wounded safely evacuated because it would require seeking Smith's permission. Indeed, one of Bonaparte's blacker days was when he ordered his chief physician to poison the sick and seriously wounded with an overdose of laudanum, rather than take them with the Army in the retreat. Once they got back to Egypt, the physician, Dr. René-Nicolas Desgenettes bitterly denounced Bonaparte, resigned his commission, and requested permission to return to France. His resignation was not accepted, and his permission to travel was denied. Bonaparte did not need any more hostile critics stirring up things back home.

The incident where Bonaparte fires his hat over the wall so at least part of him will enter Acre—I don't know if that happened or not. It was reported by several sources, but it smacks of apocrypha. True or not, however, it was too delicious a story to leave out.

The nasty letters Smith received from Lord Spencer, Lord St. Vincent, and General Koehler, were real. They were sent before they learned that Smith had defeated Bonaparte. One can only speculate on their thoughts after they learned about the victory.

Bonaparte's plan to extricate himself from Acre was an elementary one—simply declare victory and leave. The message he wrote to his troops is quoted verbatim; but leaving wasn't as easy as getting there. Smith's ships harassed them the whole way, and the march back was unmercifully brutal.

The segment involving Captains Joseph Moiret and Horace Say did not happen, mostly because Say was already dead by this time. However, I liked Say so I decided to keep him alive a little longer. However, the description of the treatment of the wounded on the march back is quite authentic.

As alluded to above, the standoff between Midshipman Richard Janverin and the Nablousians actually occurred. We don't know the details of exactly what transpired, so my description is fictional, even if the incident itself was not.

Now, I know what you're going to say, that thing about Sir Sidney subduing some bad guys, rescuing an island, being given Richard the Lionhearted's cross, and being made a Templar—you HAD to have made that up. No, it all happened. I keep telling you, I couldn't make this stuff up if I tried.

The acquisition of Richard's cross occurred as described, right down to the words used by Archbishop Chrysanthos when he placed the cross around Sir Sidney's neck. In fact, in Smith's will he "gave and bequeathed [the cross] unto the Order of the Templars, to be kept in deposit in the treasury thereof, from whence it originally came into King Richard's hands, and to be worn by the Grand Master and his successors in perpetuity."

Fireship Press has been trying to track this cross down. We know that as of 1848, it was in the possession of the Convent of the Order of St. John of Jerusalem in Paris; but there the trail grows cold. We are going to keep trying, however. Indeed, if there is a stray Parisian who is reading this book, who would like to join in the search, please let us know. We have two mysteries for you to solve. Where is Sidney Smith's cross; and, where is John Wesley Wright's grave?

Finally, I leave you with the tease that perhaps the future is not all rosy for our hero, that there are some troubles just over the horizon. Indeed, there are; and I promise you the next book will come faster than this one.

The Hottest Authors in all of Nautical Fiction
can be found at

FIRESHIP PRESS

Alaric Bond
Linda Collison
Tom Grundner
Steven E. Maffeo
and more!

THE FOURTH BOOK IN THE
FIGHTING SAIL SERIES

If you're a naval officer on the beach, you take any
job you can—even if it's with the Honorable East
India Company.

But Thomas King's first voyage on an Indiaman
proves to be far more than he bargained for.

WWW.FIRESHIPPRESS.COM
Interesting • Informative • Authoritative

Surgeon's Mate

Book Two of the Patricia MacPherson Nautical Adventure Series

Linda Collison

Patrick MacPherson is a qualified surgeon's mate; but she's not the man he claims to be.

It's late October, 1762. After surviving the deadly siege of Havana, Patrick MacPherson and the rest of the ship's company are looking forward to a well deserved liberty in New York. But what happens in that colonial town will change the surgeon's mate's life in ways she could never have imagined.

Using a dead man's identity, young Patricia Kelley MacPherson is making her way as Patrick MacPherson, surgeon's mate aboard His Majesty's frigate *Richmond*. She's become adept at bleeding, blistering, and amputating limbs; but if her cover is blown, she'll lose both her livelihood and her berth aboard the frigate. The ship's gunner alone knows her secret – or does someone else aboard suspect that Patrick MacPherson is not the man he claims to be?

WWW.FIRESHIPPRESS.COM
Interesting • Informative • Authoritative

"OLD IRONSIDES" AND HMS JAVA
A STORY OF 1812

A highly recommended must-read for every naval enthusiast—indeed, for every American!

Stephen Coonts
NY Times best-selling author

HMS *Java* and the USS *Constitution* (the famous "Old Ironsides") face off in the War of 1812's most spectacular blue-water frigate action. Their separate stories begin in August 1812—one in England and the other in New England. Then, the tension and suspense rise, week-by-week, as the ships cruise the Atlantic, slowly and inevitably coming together for the final life-and-death climax.

The Perfect Wreck is not only the first full-length book ever written about the battle between the USS *Constitution* and HMS *Java*, it is a gem of Creative Nonfiction. It has the exhaustive research of a scholarly history book; but it is beautifully presented in the form of a novel.

WWW.FIRESHIPPRESS.COM
Interesting • Informative • Authoritative